DIAMONDS TO DUST

Diamonds To Dust

A novel
by

MICHAEL DeMEIS

Adelaide Books
New York / Lisbon
2019

DIAMONDS TO DUST
A novel
By Michael DeMeis

Copyright © by Michael DeMeis
Cover design © 2019 Adelaide Books

Published by Adelaide Books, New York / Lisbon
adelaidebooks.org

Editor-in-Chief
Stevan V. Nikolic

For any information, please address Adelaide Books
at info@adelaidebooks.org
or write to:
Adelaide Books
244 Fifth Ave. Suite D27
New York, NY, 10001

ISBN-10: 1-951214-59-5
ISBN-13: 978-1-951214-59-3

Printed in the United States of America

For Bern, the best thing that ever happened to me.

Prologue

In Philadelphia, the area called Center City stretches from the Delaware River on the East to the Schuylkill River on the West. Initial settlement began with docks, warehouses, shops, and homes near the eastern river. As the city grew, it expanded west from the Delaware by adding North-South numbered streets which increased numerically in a westerly direction. These were bisected by West-East streets usually named for trees. It was, in fact, the first organized city street grid in North America. In 1854, the western edge of the city had reached 7th street, where scattered homes dwindled away into garden plots and small pastures. It was here, and at this time, that Jewelers' Row began.

Two blocks of Sansom Street around 8th Street became the first grouping of jewelry merchants in the United States. At the time, many doubted that Philadelphians would be willing to endure a six block or more excursion from their residences, stores, and offices simply to purchase adornments. Fortunately for the first jewelers, they found that customers were in fact quite eager to travel to comparison shop and especially to find bargains. In later years, New York Cities' Diamond District eclipsed it, but Jewelers' Row still attracts believers.

Chapter 1

Hassan al-Sidaan did not use his knife in the United States. He often wanted to. Especially when a particularly nasty Philadelphia driver cut him off on the Schuylkill expressway. When such incidents occurred, he wanted to pick up his dagger, grab the offending driver by the hair, and slash through his or her throat to the neck bone. He found such a manner of execution much more satisfying than killing with a gun.

Hassan also did not use his real name in the US. He was the proprietor of the medium-sized diamond store, Youkoumian's, on Sansom Street between 8th and 7th, almost in the exact center of Jewelers' Row, the diamond district of Philadelphia. His fellow merchants on the Row all assumed that he was in fact, Mr. Youkoumian, the Armenian owner of the store.

In time, he became accustomed to his new name and assumed ethnicity, and even began to think of himself in his own mind as Youkoumian.

It amused him that the pale white people with whom he dealt could seldom recognize any differences among ethnic peoples of the Middle East. He was originally from Syria and could tell instantly a person's country, and usually his tribe.

In addition to being amusing, it was also useful, for Youkoumian often had visitors that resembled himself, and these, too, were assumed to be Armenians. In fact, almost all of them were Arabic speakers and they visited Philadelphia to either deliver or receive diamonds or cash. The diamonds represented a convenient and unlikely to be traced means of moving rather large sums between countries, especially between America and the Middle East. In effect, Youkoumian was operating a money laundry for a jihadist group.

Today at his store, Youkoumian was preparing to meet two Arabic speaking group members who were waiting for him at the group's safe house. Ironically located on Christian Street, not far from the diamond store.

In his office, Youkoumian gathered together 1,000 carats of diamonds which he split into two parts. He placed each part in what seemed to be an ordinary quart-sized opaque freezer bag. The bags were not completely ordinary since each had a tiny battery and radio transmitter embedded in the bottom seam. The transmitters broadcast a signal which could be received at more than a mile and displayed on a street map by a GPS device. They were, in effect, location devices for tracking the bags. Youkoumian placed the bags in his briefcase and left the store to walk to Christian Street.

The two Arabic speakers in the safe house looked thuggish to anyone's inspection and certainly to American eyes. Youkoumian was not impressed with these new couriers. Both were partially-bearded and projected an affect which expressed their lack of interest in being there. He was sure, however, they were quite prepared to do anything required of them, up to and including murder. That much was clear from their reputations.

Youkoumian gave each courier one of the quart-sized bags. Neither was aware of the tracking device, but both knew they were each responsible for ensuring the delivery of both bags.

They would be leaving early tomorrow on a Qatar Airways non-stop flight to Doha in Qatar. From there they could make their way to the group's headquarters in Syria. Youkoumian wished the couriers well and left to return to the Sansom Street store.

Chapter 2

Gillian Andrews put on her Blackhawk ballistic vest, adjusted the shoulder holster carrying her Glock Gen 4 G27, and centered her ATF ID placard overall. She was ready for the raid.

She and eleven male ATF special agents, were participating in an operation on a local tattoo parlor in Philadelphia. Undercover agents had previously illegally purchased guns at the parlor, which provided the justification for the search warrant and raid.

The use of so many agents against a shop which usually held only two tattoo artists was intended to intimidate with overwhelming force. Experience had shown that the violent arrival of so many officers deterred any thought of resistance, providing safety for both those making the arrests and those being arrested.

In two groups of six, the agents went to front and alley doors of the shop, and, in perfectly timed synchronization, used Broco Enforcer Compact Door Rams to knock down the doors. The sudden crash of the doors, together with the inrush of shouting agents with drawn guns, almost always squelched anyone's thoughts of either fleeing or using a weapon. The tattooists were read their Miranda rights, cuffed with hands behind their backs, and escorted out to separate ATF Ford

SUVs and locked into secure back seats. The remaining agents quickly found the hiding places for the guns and ammunition being sold. As was usual in such cases, they also found controlled substances: a kilo of cocaine, and about a half kilo of what looked like heroin, indicating that guns were not the only illegal things being sold at the store.

The operation leader selected two male agents to collect and properly tag the illegal stuff. They would then transport the evidence to the ATF secure evidence room. Two other male agents were told to remain in the shop and arrange for front and alley door repair. Gillian was ordered to return to the ATF offices to start writing up the voluminous paperwork needed to report on the operation and arrange for custody and indictment of those arrested.

Gillian felt she was back in kindergarten and had been selected to pass out napkins for snack time because she was a girl. Perhaps Mother Theresa would have accepted an assignment like this without complaining, but Gillian was pissed. She noticed that several of the male agents nodded slightly at her assignment. None expressed any surprise that she had been selected for a secretary's role to take care of the paperwork chore. Still, she knew complaining would only make her look bad, so she tried to look cheerful and returned to her cubicle at the ATF offices.

Long after five o'clock, Gillian was still working on the paperwork required for the morning's raid. Some of her female agent friends dropped by her cubicle to see if she would like to go out with them for a drink. She declined, pleading the need to finish her assignment. The male agents didn't bother to ask her, knowing she would not accept.

When the paperwork was finally finished, she got on the internet to do what she liked most, data mining. Currently, the most interesting thing Gillian had found on the web was the 71st Virginia Regiment, a group of Civil War re-enactors based in the Philadelphia suburbs. They were unusual in being a self-styled Confederate organization. The usual assumption was that such groups organizing in a state would naturally follow the path taken by their putative ancestors and become either a Rebel or Yankee unit depending on that. She knew, of course, that the men in these groups tried to be as authentic about their make believe as possible, to the extent that they wore heavy woolen uniforms even at events in hot summer months. They also used black gunpowder for their rifled musket replicas. And that might be something that could interest ATF.

After all, why would a group in Pennsylvania choose to name themselves after a Virginia confederate regiment? Anomalies like that often were indicative of other interesting exceptions. Gillian resolved to attend the next meeting, even though most similar groups were almost exclusively male. Gillian had no fears about being uneasy in such a situation. And rightly so. She was a self-confident and quite capable young woman who was equipped to handle any situation in which she found herself.

Chapter 3

Youkoumians sole deviation from typical middle-class American behavior was his participation in a Civil War reenactment group known as the 71st Virginia Regiment. Like many such groups throughout the country, members dressed in authentic replica uniforms, purchased authentic replicas of Civil War weapons, and tried to recreate Civil War conditions in encampments and simulated battles.

Youkoumian was never able to fully rationalize his membership even to himself. The idea of being a rebel against the U.S. government had a certain amount of appeal as did the romance of representing a society which, in retrospect, was portrayed as respecting traditional values and culture to the extent of being willing to fight for them when threatened. There was the added benefit that it got him away from his wife for meetings and encampments.

Youkoumian enjoyed these diversions and over the years, as members fell away and new ones joined, he rose in the hierarchy of the organization. Now, he was the Colonel of the regiment, the ostensible leader, to the extent that any volunteer collection of Americans acknowledged any leader.

Youkoumian was in a good mood as he drove to the tavern where the biweekly 71st VA.meeting was being held.

The couriers he had met earlier in the week in the safe house had arrived with the jewels at headquarters in Syria. He had no problems and could enjoy himself. Being addressed as Colonel Youkoumian never failed to please him.

He began the muster by having the master sergeant perform roll call.

Among those present tonight was Hampton Wade.

Unlike all the Northerners in the 71st VA, Hampton had an actual southern heritage. He was born and grew up in Highland County, Virginia, in the mountains west of Charlottesville. Although not a "poor Mountaineer" in the traditional sense, Hampton had done a lot of hunting in Highland County. He knew how to handle guns, and had even learned how to use black powder in a rifled musket in the county rod and gun club.

Despite his lack of funds, Hampton was a prized addition to Youkoumian's regiment. In addition to his facility with the weapons used in the Civil War, he added authenticity to the re-enactments because of his weight. He was beyond thin. He resembled old photographs of Confederate prisoners of war.

As part of new business at the meeting, a newcomer named George Bailey was introduced. Since the only requirement for membership was willingness, the rest of the regiment was quite pleased to welcome him. New blood was always interesting. There was always some turnover since not everyone maintained a long-term interest in Civil War re-enactments.

After discussion of various organizational matters, the meeting concluded and those of the regiment who had permission from their wives or girlfriends talked over beers around a tavern table.

George immediately drew attention as a potential new member. He was an obviously successful young man, well dressed and well spoken. He was the standard six feet tall, with considerable muscular development in his shoulders and upper arms. He had developed this through his membership in an exercise center which featured free weights. He used them regularly because he had read somewhere that women were particularly attracted to well-developed biceps and shoulders.

Unlike almost all the current members of the 71st VA, he was unusual in that he did not live in the Philadelphia suburbs. He mentioned living in Center City which was seemingly incomprehensible to the members of the 71st. None of them would ever consider living with their wives or girlfriends in the city. This was cleared up when George indicated that he was single. All then became obvious, since Center City was the local Mecca of attractive available females to most members, even though almost all were married with families. As they put it, it didn't hurt to fantasize, did it?

To George, the group seemed quite typical of similar groupings he had attended in the suburbs. Guys around forty something drinking beer and talking sports and politics. Only two members were unusual. The Colonel, Youkoumian, who was rather swarthy and did not drink alcohol, and Hampton, who was conspicuously underfed amongst so many somewhat overweight types inhabiting cubicles in offices.

George noted the differences of the two as he exchanged backgrounds with some of the other members. Since George enjoyed an occasional drink, he did not see much connection to the Colonel, who clearly did not drink alcoholic beverages. Still, Youkoumian was something of an anomaly, apparently, an Armenian. And Armenia was somewhere in the Middle East if he remembered correctly. And he had a jewelry store in Center City. Interesting.

The other stand out, Hampton, was also an anomaly. Young, single, and, as George rapidly found out from other members, like himself, both living and working in Center City.

Chapter 4

Gillian was peeved that she had missed the latest meeting of the 71st VA, but it did give her the opportunity to discuss the whole issue with her group supervisor.

As far as Gillian could tell, the 71st Virginia Regiment was unusual in being a Confederate oriented unit in a Northern state. Despite that handicap, there were sufficient contrarians in the area to provide a membership of about forty which was a typical size for such groups. Undoubtedly many were attracted to the idea of being unconventional, going against expected paths, and just being rebels.

Gillian had plenty of scope in her present position to investigate almost anything she chose. Her group supervisor was an attractive older woman, named Gloria Wentworth, with long brunette hair, smile wrinkles around her eyes, and a curvy figure. Some of the less inhibited males in the office often tried to flirt with her and Gloria flirted right back to give them a hard time. But she was happily married, had climbed as high as she wanted to, and now was focused on her coming retirement and enjoying her grandchildren. She was fond of Gillian and gave her practically complete freedom of action to do anything she wanted. Gillian repaid this freedom by managing up. She used the often-impressive results she came up with to make her superior look good. Of course, that also resulted in commendations for Gillian as well.

Gillian walked down the corridor to Gloria's office.

"Hi Gloria, got a moment?"

Gloria smiled at her as always. "Any time for you, Gillian. Come on in and sit down."

Gillian did. "I wanted to check in with you about a new project I have in mind."

"If it's anything like the previous things you've found, I'm all ears." Gloria trusted Gillian's work implicitly.

"I've found a Civil War re-enactment group in the suburbs which has a generous supply of black powder."

Gloria thought about it. "Generally, those groups are careful about their supplies and pay a lot of attention to keeping them secure and safe. Like modern gun clubs, they want members to always assume a gun is loaded, never point a gun at another person, and never leave a gun unattended. Also, they make their own paper cartridges and insist that they are blank, without a ball."

Gillian said, "I can believe all that. I haven't found out much about this particular group of re-enactors, but I think it's significant that it's here in Pennsylvania, and organized as a confederate regiment, the 71st VA."

Gloria was interested. "That is a little out of step from the usual."

Gillian continued. "And the head of the group is an Armenian, possibly with ties to the Middle East."

"Even more unusual," said Gloria. "Is he Islamic? Or are all Armenians Christian?"

"From what I've been able to determine from the web, Armenia was the first state to embrace Christianity in 301 AD. There are in fact minority groups of Kurds and other Muslims in Armenia, but they don't appear to be a threat to either Armenia or the West. Despite the absence of any jihadist connection, I think the whole situation warrants further investigation."

Gloria considered that. "Yes, you have an outstanding facility for discovering strange connections, so you are probably right."

"So, it's okay with you if I devote some effort to it?"

"You go, girl. You've always done well for us in the past", said Gloria.

Chapter 5

Hampton Wade worked at the Rittenhouse Physics Labs at 33rd and Walnut in West Philadelphia, just across the Schuylkill River from Center City.

Hampton knew enough high school Physics to appreciate the basic principles of the research being done. He was good enough with mechanical skills to competently fabricate and assemble the equipment that both the professors and graduate students needed for their experiments. And, given enough time, he also began to understand more and more of what he was doing. He learned. And he enjoyed himself.

At noon, he usually walked through the University of Pennsylvania Campus to get lunch at the Accenture Cafe in the Towne Building. Usually on an ordinary day, but today was not ordinary.

Hampton had a good view of her back. She was leaning forward slightly on the table which was fifty feet directly across the food court from where he sat. She had her arms extended so that her back was at an angle of perhaps fifteen degrees to the vertical. Her legs were straight but the left crossed slightly over the right and created a rather interesting tautness in her short shorts. Hampton was mesmerized by the sight. But they weren't globes of course. They melded with a fair turn into a concave bare waist and terminated at a tantalizing crease at the back of her thighs. They weren't even full hemispheres. A hemisphere would have been much too artificial looking, suggestive of a Picasso nude reassembled from ill-fitting parts.

Hampton tried to think of the word for a three-dimensional section of a sphere. A line across a circle was a chord and produced a circular section. A plane across a sphere was called a what? A planoid? Did it produce a spherical section? Or a spheroid?

His analysis took too long, as usual. She looked over her left shoulder directly at him, catching him staring at her. Turning back to the table and straightening, she apparently said goodbye to her friends before turning around and starting to thread through the Formica tables and orange plastic chairs toward Hampton's seat near a pillar. It was a determined walk.

Halfway across, he recognized her from the Rittenhouse Labs. Jennifer Collins, a first-year Physics grad student. Hampton, like everyone else at the Physics labs, always felt a mild form of dissonance when he saw her at work. It was like repeatedly seeing Cindy Crawford and learning she had an honors degree in engineering. Hampton knew it was sexist, but he couldn't help the reaction. At least he never said anything about it out loud.

As she came closer, Hampton rose to his feet. Her gray eyes were at the level of his chin as she stopped. Her strikingly black hair was arrayed in a cut which Hampton did not recognize, but which set off her eyes, nose, and mouth attractively. Evidently, she was one of the few people who could confront someone without placing her hands on her hips or indeed doing anything at all with them other than allowing them their natural position by her sides.

"You didn't need to get up. I'm not about to hit you for leering." Her voice was both self-confident and pleasant. "Nor will I report you under the University of Pennsylvania code of conduct, which depending on a hearing, may result in censure or even suspension." Was there a trace of a smile under this last comment?

Hampton considered his possible responses. Injured innocence? Good old southern boy? Sexual pickup? Most of them he didn't do well and all of them didn't matter since she was out of his league anyway.

He looked into her eyes, currently a rather flinty gray. "I am not aware," he said, "of any particular stricture in the conduct code which requires me to avert my vision from another person I find attractive. In any case, I'm not a student and hence am not subject to censure or suspension." Hampton thought he detected a twinkle in the gray eyes. Or perhaps she was merely amused at his attempt to match her level of literacy.

"I know you're not a student," said Jennifer. "You're a tech at Ritt Labs and I've noticed you leering at me there as well. The code applies to everyone at the University, including faculty and staff. For a serious enough offense, you could lose your job." The flinty eyes were waiting, looking for something. Sparks, perhaps?

Hampton smiled slightly and replied, "I might say that it would be well worth it, even though I need the job to keep a roof over my head this winter."

Jennifer cocked her head slightly down and to the right, which, combined with a half-smile, led Hampton to believe he was not in serious trouble.

"A sort of backhand compliment combined with a plea for mercy based on economic need. One wonders why someone so eloquent is ogling butts in the Accenture Café."

"Please allow me to differ with your assessment of my behavior," said Hampton. "To be precise, I was merely observing and trying to remember the term for the three-dimensional figure produced when a plane passes through a sphere not on a diameter."

Jennifer smiled.at Hampton, it was quite the nicest smile he had seen in months. There was a warmth in it now. "That would be a spheroidal section. I've never had my ass compared to a geometric figure before. Some might think that assessment alone would be grounds for reporting you to the court."

Hampton knew now that it would be all right, at least for the time being. He knew getting women to smile was over half the battle. If only he knew a way to do it all the time. He said, "Then I plead guilty to an inappropriate description of natural beauty. As punishment, perhaps I could buy you a cup of coffee?"

Jennifer looked at him for over thirty seconds. The gray eyes, now penetrating, seemed to reach an assessment. "Yes, I think that would be satisfactory. Except make mine a Chai."

Hampton had time while in the coffee line to think about it. A beautiful, brilliant grad student and a lab tech who hadn't graduated college. Or even got into one. Hampton wasn't brilliant and he knew it. He hadn't made the cut to get into the University of Virginia. But he was smart enough to know that not everything is what someone says it is. Regardless of the outcome of this interaction, he was looking forward to being in the presence of a beautiful woman. At least temporarily.

Returning to the small round table with the tray containing the plain white ceramic mugs, he placed the Chai near Jennifer and a black coffee near his colorful plastic seat. After stepping to the side of the pillar to leave the tray for pickup, he turned back to see her sampling his coffee.

Jennifer grimaced. "God, how can you drink that stuff? Are you sure it's coffee? It looks like a left-over experiment from a Chem 1 Lab."

Hampton looked down at his mug, then back up at the eyes. "It's sort of a tradition at U of P... drink beer, stay up late, drink bad coffee."

"Fortunately, we didn't have that last tradition where I went to college."

Hampton looked a question.

"Universidad Latinoamericana de Ciencia y Tecnología. There, coffee like that would get you thrown out of school and perhaps up against a wall."

"That's a mouthful of a school," said Hampton. "I've never heard of anyone from there at the University of Pennsylvania. Did you like going to school down there?"

The eyes were changing color. Less flinty, more liquid. Less gray, more blue. They were smiling now. "I should have, considering I was born there and lived there all my life."

"Sorry," said Hampton. "From hearing you speak, I would never have thought you were from there. I suppose everyone tells you how great your English is?"

Jennifer was practically laughing now. "It should be, considering that my family moved down to Costa Rica from Virginia, leaving in 1882, always spoke English at home, and, except for me, has always gone North for school."

"Hmmm," said Hampton. "That's quite a resume. I have roots in Virginia, myself. Highland County."

"The Switzerland of America," said Jennifer.

"I'm surprised you know of it. There are only 2,000 people in the whole county."

"My family has a pretty good appreciation for all things Virginia, considering how long ago we moved. Sort of a tradition. Have you visited the McDowell battlefield on the Bullpasture River?"

"Uh, no. I know the river is in Highland County but I'm not familiar with the battlefield."

"You surprise me, Hampton. Stonewall Jackson's first victory in an independent command and in your home county. Tsk, tsk. People in the Labs say you are into Civil War re-enactments. As I understand it, you belong to a local outfit called the 71st VA."

"Yes, that's correct." Hampton was embarrassed. This woman knew more about the Civil War than he did and he supposedly was a re-enactor … for a Confederate regiment!

Jennifer put her hand on his arm for three Mississippi's. "Perhaps we could visit one of your regiment's meetings together."

Oh, my God, thought Hampton, she can't be attracted to me. I would be delirious if she was, but this is too good to be true.

And perhaps it was. Still, there was always the possibility that one thing could lead to another.

Chapter 6

And as usually happens, one thing did lead to another. Hampton rolled off her and lay on his back. Looking to his left, he could still see Jennifer's ass curved up and over like a perfect little white mountain as she lay face down on her stomach. As he admired the view, he remarked, "I've never done that before, but I must say I am quite taken with the process."

Jennifer shifted to lay on her side looking at him with one cocked arm supporting her head. "You really are a naïf, aren't you?"

"A what?"

"A naïf, an unsophisticated person with little experience in the real world."

"Oh, is that how that's pronounced. I've seen the word in books, but I've never heard anyone use it in a sentence before."

Jennifer smiled at him with what could only be described as a smirk. "Then that's another first for you today, isn't it?"

"Yes, things seem to be happening at an accelerated pace when I'm around you." He paused, wondering if he said too much it would lead to an end of a good thing. And it was a good thing, especially given the events of this morning. "You know, I really like being with you. It's exciting as well as interesting." God, that sounded lame, even to him. He was rather dreading her response to him.

Jennifer smirked some more at him. "Yes, I just noticed how exciting you found me."

"It's not just that," said Hampton. "I mean, that was awesome, but it's more than that." He stopped, at a loss to express himself.

"Awesome," she teased him. "Hampton, for a guy who works at a major university you sound so high school at times."

"I'm not that articulate … just trying to tell you how much I like you."

"Oh Hampton, you're way past liking. You are overwhelmingly, head over heels, baying at the moon, in love with me." Which was exactly where she wanted him.

Hampton blinked and considered that. She was right, but it didn't seem a good idea to admit it. How did she feel about him? Why the heck was all this going on? What did she see in him? It looked like she was attracted but why? If he asked her about it, would he break the spell, would she resent it, get mad at him, never see him again? He decided that he would rather know, even if it ended things. "You know, I'm still having problems understanding why you're interested in me."

"Obviously, as I've just demonstrated, I'm madly, passionately attracted to your body and couldn't wait to jump your bones."

"Have you had your vision checked lately? Most people would describe me as skin and bones if not downright anorexic. You could find any number of guys with better bodies than mine. And any of them would give their left nut to get in the sack with you."

Jennifer turned over on her back and ran her fingers through her short cut hair. "I like your skin and bones. You're nothing but hard muscle and skeletal support. And it's not your left nut that I'm interested in."

"And you could find a lot of guys with bigger penises also."

Jennifer smiled at him. It seemed that she found him amusing. Perhaps that was why he was where he was. "Is that what you call yours?" she asked. "Your penis?"

"That's the anatomical term for it. What do you call it?"

"It's a cock and it's quite big enough for the purposes I have in mind," she said, sitting up.

Hampton sat up also and looked at her. "I still can't understand what's going on. Why do we have a relationship? You're the star graduate student in the Physics Department and I'm lower than whale shit. You're one of the most gorgeous women on campus and I look like a refugee from a war zone. You're sophisticated and have a degree in Quantum Physics and I'm a 'naïf' who takes your orders as a lab tech. As the saying goes, this does not compute."

Jennifer got out of bed, locked her fingers together over her head, and stretched toward the ceiling. "Perhaps I can't resist mothering you and trying to fatten you up," she yawned.

Hampton's thought processes came to a complete halt until she finished stretching. Eventually, his brain clicked in again. *Ah ha*, thought Hampton, my theory is correct. But of course, he quickly realized that in the last few days she had never tried to cook anything for him and never urged food on him when they ate out. She obviously wasn't serious.

She turned, saw him thinking about it, and threw a pillow at him "Of course it's not that, you idiot." She bent over at the waist to pick up her jeans where they had ended up on the floor near the bed an hour ago. Pulling them on and buttoning the snaps, she said, "What I want you for is to have you construct a machine to travel between different dimensions."

Hampton stared at her. He had heard what she said but the words did not make much sense to him. "Could you explain that a little more, please." It wasn't a question.

"You know, Hampton, one of the things I like about you is *your* seriousness. If you were only a little smarter you could be a techie geek and a sweet one at that."

"Thanks for the compliment. I think. But I'd still like some context to go with this dimension stuff."

"It's actually simple, I'm from another dimension, got trapped in this one, and now I'm looking for a way back." She studied him and burst out laughing. "If you could only see your face now. I can almost see the tiny hamster running around his little wheel in your head trying to process that."

Hampton smiled ruefully. "Well, the first response most people would have after a statement like that would be, 'do you also hear voices?' "

Jennifer looked at him for a long moment. "Look, we've been hanging together for several days now. Do you think I'm mentally ill?"

"Well, no, but you must admit that ..."

"Do you think a delusional person could get into the University of Pennsylvania?"

"Well, no, although some of the professors in the poly sci department are ..."

"Then, as a Physics wannabe, don't you have to admit that there's a possibility that I'm telling the truth and shouldn't you want to hear more evidence to make a scientific evaluation?"

Hampton had no response for several seconds. It had always been obvious that she was smarter than he was. She knew more about people and situations than he did. And she certainly knew a lot more about Physics than he did. In the last few days, it became even clearer that she could out argue him as well. "OK, what's the deal?"

"Get your clothes on and we can go and get some food," Jennifer said. "As usual, you look like you're about to expire from malnutrition and I certainly don't want that to happen."

Hampton thought about it as he pulled his jeans on. At least she does want me alive. An indication of sorts. They finished dressing and went down to the sun dappled shade of the streets of the city.

Chapter 7

George Bailey was truthful in some respects. He did live and work in Center City. However, he did not work in property management. His office just happened to be in the Philadelphia Field Office of the FBI. George was a special agent.

As a special agent, George did quite well for himself, with a salary around $125,000 a year plus Law Enforcement Availability Pay (Leap) and a generous Cost of Living Adjustment. As George often put it, that was good compensation for someone who's most dangerous contact with a weapon was a yearly qualifying shoot at an indoor range. And as he also put it, not bad for a guy with just a Bachelor's degree in Criminal Justice.

He walked down the hall of the Field Office and stopped just outside the office of the special agent in charge, the SAC, Dan Corolli. He leaned over and peeked in the open doorway.

Dan Corolli was a huge man, not fat, but big enough to play Little John in a Robin Hood movie. The adjective most likely to be used to describe Dan was burly. His face included bushy untrimmed eyebrows, a hooked prominent nose, and a large mouth which often could be heard bellowing in the office halls. He had little hair left other than a wiry salt and pepper fringe just above his ears.

"They stink!" he said as he threw his copy of the Philadelphia Inquirer down on his cluttered desk.

George entered Dan's office and closed the door behind him and took a chair in front of the SAC's desk. "And what group, organization, or entity is emitting foul odors today?" he asked.

Dan stared at George incredulously. "The Phillies of course, who else! Two in scoring position with one out in the ninth, and couldn't get a run in to tie it. No hitting. Never had any, never will."

George viewed his boss with a slight smile on his face. "Dan, you transferred here four years ago, right?"

"Yeah, so what?"

"So how can you get so emotional about the Phillies when you're not even a native Philadelphian."

Dan looked at George as if the answer should be obvious. "What the hell, ya got to identify with where ya live right? City, teams, people, places, whatever. Breathes there a man with soul so dead who never to himself has said, this is my own, my native land ... and so on and so on." Dan looked sternly serious about the issue as if daring George to contradict him, even though the quotation did not actually apply to him. Since George knew that arguing with a boss was a lose-lose, he decided to retreat.

"When you put it that way, you're right, Dan, they do stink."

"Damn right!" Dan's mouth moved as if chewing a cigar he was no longer allowed to enjoy in his office. The motion provided him a satisfactory coda for his point.

"Anyway, I came in to go over this proposed investigation on ...."

Dan groaned. "Not the damn probe into the Civil War kooks again, haven't we thrashed this ...."

"Yeah, but wait, they are a Confederate outfit in a Northern state, the head of it is an Armenian, of all things. I've been to one of their meetings and there's something not quite right with the whole group. And any outfit that deals with black powder ...."

"Is well worth investigating, yeah, yeah, I've heard it before and I don't want to hear it again. Don't we have enough mafia and corrupt politicians in Philadelphia to keep you busy? If you haven't got enough to do, Gentry can use some help."

George raised his hand to shield himself from the threat of Gentry. "Okay, okay, I get your point. I'll come back when I have more to go on."

"Damn right!" said Dan, chewing his imaginary cigar.

As George retreated down the hall to his office, he thought about how he might develop new information on the black powder guys. He was convinced that he had a legitimate area of inquiry: an organization of grown people running around playing make believe war as if it were 150 years ago. It was even more suspicious that they were Confederate reenactors in the Philadelphia area. What was the point unless it was a diversion of attention from some more criminal activity? And these reenactor groups had supplies of black powder for their musket rifles. He wondered if anyone from Alcohol, Tobacco, and Firearms, ATF, was checking out the 71st VA.

Unfortunately, the logical place to start to answer that question was to contact someone in the local ATF office. Unfortunate, because the agencies did not enjoy "buddy" status with each other, and even asking for information might be seen as an admission of weakness. George had never had dealings with the local branch of ATF, and so had no contacts to get in touch with informally. Too bad, since he would undoubtedly have been interested in Gillian Andrews, who was not only an ATF agent in Philadelphia but, in George's terms, was quite a hot chick.

Chapter 8

Occasionally, ATF worked with the FBI. Of course, some fibbies tended to look down on the ATF special agents. Gillian never let such patronizing affect her. In some ways, she relished it, knowing that the superior attitude pigeonholing her gave her more scope to turn heads when she produced significant contributions to the work at hand. And she had no trouble contributing. Occasionally an FBI special agent, sufficiently secure in his own skin, would notice her talents and suggest that she transfer. Gillian always declined. She intended to eventually head up a combination of all the Justice Department investigative agencies, including the FBI, by standing out in ATF.

Just now, she was not feeling likely to reach that goal anytime soon.

She had been relegated to an ATF surveillance van which was observing and recording visits of customers to an ATF "shop" in North Philadelphia. The van taped the arrival and departure of customers and was also collecting video on what went on in the store. Ostensibly selling T-shirts, the shop was a sting operation which bought unregistered weapons. The transactions were recorded and transmitted to the van. The purpose of the sting was to get felons to sell their guns to the government. Forensics could then often use ballistic testing to link the handguns with the crimes associated with them. The surveillance videos could then occasionally reveal a link to an individual. Sometimes the evidence would be strong enough to result in an arrest, indictment, and conviction. Gillian, like all the ATF agents working this shop, knew about the problems this kind of activity, known as Operation Fearless, had brought down on ATF in the past.

Despite the problems, ATF still felt this was an effective way to get unregistered hand guns off the streets, occasionally tie a perpetrator or accomplice to a crime, and sometimes ensure justice for victims of the crimes. This shop had been in operation for four months and had already removed 67 weapons from the street, arrested 32 persons for illegal weapons possession, and collected a large amount of controlled substances.

During a lull in shop activity, Gillian brought up the subject to her older fellow agent, Tom, in the van.

"Tom, you were involved in "Operation Fearless" in Milwaukee, right?"

Tom, with an askew smile, said, "Typical ATF operation, SNAFUs and FUBARs everywhere."

Gillian said, "So, give me an example."

Tom leaned back. "One of the worst was when one of the Milwaukee agents left an ATF SUV in a coffee shop parking lot. Then he got driven to the sting site by another agent in an unmarked car. Unfortunately, he left three ATF weapons, including an M4 .223 caliber rifle in the car. When he returned later that evening, he discovered that the car had been burglarized and the weapons stolen.

Gillian said, "Embarrassing."

Tom said, "Yes, but that's not all. The next day the thief brought in one of the guns to the sting site and sold it back to us. He promised to bring in the other two, but he never did."

Gillian said, "Wow, so they wound up buying back their own weapon that had been stolen. Ironic."

Tom linked his hands behind his head and continued. "Another time, a known felon offered to sell the sting shop a silver revolver for $250. The agents were ready to pay it, but the felon wouldn't sell at that time because he was planning to use it to retaliate against some people that had shot his cousin. He left the store with the gun. Unlike the setup for this shop, there was no outside cover team to follow the guy and stop his planned crime."

Gillian just shook her head. "Not much in the way of planning for unexpected contingencies."

Tom said, "Not much planning for anything. About this time, the higher-ups decided to close the operation down. While it was closed, it was burglarized to the tune of $39,000 worth of ATF equipment, including an ATF tactical ballistic shield. Additionally, it was vandalized and the ATF had to compensate the store owner for $25,000."

Gillian ruefully said, "Kind of discouraging to learn of stuff like that."

"Yes," said Tom. "I've definitely had enough of ATF. In four more years, I'll have my twenty in and I can retire and get a job in private security."

This conversation discouraged Gillian. She had been counting on rising in ATF and accomplishing things. Now it began to look as if rising in ATF would be like being a rising raisin in a collapsing loaf of bread. You might well wind up lower than when you started.

As in any organization, ATF had its own hierarchy of prestige positions. In Philadelphia, Group V (Intelligence Group) was the choice place to be. Special Agents from that group had a noticeably higher probability of getting to

National faster than any others. And so, Gillian had spent her nights and weekends mining the Internet for leads, correlations, inconsistencies, anything that might lead to something big which she could use as leverage into Group V. It was beginning to look to her that all that effort would not achieve what she wanted.

Chapter 9

A new set of couriers had arrived in Philadelphia from Doha. As was usual procedure, they went immediately to the safe house on Christian Street. When they called to report that they were in the house, Youkoumian went to his office to prepare new shipments which they would take back with them the next day on the morning non-stop flight to Qatar.

Some large contributions from various Islamic organizations in the U.S. had arrived at the diamond store and they had been used to purchase over 2,000 carats of diamonds from different sources. Youkoumian divided the jewels into two roughly equal parts and placed them in two of the group's special zip lock bags. He placed the bags in his briefcase, informed his store manager that he would be out for a short time, and started to walk to Christian Street and the group's safe house.

As he walked, he thought about the city he was walking through. Philadelphia was a sinful city. The shameless behavior of women, the lack of respect for religious and spiritual concerns, the unending quest for more and more material goods was certainly an ungodly ambiance in which to live. The sole factor that made living tolerable in such a morally bankrupt atmosphere was the consolation that he was, on good authority, performing the will of Allah by his activities.

Reaching the safe house, he greeted the two new couriers. Since this was their first trip, he decided he should make sure they understood the gravity of being a courier. As was usual, the first thing the couriers had done, upon arrival, was to turn on the internet connected computer kept in the house, selecting porn sites that previous couriers had informed them about. Youkoumian noticed the sites selected featured Muslim looking women in completely subservient roles.

"Turn off that trash while I am here," he ordered. The couriers were not happy about it but did obey his command. "You would both be better off watching TV or western movies to improve your English skills." The men did not respond to this.

"Show me the H1-B visas and your passports." Both men produced their visas and passports readily. To his eye, the pictures on the visas did not match the passport pictures, and no picture looked much like the men who were using them.

Youkoumian asked, "It is hard to believe you had no problems coming through immigration with these."

"The officers barely looked at them. We all look alike to the Crusaders."

Youkoumian himself did not label the people of the West as Crusaders. After years in the country, he was convinced that Westerners were not interested enough in principles to sacrifice any of their comforts to enlist in a cause like a Crusade. The present danger to Islam did not come from deeply felt religious convictions but arose from an unthinking and mindless people that, while pursuing selfish lusts and hungers, trampled on the established customs and beliefs of right-thinking people everywhere.

Youkoumian returned the documents with instructions. "Always make sure that when presenting them the visas match the passport. If they don't, some agent might notice and investigate in more detail."

"We always check each other's papers before we board and before we go through immigration controls."

"That is well. You should continue doing that." Youkoumian produced the zip lock bags of diamonds and gave one to each man. "You of course, are aware that both of you are responsible for the safe delivery of both bags to headquarters."

They indicated assent to this, even though the implications of this were that they were not individually trusted to deliver the bags as instructed. Youkoumian then produced an airline envelope for each courier "Here are your tickets for tomorrow morning's Qatar airways flight to Doha. I wish you a safe journey."

Walking back to the store, Youkoumian wondered if either man would ever try to use the contents of his bag for himself. Probably not, for each of them was aware of the ruthlessness of the members of the group. An unsuccessful attempt to steal from the bags would be unpleasant for the one trying to do it. And for his partner.

Chapter 10

Later, when Hampton and Jennifer were eating breakfast at Sandy's Diner at 24th and Spruce, his thoughts about her comments on dimensions finally came out. He asked for some clarification.

"Let's talk about it while we walk back." Jennifer got up, gave him her half of the check, and started out of the diner. Hampton added his share, paid Sandy, and they started walking back to campus.

Jennifer studied his face as they passed in and out of the dappled shade of the tree lined streets. "It's simple. In my dimension, some physicists ran with the multiple dimension hypothesis and came up with a practical device to transfer between them. I was a grad student there and volunteered to be the one to travel."

Hampton looked at her. "And you did this without having a guarantee that you could return? I may not be so smart but even I've seen the cartoons about the guy who took his machine back in time and then couldn't find an electric outlet when he wanted to return."

"This isn't time travel, just transposition between alternate dimensional universes, all of which started with the big bang, and all of which are pretty much at the same level of development. My professors were convinced that any dimension to which we transferred would have developed the equipment to allow me to travel back."

"And clearly they were wrong."

Jennifer frowned. "Yes, it appears that not all of the dimensions are identical in development. Probably some difference in the sixth decimal place means that dimensional travel hasn't been developed here yet. But I know enough to put together a device that will allow me to return. And that's why I need your help."

"But why me?" asked Hampton. "Why not go to the head of the department and get a lot of people working on it."

Jennifer stopped short. "Yes, that would really work well, wouldn't it?" she said sarcastically. "Your first reaction was that I was nuts, but you at least have a mind open enough that you can consider the idea. If I went to one of the professors, they would have me on medical leave of absence in a heartbeat."

Hampton stopped and turned to look at her. He shook his head helplessly. "Is there any way you can provide some evidence of your being from another dimension? Did anything make the transition with you? Do you know stuff from your place that we don't have? If you had something like that they would have to consider it."

Not wanting to have to show something that she didn't have, Jennifer improvised on her feet. "No, nothing comes across except living tissue. You make the transfer naked. And get that leer off your face. You're just like every other male in both dimensions."

"I can't help thinking" muttered Hampton, "that there are a lot of coincidences if there are multiple dimension universes and you came from a different one. I mean I can testify that physiologically you're the same as people here, you speak American English, and you are acclimated to living here. If you are from a different dimension, what's different about it?"

Jennifer looked carefully at him. She had an answer for this as part of her plan. "Well, for one thing, where I came from, the South won the Civil War." She waited for a reaction which was not long in coming.

"And just how the heck did that happen?"

"Basically, by refusing to give up. Everyone who writes about the Civil War here speculates on how the South might have won by doing things slightly differently in one battle or another. I saw a book recently that claimed that Picket's Charge at Gettysburg was a stroke of genius on the part of Lee which could have won the war. Others claim the South could have won by emphasizing a different aspect of strategy. Or concentrating their forces better. But in my dimension, they won, despite being inferior in manpower, resources, manufacturing, and transport capability, like almost every other underdog in history has won: by not giving up. They gave up trying to beat the North in pitched formal battles and began to rely on guerrilla tactics ... not unlike those used in the Revolutionary War against the British. Eventually, the North decided it wasn't worth the cost and walked away, leaving the CSA to itself."

Hampton thought about it. "Let me guess, in your dimension you were from the South."

"That's right. I was at the University of Virginia at Charlottesville. The premier location for Physics research in North America."

"I guess the South winning had a big effect on subsequent history. I mean, are there still slaves?"

"No, of course not! The CSA abolished slavery a year before Brazil. And my dimension is close to this one. In every universe, there's a natural equilibrium point, like a saddle point, that damps out changes and moves every dimension to its most probable state. In general, they are all expected to be quite similar at any point in time. That's why my professors expected me to be able to find the necessary equipment in this dimension to return."

"And what kind of equipment do you need?"

"Most of it is electronics, both standard and state of the art here. But there's one component that's going to be the hardest."

Hampton smiled. "A flux capacitor?"

"Very funny. No, we need 10,000 carats of brilliant cut, high-quality diamonds."

Hampton looked at her blankly. "10,000 carats of diamonds."

"Brilliant cut, flawless, grade VVS1 or better, and color D." Jennifer coolly waited for him to catch up. "You have questions?"

"I don't know where to start", said Hampton. "Why do you need so many diamonds? What do they have to do with dimensions? Where could we possibly get so many?"

"Whoever we get them from will get them back. They're not consumed or harmed by the machine. We just need to convince someone to lend us the diamonds for a short time. They're the basic part of the machine that makes the transformation. Once we have them it's relatively straightforward to assemble them properly. It needs to be done with precision but I've watched you in the lab. I can see that it's something you could handle without any problems."

"I'm glad you have such confidence in me", said Hampton. "Now we only need to find someone with enough faith to trust us with about ten million dollars' worth of diamonds. I sincerely doubt that the University Physics Department would pass a purchase order for 10,000 carats of diamonds."

"The only place to get them is from someone in the business. Somehow we need to develop a connection with someone who deals in diamonds."

"And why do we need these again?"

Jennifer gave him a look. Hampton hoped it was a fond look. She said, "Do you think you would understand the theory behind the whole thing?"

"Well, I would at least like to get an inkling of the process. If I work at it long enough and ask enough questions about it, I can usually get a pretty good feel for the way things work."

"All right", said Jennifer. "It all stems from string theory."

"I've heard of that. Developed by a consortium of cats, I believe."

Jennifer gave him a pained look. "Very funny. OK, what's your understanding of it?"

Hampton thought about it, not wanting to appear even more of a dolt than she now thought him. He wanted to give at least a coherent word description. "Up until not long ago, Physics has explained things by simplifying components to particles... basically points. And a point has zero dimensions. Then someone had the bright idea to speculate about strings... which are one dimensional. So, they can vibrate, like a guitar string. So, the speculation is that a one-dimensional object can have changes relative to itself, unlike a point. Reality, at the most fundamental level, below atoms, below electrons and neutrons, below quarks and all of that, consists of small vibrating strings. That part is okay, but somehow the math needed to describe strings depends on there being six or seven extra dimensions. I mean six or seven more that the familiar ones of length, breadth, depth, and time. We never experience them because our senses are only set up to perceive the traditional four dimensions.

Using the math they use, and making some assumptions about the extra dimensions, the theorists can derive equations for the fundamental forces of the universe: gravity, electromagnetism, the strong force, and the weak force. It sort of provides a theory of everything."

He thought a little, decided he couldn't add anymore because he didn't know any more, and asked, "How's that?"

"Pretty good for someone who's highest progress in Physics was a C in high school."

"I should never have told you that. Now you think I'm a complete box of rocks."

"Sweetie, I knew what you were before you told me about your high school. I didn't hook up with you for your mind. For our machine, the important part of string theory is the size of the extra dimensions. The strings, if they do have some physical reality, need to be of a size that's so small that no one has observed them in any current high energy experiments."

"Yeah, I remember that. Strings have to be smaller than cm."

"For the same reason, the extra dimensions have to be smaller than that as well. And that's where our machine comes in. We have to stretch one of the dimensions to the next higher state and then one of the three ordinary dimensions in this set will collapse, leaving us in the alternate dimension."

Hampton shook his head. "I don't understand any of that, but I can accept it. How do you stretch a dimension?"

Jennifer smiled. "That's where the diamonds come in. The speed of light is a constant but light slows down when going through materials. And it slows down more in materials with a higher refractive index. And what substance has the highest known refractive index?"

"It's right on the tip of my tongue, but I can't quite get it."

"Idiot, you don't know and I don't expect you to. It's diamond. If you slow a phased coherent laser beam passing through diamonds enough it affects the dimensional stability, and bingo, the next dimension."

Hampton smiled. "Yes, it's quite obvious when you think about it."

She bopped him upside his head.

Chapter 11

Hampton was not stupid, even though he didn't mind people considering him slow. As many before him had found, being underestimated had distinct advantages. And sometimes big benefits. He took his time thinking about any situation or problem and tried, to the best of his abilities, to develop more information about it. In fact, despite lack of professional credentials, it could be said that he approached problems using the scientific method.

The problem of the diamonds occupied him as he and Jennifer took the suburban commuter train to the small town where the next meeting of the 71st VA. was being held. After considering many approaches, it appeared to him that the only way to get a loan of many diamonds was through a jeweler. And the only jeweler he had even a passing acquaintance with was Youkoumian. It amused him to think about a conversational approach to the topic.

"Say, Mr. Youkoumian, I happen to have a girlfriend who's a traveler from another dimension and she'd like to borrow 10,000 carats of diamonds so that she can get back home."

Mr. Youkoumian would smile politely. "Hampton, that is most interesting. What period is your girlfriend from, perhaps the future? Perhaps she might provide us with profitable insights into business matters that will develop?"

"Well actually, she's from a parallel dimension in which the South won the Civil War. She doesn't have any knowledge of what's going to happen in this dimension in the future."

"That is indeed most fascinating. Perhaps she can give us a talk at the 71st about how it happened that the South was victorious."

Hampton shook his head over the scenario he imagined. Still, Jennifer wanted to meet Youkoumian, presumably because he was a jeweler with access to diamonds. And Youkoumian had urged him to invite Jennifer to a meeting of the 71st, so perhaps there might be an opportunity for them to talk in private.

As Hampton and Jennifer entered the tavern back room they joined the 71st VA. Colonel Youkoumian's group consisted almost entirely of men. Women were not prohibited, and in fact were always welcomed. There were a few wives and girlfriends which occasionally participated in the re-enactments as camp followers, but their roles tended toward cooking and washing. Since they were doing most of this in their relationships with the male members of the group anyway, repeating these chores in the realistically uncomfortable setting of the 1860's was not an attractive prospect.

Hampton recognized George Bailey, and, unusually, a female who seemed to have no prior connection with any of the males in the outfit. Hampton was informed that her name was Gillian Andrews.

Of course, after the meeting most of the members were attracted to her and Jennifer. George and Hampton observed the gravitational field from a distance. A little like planets orbiting binary stars, thought Hampton.

George shook his head ruefully. "If I'd known what a babe magnet this group was, I'd have joined a long time ago."

Hampton said. "Gillian is quite attractive, but during my time here, she's the first unattached women to ever show up."

"Your babe, Jennifer, is no slouch either."

"I don't think she would appreciate being called my 'babe', but she *is* quite gorgeous and smart to boot," said Hampton.

George shook his head, "Not a good combination. What you want is drop dead beautiful alright, but not smart."

"Jennifer is definitely smarter than I am."

"George kept shaking his head. "My friend, you rate yourself too low. You are far too humble." He looked over toward Jennifer who was now talking with Youkoumian. "Although I could pretend to be humble for some of that, too."

Hampton thought George was something of a hound, but decided arguing with him would not be profitable for either side. He wondered how Jennifer was doing with the Colonel. George took the opportunity of the cessation of their chat to wander off toward Gillian as well.

Inserting himself into the swarm, George introduced himself to the attractive young woman.

"George Bailey, I'm new in the group like you."

Gillian shook his hand, "Gillian Andrews. Do you live around here?"

"No, I both work and live in Center City."

"Same here, I work in insurance and live in SOSO."

"SOSO?"

"South of South Street, or in my case, South of West South Street. 'SOW-SO' "

"Not a flattering designation for such a pretty woman", said George.

Gillian looked him over. "I appreciate the compliment. But the more immediate question is, are you already married, in a relationship, or otherwise committed?"

George laughed. "I can imagine how many married guys are hitting on you in this group. Let me apologize for them and assure you I'm just being friendly, not hitting on you, and currently not attached to anyone." He took her arm and guided her away from the swarm. He gave her his most sincere smile.

"OK, that's a good start", said Gillian, "have you talked to her?" She nodded toward Jennifer.

George took a swig from his bottle. "Her name's Jennifer Collins. You two are definitely in the same league, but she came with Hampton, the thin guy over there."

"And I suppose the unwritten male code involves no poaching on other guys' property."

"Well, women are not property, but it's not something one would do without considerable motivation."

Gillian checked out Hampton. "He's kinda cute. I take it he's unattached. What's his role with this group?"

George looked her over. "Apparently, he looks after the black powder supply for the regiment."

Gillian smiled and said, "Interesting." Hampton was almost certainly a good person with which to begin her investigation. "At least he looks appropriately underfed for a Confederate organization."

George raised his eyebrows, "So, no female code about poaching guys from other women?"

Gillian smiled also. "As far as we're concerned, all's fair in love and politics." Gillian wasn't sure whether she subscribed completely to that tenet. So far, she had not encountered a guy who was both committed to someone else and worthy of stealing. She thought she probably would never be the 'other woman' but was honest enough with herself to admit that such a situation could arise. "He looks a little forlorn over there."

George considered her eyes. "A little maternal instinct kicking in there?"

Gillian looked right back at him, and thought 'he's certainly not afraid to speak his mind'. And his whole affect was relaxed and as upscale as his clothes and shoes. He could be a possibility.

George said, "Scratch that, dumb thing to say. Come on over, I'll introduce you to Hampton directly."

From the corner of her eye, Jennifer noted George and the new attractive girl walking over to Hampton, but she returned her attention to talking with Youkoumian.

"Hampton, Gillian would like to talk to you," said George.

Gillian gave George a miffed look, and returned to look at Hampton. "I can imagine you as a Confederate soldier. All you need is a slouch hat and a blanket roll."

"That pretty much describes my uniform for re-enactments", said Hampton. "I can't afford a rifle."

"And I understand you're in charge of the powder supply. Isn't that dangerous?"

Hampton rather liked this young woman with the short blond hair and trim figure. "Not if you're careful. The powder is kept in small drums which can be sealed tight with rings. And they have desiccant inside to take care of moisture. The only real danger from powder is an open flame. And there aren't too many of those around. Nobody smokes anymore."

"Well, this looks like a cozy group", said Jennifer as she joined them, apparently finished with Youkoumian. Hampton got the flinty stare. But I haven't done anything, he thought. She couldn't possibly be mad at me. Besides, why would I spoil such a good thing?

Jennifer turned her attention to Gillian. "Hi Gillian, I'm Jennifer Collins. Can I rescue you from these overloaded male chromosome bearers? I think this regiment can get a little pesky around unattached females. Especially attractive ones."

Gillian checked out George and Hampton. "I think I'm pretty safe with these two. But thanks for the thought."

Jennifer took Gillian's arm. "I need to take a pee. Come on with me to the john."

Hampton watched them walk away. It reminded him of what Oscar Wilde had suggested in "The Importance of Being Earnest". Two attractive women could begin by despising each other and later wind up calling each other sisters. But only after they called each other a lot of other names first. He rather thought that might be the next thing to happen.

Meanwhile, George Bailey brought up the subject of Youkoumian with Hampton. "You seem to be quite in with the Colonel", said George. "Both you and your girlfriend."

"Mr. Youkoumian may be able help us with a special .... Physics project", said Hampton.

"I wouldn't think he would have much to contribute to a scientific experiment", said George.

"He may help us out with some of the special materials we need", said Hampton. "Stuff we can't get through normal channels at U of P."

"Interesting" said George. "And this experiment is being conducted at your Labs?"

Hampton smiled ruefully. "That's another one of the problems. Because of the confidential nature of Jennifer's work, I think we probably will need to find a private space where we could set up."

"And does this experiment involve anything like the black powder you supervise for the 71st?"

"Oh no, just lasers and ...optical equipment and materials."

"Interesting" said George again. "And how much space would you need?"

"Not really that much. A space of about fifteen by fifteen would probably do it. If it's private."

George smiled and said. "You know, I might be able to help you. Property management is usually boring but it does give you temporary access to a lot of spaces."

Hampton cocked his head. "That *would* be helpful," he said.

George said, "Let me check it out and I'll get back to you later this week.

In the john, Jennifer paused for a perceptible heart beat and then said, "Sorry, I never got a chance to welcome you into the group." She gave Gillian her glorious smile and offered her hand. "I'm Jennifer. I'm a Physics grad student at the University of Pennsylvania."

"Thanks, I'm Gillian. I work in insurance in Center City. It's good to see another woman amongst these married geeks."

Jennifer smiled at that. "They seem to be pretty harmless, although geeks is a pretty good term for them. They tend to get somewhat technical with their make-believe soldiering."

"That George seemed a little above average, not a geek or always on the make," commented Gillian.

"This was the first time I met him, so I really can't say."

"I would suppose Hampton is also not so bad. I understand you and he are an item."

Jennifer turned to check her hair in the mirror. Turning back, she presented a wistful smile and said "Well, he is cute and ferociously firm and hard, but a little short in the smarts department."

"He seems like quite a babe and quite sweet. I could get interested in him," Gillian said as she watched Jennifer carefully.

She was interested in how Jennifer would react to her showing interest in Hampton. It was already clear to her that Jennifer was quite confident and self-assured. Clearly a woman who controlled situations rather than reacted to them.

Jennifer returned the careful look. "Be my guest," said Jennifer. "However, I'd appreciate it if you didn't distract him too much for a while. We're working on a Physics project together." Although Jennifer was smiling at her, Gillian clearly got the message that Hampton was her property.

"Oh boy", said Gillian, "I nearly flunked Physics in high school. Is what you're doing anything I could understand?"

Jennifer laughed. "Well if you almost flunked Physics, it would be hard."

"I can accept that "said Gillian. "Perhaps I could see it sometime just to get a flavor."

Jennifer shook her head. "We haven't started yet. But when we get it going you're welcome to come and see it."

'Yeah,' thought Gillian, 'like that's going to happen. I have zero chance of learning anything through you. You are a closed book. And you basically would never allow Hampton to be alone enough to talk to me. So, trying to get details out of him seems like a lost cause.' She would just have to be alert for other opportunities to learn more about the anomalies associated with the 71st VA.

As Gillian and Jennifer exited the women's room, they saw the gathering was about to break up. Gillian said goodbye and went out to the parking lot for her car.

George offered to give Jennifer and Hampton a ride back to Center City, but they declined since the suburban train was much more convenient, allowing them to get off at 30th street station, and from there it was a pleasant walk along the Schuylkill River Pathway to Hampton's apartment.

For her part, as Gillian drove back to center city, she was thinking about the situation she had just left. Most of it was straightforward. A bunch of white suburbanites indulging in make believe about being in the Civil War. Still, there were interesting anomalies: the connection between Hampton and Jennifer was an obvious one. And so was the connection between Youkoumian and Hampton and Jennifer. What were they all doing together? What could motivate them?

Chapter 12

After the meeting, Jennifer and Hampton walked to the commuter station to catch a train back into Center City.

Jennifer was thinking about her progress toward getting her hands on a considerable quantity of diamonds. But not for use in a machine for travelling between dimensions. She had other plans for the jewels.

Jennifer *was* born in Costa Rica, but her actual name was Jennifer Lopez. She had had the advantages of being raised in a well-off family. In the top one percent of Costa Rica. Her father was a deputy secretary in the government's Ministerio de Comercio Exterior. More importantly, her mother was an assistant professor of Physics and Math at the Universidad Latinoamericana de Ciencia y Tecnología. Jennifer thought her mother was the smartest person she had ever met. Yet, her mother never achieved a position more notable than assistant professor. Despite the lack of recognition, her mother was not bitter. She was resigned to the clear fact that Costa Rica, like many Latin American countries, was run on patriarchal principles. Women had more of a glass ceiling there than the one that existed in the U.S. As Jennifer's mother put it, the only way a woman could get respect in Costa Rica was to be independently filthy rich. Jennifer was working on her own plan to accomplish this.

Hampton was waiting for Jennifer to tell him about her talk with Youkoumian.

She seemed to be musing about it and finally spoke up.

"Okay, I interested him enough so that he'll see me privately in his store. Five PM tomorrow afternoon."

"You're amazing. Did you ever have your IQ tested in your dimension?"

She bopped him upside the head. Which also seemed to be a recurring part of their relationship. "You are such a nerd, concentrating on numbers all the time. Listen to what I'm saying about Youkoumian."

"How did you get his interest?" asked Hampton, rubbing his head. "You didn't get into discussing dimensions, did you?"

"Not yet. Eventually I'll have to explain dimensions to him to justify borrowing his diamonds but I'd rather do it privately in his office tomorrow. The fewer people that learn where I came from the better." Jennifer looked at Hampton. "Basically, I just suggested to him that I have quite a lot of knowledge about the Civil War including some secret things in which he would be interested. Apparently, it was mysterious enough to intrigue him and he agreed to see me tomorrow."

She put her hand in his. This was a rather new and endearing gesture on her part. Hampton was pleased at this sign of affection. For a short period.

"Now what about that Gillian you were flirting with?" she said, digging her nails into his hand.

"Owwie," he said. "I swear I wasn't flirting with her." He looked at his palm. She'd drawn blood.

"Oh, really. And you're telling me you didn't think about getting her in the sack?"

Busted, thought Hampton. How could she know what I was thinking? But of course, she was smart enough to know what most young men were usually thinking about whether they wanted to or not.

As usual, Hampton took a little too long to respond. "Of course not! I'm just glad you like being with me. You're much more attractive than she is and I'm sure you are much more exciting to be around. I would be pretty stupid to throw that away." He put on his most sincere look and plaintively looked at her.

"Don't give me those puppy dog eyes." Jennifer stared at him. "And don't underestimate your stupidity, sweetie."

Hampton was finally beginning to accept that not only was she smarter than him, and could out argue him, she had total control of their relationship. How did that happen? In the past, while he had never wanted to control a relationship, at least he felt they were more equal, more give and take. In this one, he was outclassed.

He still was not convinced that she was from a parallel dimension. The whole idea of being able to easily transit between them did not make much sense to his limited knowledge of Physics. But then, most of what he read about modern Physics did not make a lot of sense to him. Without any easy way to discern the truth, it was simpler to accept what she said, especially considering the benefits. What possible reason could she have to make up the story?

It seemed remarkable to Hampton that she had convinced Youkoumian to meet with her. He himself, could not imagine how to bring up the subject without sounding demented. In addition to everything else, she could take charge of any situation she found herself in and become the alpha dog. Hampton had never particularly wanted to be the alpha dog, but it was disconcerting to have his beta status pointed out so obviously and so often.

Jennifer looked over at him. "Oh, come on, don't look so hurt. You know I'm not mad at you. I just got a little jealous when that Gillian started hitting on you."

Gillian was hitting on me, thought Hampton. Why didn't I catch that? Probably because I'm 100 % involved with Jennifer. Gillian probably had some reason of her own for showing interest in me. But Hampton could not imagine what that reason could be.

Jennifer said, "And I depend on you for the tech work to get me back to my dimension. I don't want to lose that." Jennifer refrained from informing him about what she intended to do with the diamonds. She didn't think he was smart enough, certainly not smart enough to appreciate the value 10,000 carats of diamonds could provide.

Well, that's something, thought Hampton. At least she needs me for something more than sex. "So, what happens when you do get back? I'll still be here and never see you again." He sounded rather wistful about that.

"Don't worry, sweetie, I'm going to take you with me when I go. You have valuable assets other than your mechanical ability", said Jennifer. She was willing to say anything that would keep him working on the prototype.

Hampton wryly said, "Am I correct in assuming you value a particular one of my mechanical assets, in addition to plain technical skill?"

"It's the whole combination that I find attractive." She gave him a fond look. "And you're going to prove it when we get back to your apartment." Jennifer thought he was useful in other ways than assembling equipment.

"You make me sound like a 'boy toy' "

Amused, Jennifer checked him out. "Every guy I've ever known has secretly wanted to be a boy toy. It's the hidden desire of all males to excite uncontrollable lust in their women." She smiled at him affectionately. "I sometimes lust after you but not uncontrollably."

Hampton could well believe that Jennifer was always in total control of herself in any situation that she was in.

It would in fact be interesting to have a female as hot for getting me in the sack as I am for her, thought Hampton. It would be unusual and somewhat nice to have a girl friend who couldn't keep her hands off me. But would it become annoying? As something that had never happened to him, Hampton decided to put off any thought about that aspect. After all, it's clear that Jennifer had complete control of both him and their relationship. What more did he need?

But she's right about guys and women, thought Hampton. What guy would not be flattered by a female treating him like her prized sexual possession? The uniqueness of that would probably appeal to a lot of guys. It certainly did to him. Still, it might get a little impersonal without some genuine human affection. Perhaps that's what women were talking about when they discussed guys who were after just one thing.

As if she knew exactly what he was thinking, and she probably did, she put her arm through his and drew him closer. "Come on, you know I'm right, you totally love me, don't you." It was not a question. She knew she owned him. He would do anything she asked.

Hampton thought about it for a few seconds. She was right, he was enthralled by her. Maybe he was just totally in lust for her, but he didn't feel capable of defining the difference, if any. There was no sense denying it. Hampton admitted it. "Yes, you are correct."

A city bound train was just pulling into the station as they arrived there.

"And I love you. So, let's get back to your apartment."

Chapter 13

The next day at her office, Gillian was thinking intently about her first foray into the 71st VA. As expected, most of the members appeared to be just overweight suburban guys looking for a way to get away from their families for short breaks.

The men ranged in age from 20 to 50, and had two outstanding characteristics: they had both the interest and resources to devote to the hobby. Of the two, resources were a bigger factor, since an authentic reproduction of a Civil War rifle could cost as much as $2500. The 71st 's weapons were reproductions of U.S. government model Springfields and the group liked to joke with Northern re-enactors that they equipped themselves from the discards of Yankees fleeing from "Southron victories". Uniforms for the 71st were much less expensive than for their Northern friends. Confederates, while nominally wearing Grey, in practice wore clothes common to farmers and workers in the mid-1800s in the South.

But there was something decidedly out of kilter in seeing the swarthy Colonel, Youkoumian, talking intently with the drop dead gorgeous grad student, Jennifer, who was obviously sharp.

The walking refugee, Hampton, clearly didn't fit in with the suburban types either. It would be worth her while to talk to him some about the regiment's black powder supply. The problem was Jennifer, who seemed to take quite an ownership approach to Hampton. She claimed to think he wasn't too smart and tried to seem unconcerned about Gillian talking to him. But Gillian knew it would be difficult to find out more about what was going on with their project when she was around. And she seemed to always be around Hampton, at least at meetings.

Gillian was not buying Jennifer's casual acceptance of her, Gillian's', interest in Hampton. Jennifer's whole affect projected a proprietary aspect in Hampton. Which was OK, because he was kind of cute and appealing in a lanky kind of way. She had a right to her boyfriend. But Gillian was certain that Jennifer would completely block any attempts to get any information out of Hampton. Why? There was something a little strange there. She talked about him as if he was of limited intelligence, but Gillian did not think a stupid person could work himself into a position in the Physics Department of the University of Pennsylvania.

And the attractive young guy, George Bailey, was also an anomaly. He claimed to be unattached and showed up on the web as living somewhere in center city. But where he worked was not apparent. He also seemed to be close mouthed. Was it possible that he was clandestine? An op of some kind for some criminal organization? That would make the whole thing much more interesting.

However, it was not apparent why any criminal group would take a lot of interest in a Civil War re-enactment gathering. Except, of course, for the black powder. That's what had caught her attention initially and there was no reason someone criminal might not have noticed it as well. She concluded that considering it further was a worthwhile project. It didn't look like she would get much out of Hampton with Jennifer so protective of him. That left George Bailey as a possible point of contact to learn more.

She decided to consult Gloria about it. She walked down the hall to Gloria's office and tapped lightly on the door frame.

As was usual, Gloria smiled as soon as she saw Gillian in the doorway. "Come on in, dear, and take a seat." Gillian did so. Gloria leaned back a little in her swivel chair. "So, what's up?"

"I'm still working into the Confederate re-enactor's group. I went to a meeting last night and found out some interesting stuff. I haven't told anyone in the group about my connection to ATF, but I have talked with the guy who takes care of the black powder supply. The problem is his girlfriend who is protective of him. She's a graduate student in Physics at the University and apparently brilliant. It's clear she doesn't want me to talk to him."

Gloria thought about it. "So, she has some motivation for keeping their connection secret."

"It certainly seems that way. Apparently, she, the black powder guy, and the head of the reenactor group have some kind of secret project going on. There is a single guy in the group who seems to be friendly with both the black powder guy and the women grad student. I'm wondering if it's a good idea to cultivate him as a source to what they are doing with this project of theirs,

"Well, if anyone can 'cultivate' a guy it's you. If you work on him, I'm sure you could have him fetching sticks for you in no time."

"That's kind of the encouragement I was looking for," said Gillian.

"If anyone can do it, you can, girl. So, is this single guy nice?"
"Nice?"
"You know, not a jerk."

"Well, he's a little more human than most of them. He seems to be a little more sensitive."

"Ah ha", said Gloria, "do I detect a glimmer of interest there?"

Gillian felt her cheeks reddening a little. "He *is* kind of cute."

Gloria smiled knowingly, "OK, keep on it, and keep me posted on what you learn. And keep me posted on your new boyfriend."

Gillian thanked Gloria and thought about it as she walked back to her office. She did get a kind of tingly sensation when she thought about George. He *was* cute, and expressed good attitudes about women. She wondered if that was an act or if he was sincere.

In retrospect, it appeared to her that she perhaps had sought out Gloria mainly to get someone's approval to see George again. Which didn't seem at all like herself. Apparently, she needed outside affirmation to acknowledge to herself that she liked someone. It seemed rather a strange deviation from her naturally rational decision making.

Despite that, the more she thought, the more it seemed that it was rational to think that her path to finding out more about the 71st VA. and its black powder was currently limited to working through George Bailey.

Why exactly was he hanging around the re-enactors group? It would be interesting to find out. It seemed essential to make further contact with George.

Gillian recognized George as a guy primarily interested in getting into her panties. That didn't bother her. With an ironic smile, she admitted to herself she might even enjoy it. At any rate, she knew she could handle him. His attraction to her would probably be enough for her to arrange a date for a drink with him.

Chapter 14

George knocked on the SAC's open office door.

Dan looked up and grimaced. "What now?"

"New developments with the Civil War confederates" said George as he took a chair. "I've been going to their meetings and interacting with some of them and getting some tantalizing hints about their activity."

"That's surprising," said Dan. "I wouldn't have expected them to be talkative with an FBI agent."

"They don't know I'm with the bureau. It seemed to me I could find out more if I didn't announce that. As far as they're concerned, I'm in property management in Center City."

"That should discourage them trying to find out more about you," said Dan.

"The only thing better would be insurance, and I don't know enough about that to fake it. Some of the guys in the regiment actually work in insurance in Center City."

"No wonder they look for some amusement in a Civil War group. So, what are the new developments?"

"Some of them, including the head of the group, are working on a special project involving some high-power Physics. The head of the group is an Armenian who has a jewelry store on Sansom St. The others are a guy who's a Physics lab tech and a female who's apparently the smartest grad student in the Physics Department at the U of P.

"U of P?"

"University of Pennsylvania, across the river."

"And this is our concern, how?"

"Apparently, it involves a lot of electronics, optics, and lasers and it's so hush hush that they need a secure secret place to work on it." said George.

"I don't get it", said Dan. "Why don't they just use space at the university?"

George said. "That's a question they seem to be evading. Which is an indicator, I think."

Dan thought about it. "So, something they don't want made public at the University but want kept secret in some private space."

"Yes, that seems to be the case."

"So, what could they be concerned about?"

George shrugged, "Well we've got a guy who deals with black powder for the reenactor group. He's a lab tech, so we can expect he's good at building things and putting them together. Then there's the brilliant grad student, the female, who is up on electronics and other advanced stuff. And finally, a Middle Eastern type, the Armenian, who is also involved. What's your conclusion?"

Dan thought about it. "Armenia is somewhere in the Middle East, right?"

George nodded, patiently waiting for Dan to make connections for himself.

"Are these Armenians Moslems?"

"I think they're mainly Christian, but nowadays that's no guarantee of their peaceful intentions."

Dan nodded sagely. "I see your point. It does sound suspicious. So, what are your ideas about how what we should do?"

George was ready. "I'm already able to talk with them at their meetings. I'm thinking I could be able to get more inside information on these special members if I can supply them with the space they need. It would give me special access to anything they are doing."

The SAC frowned. "Why would they think you could supply space?"

Inwardly George grimaced. This could be a slow process. "Like I said, I've sort of intimated that I'm in center city property management as a cover. I certainly didn't want to let them know I was in the FBI."

Dan nodded, "Ok, I see that point. I see why your property management cover could make you a plausible source of space. That makes sense, but where would you get the space from?"

George had a ready answer. "We still have access to the loft we took over after the Meth sting with DEA last year. The lease holders are not going to be able to object to what we do with it for a long time. I can make believe I manage space, like that loft, which could be made available for a short period."

"And you're sure it would be a short period?"

"The lab tech indicated the project could be completed in a matter of weeks."

The SAC twirled in his chair and pondered it. "Well it is an anomaly. What ethnicity are these people from the university? They're not Middle Eastern, are they?"

"No, the ones at the university seem to be typical Americans."

"No connection with Islam?"

"None of them appears to have any interest in any religion. I checked the social media and they don't even use it."

Dan thought about it "That's also unusual for young people. Well, it would be more interesting if there were some more threads in the right direction."

George repeated himself again, "The Lab tech is the custodian for the regiment's black powder supply. That in itself is interesting."

Dan said, "I guess you're right. Could someone have an interest in the group to get their hands on some powder?"

"As far as I can tell, the only guy with Middle East connections is the Colonel of the regiment, Youkoumian. He's some kind of Armenian which is somewhere in the Middle East. And he's involved in this project also."

Dan said, "You'd think that as head of the group, he could get all the powder he wanted himself."

George thought he finally needed to explicitly suggest the connections he wanted Dan to make. "Maybe it involves using the electronics expertise of the Lab Tech and the grad student." George thought letting the SAC to gradually come to his own conclusions would produce better support for what he wanted to do. But he was a little irritated that it was taking so long.

Dan nodded, "Yeah, that makes sense. With electronics, it could have something to do with a bomb or a remote-controlled device. I think you're on to something. Go ahead and set it up. It doesn't cost us anything and doesn't seem to have any downside.

"Now what about those Phillies? They actually won a tight game last night!"

George escaped after five minutes of boring baseball talk. The price he paid for having a boss who liked the game. At least he was now ready to contact Hampton with the offer of a place.

Chapter 15

Most Americans can at least recognize the initials of the most common federal investigative agencies ... FBI, CIA, ATF, DEA, among many. Few would consider the acronym DHS as part of this group. Probably they would think this stands for the Department of Human Services.

In actuality, DHS now usually stands for Department of Homeland Security, and it encompasses 24 distinct entities ranging from the Coast Guard to the Federal Law Enforcement Training Center. There are over 170,000 full time employees, among whom, Aban Hassad, a third generation Arab-American, was progressing swiftly in the organization.

Aban was born and raised in one of the posh New Jersey suburbs west of New York City. His father supported the family from the proceeds of a successful office supply store. The family attended a mosque in the suburb without incidents of any kind. As Aban matured, he was compared to Rudolf Valentino of 1920s silent film fame. He was as darkly handsome as Valentino, with some of the same magnetism that film star had for women of all ages. When younger, he had enjoyed the attention it provided. When he got married, his wife insisted that he tone it down around females other than her. He had complied to please her.

Aban was normally based in New York. It has a much bigger Arabic presence than Philadelphia, both in terms of resident and floating populations. Air traffic from Arabic countries was also much greater, but it was harder to discern any particular threads in such a large tangled skein of them.

In the case of Philadelphia, computer analysis of travel of Arabic speaking persons of interest showed a much greater percentage visiting Philadelphia than could logically be accounted for by either native Arabic speakers in the area or locations attractive to Arabs. Currently, it was Aban's assignment to discover why, over the last five years, there was an above average number of young Arabic speaking male nationals in Philadelphia at any given time. What was most interesting was the fact that some of these young Arabic males often travelled in pairs. Currently, this was the topic that engaged Aban's presence in Philadelphia.

In particular, in this instance, he was trying to track down the presence of two young men with Egyptian passports who entered the U.S. recently and who did so frequently. This in itself was perhaps not unusual. What did engage Abad's interest is that the persons were able to enter and depart regularly with little notice because they had H1-B visas.

The H1-B visas were instituted by the Hart-Cellar act of 1965. Once granted, they were valid for at least 6 years and sometimes longer depending on circumstances. Unlike some regular visas, there was never any problem for the individual in getting back into the U.S. even after they had left it temporarily. The basic requirement for an H1-B was to be employed by a U.S. company in a capacity that required the equivalent of a U.S. Bachelor's degree.

The visas Aban was focusing on in Philadelphia were somewhat unusual in that the employing company was a jewelry store on Philadelphia's Jewelers' Row, Youkoumian's. Aban was quite curious as to why a company selling diamonds needed to employ foreign Arabic speaking workers.

It also seemed to Abad to be a little out of the ordinary that a Bachelor's degree or equivalent was needed to work at a jewelry store. Perhaps it could be argued that the skills necessary to evaluate jewels or design settings required the equivalent knowledge of such a degree. However, could it actually be true that an American jewelry store could not find any suitable workers among the current U.S. population? Aban's superiors were also skeptical and he had been assigned to check out the situation.

As a courtesy, upon arriving in Philadelphia, Aban checked in with the Philadelphia police unit which covered the area of Jewelers' Row. At the 6th Precinct headquarters on north 11th street he presented his credentials to the lieutenant heading the detective unit and explained what he was looking for. The Philadelphia police were a little surprised that he had begun by talking with them before starting his investigation. Other federal agencies, such as the FBI, were notorious for doing whatever they wanted in local jurisdictions without any consultation at all. The result of the early contact was good feeling all around.

But Aban learned something as well. The company that sponsored the H1-Bs he was tracking was Youkoumian's Diamonds. The 6th precinct detectives were quite familiar with it and its owner. He was a well-known Armenian who was generous in subscribing to police sponsored events and other charitable activities. In general, they considered him a solid businessman in their community and were surprised to find that he needed to employ Arabic speaking employees from the Middle East.

Aban was also surprised at this anomaly. Why would an Armenian be involved with Arabic speakers? Most Armenians of course spoke Armenian. If they spoke another language it would most probably be Turkish or Russian. And most of them were Christian. It was certainly possible that there were some Armenians who were Moslems and even more could possibly be Arabic speakers. But he considered those possibilities to be vanishingly small for Armenians who were living in the US. On the other side, why would Arabic speakers find it attractive to work for an Armenian in Philadelphia? How would they even make contact to find out about employment possibilities? There might well be some simple answers for these questions. But it would probably require considerable investigation to find them. Aban intended to find those answers.

Chapter 16

Like almost all jewelry stores in large U.S. cities, Youkoumian's door was kept locked at all times. Customers were welcomed in but only after careful scrutiny. Since she appeared to be not only not a threat, but an attractive example of the affluent customers who typically purchased diamonds, the interior guard was happy to open the door for Jennifer.

The place appeared to be a typical jewelry store. Waist high glass cabinets displaying all manner of rings, and watches, and jewelry. Reasonably plush carpets. Sitting areas at desk displays where couples could look at rings together. Quite a selection of rings, bracelets, necklaces and all manner of adornments were all attractively displayed. Several obviously well to do female customers were attended to by well-dressed staff persons. One of those politely directed Jennifer back to Youkoumians office in the rear portion of the building.

He graciously welcomed her. "I am quite pleased to see you, Jennifer. Hampton has told me that you are one of the most brilliant graduate students in Physics at the University of Pennsylvania, "said Youkoumian. "Please have a seat."

"Thank you, you have a beautiful store and office," said Jennifer.

"Thank you," said Youkoumian. "We have a fairly successful business here." He had been rewarded for his services in the middle east by being made the ostensible owner of the store. These past services included a number of actions against Christians, Jews, and even Moslems in various states of the Levant. The consequences for those Christians, Jews, and Moslems usually included suffering and death. Beheadings, knifings, shootings, and other forms of mayhem were considered appropriate responses to those in the house of war.

Youkoumian was quite willing to adopt the Moslem division of the world into two houses: those who submitted and those in the house of war. Although happening in his younger days, Hassan had not hesitated at torturing, killing, and mutilating those who did not accept Mohammed as the prophet of Allah. Even those who claimed they were followers of the prophet were sometimes treated in this way if they were judged to be not sufficiently supportive of the proponents of the messenger of God.

Youkoumian cleared his throat. "Hampton has mentioned that you have quite an interest in history, just as we do in the 71st VA."

Jennifer put on her most charming smile. "That is the reason I wanted to speak with you privately. I'm not sure what Hampton has told you about me, but I do have a lot of interest in the Civil War."

"Yes, he certainly mentioned that. Also that you position yourself firmly on the side of the South."

"It's rather more than that, Mr. Youkoumian." She paused before taking the plunge. "You see, I am from another dimension in which the South won the Civil War and became independent. And I need your help to get back to it."

Youkoumian looked extremely carefully at the young woman to see if she was serious. "That is rather a difficult statement to absorb. Are you trying to tell me that you came here from the 19th century where everything is like it was 150 years ago except the South won?"

"No," said Jennifer, "time has progressed where I come from just as it has here. Time is an invariant, but different dimensions have different situations in some details. Modern physics has postulated the existence of multiple dimensions existing simultaneously. Each grouping of the possible dimensions of length, breadth, and depth constitutes in essence a different universe with a unique history and development." She waited for a reaction, but it was apparent that Youkoumian was still digesting her remarks.

Youkoumian finally responded. "I have no knowledge of Physics. The idea of different universes seems extremely hard to believe."

"Yes, I can imagine that."

Youkoumian cleared his throat. "Is there any way you can demonstrate what you are saying? Do you have any thing that could prove it?"

Jennifer shook her head. "No, only the differences between the two dimensions, such as the South winning the Civil war. I can give you other examples. There is one difference that might interest you. The Armenian Genocide of 1915 never happened in my universe."

As a Syrian, Youkoumian's tribe had once been subjects of the Ottoman Empire. Almost everyone in it, then and now, had no concern about alleged incidents that reputedly occurred 100 years ago, and most certainly were not interested in what happened to Armenians at any time. Most middle-eastern natives of Moslem countries felt the same way. Indeed, it is still a crime in Turkey to discuss the so-called genocide. The offense is described as "insulting Turkishness".

"Armenian genocide?" Youkoumian appeared briefly puzzled. And then relaxed his face. "Yes, yes, a terrible thing and a good thing that it didn't happen."

He relaxed slightly in his chair and then said. "I suppose there were even more changes in the history of the Middle East? For example, what is it like in Syria and Palestine? Did the Jews take over Palestine as they did here? Is there conflict between Arabs and Jews as there is here?"

Jennifer paused to reply carefully. It's rather strange that he was not interested in Armenians. Was it possible that he was Arabic or Jewish? She knew she would have to tread carefully to avoid alienating him. This could be the crucial point in obtaining access to the diamonds she hoped he might supply. "Ah, there is conflict between Arabs and Jews ... not on the scale of this dimension. You would appreciate the reason for that. Armenians spread throughout the region to become the insulators between ...."

Youkoumian interrupted her, "Yes, yes, quite nice, but it's hard to imagine Jews and Arabs coexisting in peace, even with Armenians separating them. Surely one group or the other has become dominant."

Jennifer paused and thought carefully about it. His interest in Arabs and Jews made her think he was either Moslem or Jewish. Which would be more likely to have Armenian antecedents, Moslem or Jew? She decided to gamble on Moslem. She said slowly, "Well, if anything, one could say that the Caliphate of Damascus exerts the most influence in the area, and its protectorate over Palestine allows everyone to exist together in relative peace."

"The Caliphate of Damascus", said Youkoumian. "Very interesting ... interesting indeed. I would like to hear more about your world. I would be most interested in learning more.

Allow me to order some coffee and you can tell me about the middle east in your dimension."

Over coffee, Jennifer related many of the developments in her dimension which differed from those in the current one. Following Youkoumian's obvious interest, she concentrated on Moslem aspects. She elaborated on the status of the Caliphate and various Arabic speaking peoples in the Middle East.

"One of the most striking contrasts," said Jennifer, "is that, after the Caliphate was established following the First World War, it became one of the most technically advanced countries in the world. Once free of the rather stultifying control of the Ottoman Turks, the way was clear for those with modern ideas and with the spirit to improve the lot of everyone in the area. The caliphate established western style technical schools and universities which helped provide the expertise to improve the economies in that region. After the Second World War, everything was ready for the boom produced by increasing world demand for petroleum. The Caliphate is the major influence in the area and one of the most influential states on the world scene." Jennifer could see him almost beaming at this revelation. She congratulated herself on her ability to make up a tale which would interest him. It looked like she could make this work!

"Fascinating," breathed the Colonel. Youkoumian did not consider himself an evil man. On the contrary, it was quite obvious, both to himself and to his most intimate associates, that he was in fact doing God's work even in the godless environment that he found himself. "Allow me to refill your cup while you tell me more."

She did, and after a time, his immediate interest appeared to be satisfied. He leaned back.

"Your experience is most interesting, Jennifer, but, since I know nothing about Physics, I do not see how I could possibly be of assistance to you."

Jennifer took a deep breath. Internally she was quite excited. She felt she had baited the hook enough. It was time set it home. "You could be of the utmost assistance, Mr. Youkoumian. You see, in order to return to my world, I need to borrow 5000 2 carat diamonds to temporarily use in a device which facilitates travel between dimensions."

"Ah, I see why you needed to speak to me, one of the larger diamond merchants. For most owners, such a request would be quite unusual. Definitely a substantial amount of capital, and not every jeweler would be able to even consider it. Even I would have to borrow from other establishments to obtain such a number."

"I'm hoping that, since it would only be a temporary loan of the diamonds, that you might be willing to entertain the idea. The device will not harm the diamonds or affect their value in any way." Jennifer could say this with great sincerity, since her plans for the diamonds depended on their remaining valuable. Especially to her. "We would take good care of them. You're familiar with Hampton, and I'm sure you would consider him trustworthy."

Youkoumian agreed. "The idea of Hampton doing anything bad with anything he was entrusted with seems most far-fetched. Still, arranging the loan of so many gems based solely on your story would be hard to justify without tangible evidence."

Jennifer thought rapidly, and without missing a beat, said "I think I can provide all of the evidence anyone would need by constructing a small-scale demonstration device. That would allow moving an object from my dimension to this one. I can do that with a loan of 250 diamonds." The idea of a prototype device that would demonstrate the possibilities of dimensional exchange was a good testimony to her ability to quickly improvise on her feet.

Youkoumian smiled slightly. "That is far more feasible. How long would it take to construct such a device?"

"I'm confident that Hampton could construct it in less than two weeks."

Youkoumian thought about it for at least a minute. During the time, which seemed agonizingly long to Jennifer, she tried to appear calm and collected. In reality, she was at a high pitch of expectation from being so close to her goal.

Youkoumian finally refocused on her. "I think that the whole idea of another world in another dimension is quite hard to understand. But it also is also intriguing. If you wish, I will look into what would be required to loan you the smaller number of diamonds for such a period."

Yes! Jennifer said internally. Jennifer's relief was palpable. She felt her hands might begin to tremble noticeably. She rose and restrained herself from giving him a hug. "That would be excellent, Mr. Youkoumian, I will be extremely grateful for your help."

Very shortly after Jennifer left, Youkoumian returned to consideration of an Islamic state in another dimension that was as economically advanced and technically proficient as western societies in this dimension. That would be an ally to have on your side! Could it be true?

He got onto the internet to email his superior, Amin al-Tunji. It was unfortunate that the code book used by both sides did not include any innocuous sentences about jewelry that could be used as code for physics or multiple dimensions. However, there were enough appropriate phrases that he could arrange a face to face meeting in two days with al-Tunji. This was much superior to attempting to have a conversation over satellite phone, which, of course was subject to so much interception and meta-data gathering.

The bigger problem, thought Youkoumian, when he was finished, was how to talk with his superior about the possibility of aid from an Islamic state in another dimension. Outlandish, yes, but perhaps a possibility in a world where western scientists seemed to be able to effortlessly produce tools to dominate Islam. If there was such a dimension, and there was a functioning caliphate there, surely, they would be motivated to help their brothers in

this dimension. At any rate, he would certainly place the idea before al-Tunji in person, get his thoughts about it, and hope that al-Tunji saw the same possibilities that were so appealing to him.

Chapter 17

George waited for Gillian at the large rectangular bar in the restaurant Devon on Rittenhouse Square. In all honesty, he thought, she picked a good place for a drink. Lots of light from the windows facing the Square, lots of trees doing spring-like things in the square, lots of wood paneling and older club-like tables and chairs around the periphery of the bar. I can imagine a Men's club like this, he thought.

So, evidently, she picked a place to make me comfortable, he mused. That's something of a change from the first time we talked. I had her pegged as the original Ice Maiden. I wonder which Gillian will show up this time.

In any case, George thought it was worth it to meet with her, primarily because she was enjoyably attractive, but also because she may have learned more about the black powder guys than he had. Especially Hampton and the Colonel.

George thought about the Colonel being in a bar like this. It seemed unlikely. It appeared Youkoumian enjoyed social-izing with the members, but drank no alcohol. No one con-sidered this a practice worthy of notice. Everyone had friends who drank too much, and some friends were virtually alco-holics. Anyone who abstained was quite understandable. And probably a good object lesson that they themselves should cut down on their consumption.

Gillian appeared as he was pondering Youkoumian.

"Hi there, sorry I'm late", she said as she took the stool next to him.

"Don't worry, that's definitely a gorgeous woman's prerogative."

Gillian smiled at him. Not the Ice Maiden this time. "You are quite the courtier this evening. An excessive compliment, deference to feminism, and correct pronunciation of 'prerogative' all in one. Most guys would have said 'girl's per-rogative'."

"Well, we're not all morons. At least, not all the time."

Gillian laughed at that.

The bartender chose that moment to approach them to ask if the lady would like a drink.

"Sweet vermouth, on the rocks please."

"Why does that give me a feeling of déjà vu?" George asked.

"One of my favorite movies", said Gillian.

"Now if I was Bill Murray, I would say mine too!"

"You have more hair than Bill Murray. Better looking, too."

Oh, my god, thought George, the thaw is in. I don't care if we ever talk about black powder, I think I've gone to heaven. He looked at her as she received her drink. Worth the effort, He thought.

The two sipped their drinks. Interestingly, they both were content to sit together for a while without the compulsion to fill in with words. George admired this self-composed and evidently competent young woman sitting next to him. Gillian broke the silence first.

"I'm interested in your take on the 71st VA." she said. "How did you find out about them?"

George was not about to reveal that he found out about the group from research at his FBI office. He saw no point in revealing his FBI status to anyone associated with the re-enactors. "I saw a notice about an encampment they were having earlier in the spring and decided it might be fun to see what one was like. It was sort of interesting how much effort they put in to try to be as authentic as possible, even to the extent of wearing heavy wool uniform replicas during hot spells. Also, they seemed like a friendly group. How about you?"

Gillian cocked her head, "Typical female urge to go where the boys are," she said. "Unfortunately, almost all of them are already attached."

'Sure', thought George, 'the idea you need to go where the boys are is completely believable. It's much more likely that you need a stick to beat them off.' "So, you're not likely to continue to go to many more meetings, I guess."

"Not necessarily", she smiled. "You're not attached, which is nice, and that guy Hampton seems kind of attractive in a home spun corn-fed kind of way. And it's interesting that Jennifer has some kind of Physics project going on with him and the Colonel."

"Yes, I heard about that. No details except the Colonel may be supplying them with special materials."

"Any indication what those would be?"

"No but the whole deal sounds pretty high end technical. Hampton mentioned lasers, optics, electronics, stuff like that."

Ah ha, thought Gillian, I did learn something from this date. She was surprised that she admitted to herself that it was a date. But George was more relaxed, easier to interact with than most of the young men she occasionally dated, and did not immediately make it obvious that his major interest was in having sex with her. Although his thoughts on that subject were usually not far below the surface.

It was kind of fun to talk with him.

Gillian smiled and said. "I wouldn't have thought that Youkoumian would be of much help with high end technical equipment."

George agreed, "I had the same thought."

"Do you suppose it has anything to do with the black powder that Hampton oversees? Could he need the Colonel's approval to get bigger quantities?"

George thought about it. "I suppose that's possible, but Hampton's tone indicated something that only Youkoumian could supply. I get the impression that Hampton has a lot of freedom of action in dealing with the black powder. I think he could order as much as they might need on his own hook. No need to involve the Colonel."

Good, thought Gillian, I'm learning more and more about the situation because of this outing. But if it doesn't involve black powder, what was it about. "So, have you seen what their project is like, what it involves?"

"No, apparently, it hasn't gotten started yet. They still need a place to set it up." George was tempted, but resisted the urge to tell Gillian about the space he was going to offer to Hampton and Jennifer. Something about Gillian suggested that she had depths and motives beyond those she spoke about. There was no need now to let her know what he was doing in detail.

Gillian said, "I asked Jennifer if I could see their project but she said it was a long way from being presentable. Also, that I probably wouldn't be able to understand it."

George said, "That seems pretty unlikely. You seem able to pick up on any nuance or suggestion made in your presence. If you do learn anything about their project, I would be interested in finding out what you discover."

"If I get some information, I'll be glad to discuss it with you. And the same with you. The whole thing is kind of mysterious and I'd definitely like to learn the details."

Content with her start on gathering information, Gillian was willing to let go of her inquiry into the 71st VA. and just respond to small talk. Surprisingly, she enjoyed it during the remainder of their drink. It was rather nice that George was unattached and in the group she was investigating. He obviously didn't think he was God's gift to women. At least he did not immediately present with that aspect. He had more potential than most guys she met in Center City.

They parted with smiles as they exited Devon.

Chapter 18

After her meeting with Youkoumian, Jennifer met Hampton at Parc, a restaurant just adjacent to Devon. They just missed seeing George and Gillian exit Devon as they entered Parc.

Both Jennifer and Hampton rather enjoyed Parc, which approximates a large Parisian Brasserie. Well attended, it attracted many young people, and was quite lively.

They also were going to have a drink. Once their orders were placed, Jennifer filled in Hampton with the results of her meeting.

"It went well." Jennifer said to Hampton. "First, Youkoumian didn't dismiss the idea out of hand. He was gracious and accommodating. Almost courtly. When I told him I was from another dimension, he was skeptical but didn't reject the idea entirely. And then I thought he'd be interested in stuff about Armenia in my dimension, but he basically ignored everything I had to say about that."

"He's never mentioned anything about Armenia in all the times I've ever talked with him," said Hampton. "Maybe he's been here so long that it's no longer of interest to him."

With a thoughtful look, Jennifer mentioned how much he wanted to know about Jews and Arabs. "Couldn't get enough of that," she said.

"Well, it is pretty much the biggest issue in that area. Although you might think it would be of less interest to Armenians.

"The Caliphate of Damascus fascinated him."

"I take it that's an Islamist state in your dimension?"

"Yes, they practically dominate everything in the old Levant, the old territories of the Ottoman empire on the Mediterranean. He was especially interested in how scientifically advanced they were."

"And I take it they are?"

"Yes, it seemed to please him that they administered Palestine including whatever Jews were living there. Also, he was quite glad to hear that their scientific and technical capabilities are equal to the West."

"Did you get a chance to discuss diamonds with him?" asked Hampton.

"Yes, he's going to help," Jennifer said.

"You are amazing. He's going to lend you 5000 2 carat diamonds just like that?"

Jennifer smiled and said, "Not quite. But he is considering letting us use some for a small-scale prototype. I promised him you would make a demonstration unit which would prove that what I have been saying is true and that travelling between dimensions is doable."

Hampton smiled wryly, "O… Kaaaay …. I would like to see that in action myself. Now all you need to do is show me the design for the thing and we can get started. I still don't get how all of these diamonds warp dimensions to get to the one you want. Something to do with slowing down light you said."

"One more time for the slow learners," she said. "You're OK with the idea that light slows down when passing through a denser substance. So. What we're going to do is pass one half of a coherent laser beam through every diamond we can get our hands on, and then recombine it with the original. The two beams will be tremendously out of time synchronization at that point and the resultant slow down means that one beam will be travelling at much slower than the speed of light relative to the other. Because of that, one of the small coiled up dimensions of the eleven in string theory will pop up into a normal dimension to bring the beams into coherence. Since we can only perceive three dimensions at a time, one of the three usual dimensions in this universe will pop down, and whatever is enclosed in the space will be in an alternate dimension. Quite simple. It's surprising no one in this dimension hasn't thought of it already. Any questions?"

"Perhaps a few," said Hampton. "Does this popping effect apply to everything in this dimension? Will our whole dimension transit to yours?"

"That would hardly be practical," said Jennifer. "The effect is limited to an ellipsoidal shape defined by the paths of the light beams. The beams have to fully enclose some volume in a geometric shape."

Hampton thought about it. "My guess is this prototype you have in mind is substantially smaller than the volume necessary to enclose a human. How is the prototype going to prove anything?"

Jennifer smiled like a satisfied cat. "I'm going to use it in Youkoumian's presence to transfer something from my dimension that will really impress him … a gold coin minted in the Caliphate of Damascus."

"That would probably convince him alright." 'It would certainly convince me,' thought Hampton. "How are you going to get that to happen?"

"When you've finished the prototype, we'll get Youk-oumian to look at it, I'll transmit a note to my dimension asking for the coin, and in a short time, my professors back at the University of Virginia will transmit it to us here."

Hampton made a face. "Arthur Clarke once said 'Any sufficiently advanced technology is indistinguishable from Magic.' "

"He said that in my dimension, too."

"There's an Arthur Clarke in your dimension?"

Jennifer took his arm as they left Parc. "A lot of people are represented in every dimension"

"So somewhere in this dimension there's a Jennifer Collins just like you?"

"Could be."

"Weren't you curious about her? Whether she's like you, and so on?"

Jennifer gave him an ironic look. "I've had all I could manage getting into the University of Pennsylvania Graduate School without having any antecedents here. I haven't had time to try to track down my hypothetical twin in this dimension"

Hampton pondered the idea of two Jennifers in the same room and gave a little shudder. It would be something to see them both trying to take over and run the situation. A little like Godzilla confronting King Kong.

He wondered if there was a Hampton like himself in her dimension. He rather thought it would be fun to meet himself. Almost like having a twin brother. He had two younger sisters but had always thought it would be nice to have a brother.

Jennifer noticed his look … he was thinking about something. "I can see you're getting confused about the whole idea of dimensions." Said Jennifer. "Don't worry your pretty little head about it, sweetie. All you have to do is worry about constructing the demo device I'll design. Once I've got the plans laid out, you can put it together."

"And where are we going to accomplish this feat ... I was thinking it might provoke some interesting questions if we tried to use space and equipment from the Ritt Labs."

Jennifer frowned slightly. "I see your point. We need to find a space secret enough to work in without arousing any suspicions. Why don't you work on that while I detail the design?"

Chapter 19

Aban Hassad was still carefully planning his investigations into the whereabouts of the H1B visa holders. He was not quite ready to pursue his investigation directly into Youkoumian's jewelry store. He preferred to first get as much information as he could before possibly alerting the owner by confronting him directly. He was trying to find and follow recently arrived Arabic speakers by checking names recorded from the H1-B visas. He initially tried to find the names at the address they had listed upon entry. Unfortunately, that address was nonexistent. He then checked hotels and other likely places of residence in center city. For several days, he had no luck, but was not discouraged. He was reasonably certain that the pattern would repeat and that he would be able to track the holders of the H1Bs into Philadelphia to where they were active. Once he knew where the holders were staying, it would be possible to observe what their activities were and how they related to Youkoumians.

Aban considered himself a Muslim, but it is unlikely that Youkoumian would have approved of Aban's involvement with Islam. Aban did not attempt to support other nations which were primarily Islamic. He did not donate to Islamic causes. He did not even require that his wife wear a hijab. If he had tried to make her do that, she probably would have thought he was delusional, since both were quite comfortable with a more relaxed attitude toward religion. They were believers but not belligerent. Their religious feelings were not unlike the attitudes of some of their Christian and Jewish friends in the suburb where they lived. They were all, in effect, secularly religious.

Neither Aban or his wife felt the need to conspicuously assert their Moslem religion. For her part, his wife felt no need to wear a burqa or even a hijab. Many Islamic scholars indicate that these are not compulsory for females, but the myth persists that they are a requirement of Islam.

Aban briefly thought about trying to check with local masjids in Philadelphia to see if any Arabic speakers had suddenly began attending prayers. None were reasonably close to Jewelers' Row and hence unlikely to be visited by anyone connected with Youkoumians store. While he was still pondering the question of trying to find the H1B visa holders, He got notification from INS that the Visa holders had left the U.S. for Qatar. It appeared that he would not be able to narrow down where the visa holders were staying in Philadelphia on this visit. That did not discourage him either. The pattern of entries and exits for these visas showed recurring visits to Philadelphia from Qatar on roughly a weekly basis. He got clearance from his superiors to stay in Philadelphia and meet the daily arrival flights from Qatar until the visa holders showed up again. Using this approach, he began meeting the daily non-stop flights from Qatar at the Philadelphia International terminal. Not exciting work, but likely to provide avenues to find out more details about what was going on.

Chapter 20

The next day George called Hampton with the offer of space. It was arranged that he would meet Hampton and Jennifer at 2nd and Arch streets in Old City Philadelphia not far from the Delaware River.

George was smiling as usual as he walked up to them. "Hello, Jennifer. And Hampton. The place I can get you is in the second story of an old warehouse down on Front Street."

"This is certainly an old part of Philadelphia," said Jennifer.

"Yes, it certainly is," said George. "A lot of these old warehouses and stores are being converted into luxury condos. A lot of money involved." He stewarded them down 2nd Street. "We can cross over to Front through Elfreth's Alley." George pointed out the sign on the little cross street: "The oldest continuously inhabited street in North America."

Hampton wondered how they could possibly know it was the oldest. The houses along the alley definitely looked old enough to date to colonial times. But weren't both Plymouth Massachusetts and Jamestown Virginia founded before Philadelphia? Also, wasn't the tip of Manhattan settled by the Dutch before Philadelphia? Hampton thought it probably was a chamber of commerce type claim trying to add distinction to the area. ampton looked over the historical sign.

They turned left onto Front Street, stopped before an old looking building, and George unlocked a door that provided stairway access to upstairs.

"It smells sweet in here." remarked Jennifer as they climbed the stairs.

George casually said "A lot of these old buildings have accumulated unusual smells over the centuries. I think some of them might have been used to store sugar and rum imported from the Caribbean Islands in colonial times. Here we go," he said, opening the door to the second-floor loft area. The second story was one room about 15 feet by 15 feet with lots of light from front and rear windows.

"Looks big enough," said Hampton. "I like the natural light for working on small stuff. Plenty of room for electronics racks. I assume all of the electrical outlets work?"

"Yeah," said George, "I'm pretty sure everything is in working condition, even this big drainage sink."

Hampton said, "I don't see a use for the drainage sink, but that doesn't matter."

"There are even some 220 volt outlets but I don't think you can use all of them at the same time," said George.

Hampton said, "We won't be using that much power at any one time, at least at first" He scanned the room. "The big lab counters will be handy for working on stuff."

Jennifer asked "What was it being used for before your company got it?

George gave the appearance of thinking about it. "You know I'm not sure but, but judging by some of these stands and glass ware, it looks like they were doing some chemical stuff."

Jennifer already knew that the previous occupants were doing chemical stuff. She'd recognized the sweet smell as the distinctive tang of a meth synthesis operation. She recognized it because, when she first entered the U.S., before getting herself into graduate school, she had worked for some Costa Ricans in New Jersey who were making bundles of cash producing crystal blue Meth. She had been hoping to do the same with them, but their operation was busted before she was able to accumulate much cash. For some reason, she had not been charged with the other Costa Ricans who were bagged in the bust. Privately, she thought it was a justifiable perk of being superbly attractive, and thought the male law officers on the case had not put her on the charge sheets because they were hoping for extracurricular benefits from her. Her shameless flirting with them probably helped with that impression. At any rate, she suffered no consequences from the bust and subsequently had no problem enrolling in the University of Pennsylvania Physics Ph. D. program.

Based on her prior activities, she was certain that George was giving them access to what had been a Meth Lab. So far, she didn't see any immediate problem with that. Except that it reflected on George's motives for offering the space to them at all.

She was also certain that George knew the previous occupants were running a Meth Lab. His evasions and fake pondering were pretty obvious. Was he trying to mask the previous use to cover his involvement? Was he involved in the lucrative business of producing crystal Meth? Did it matter? Jennifer was willing to go along with it until she could determine the lay of the land. She decided to wait before bringing up the issue with Hampton.

"If they were doing chemical stuff, that would probably account for the sweet smell", said Hampton.

He looked around the room at the walls. "It looks like they had 100 amp service based on that circuit panel by the door. A lot of power for the room size."

George said, "You know, the more I think about it the more I remember that they were doing work with glass tubing and chambers and heaters. Perhaps some kind of testing service for materials."

"We can definitely make use of the left-over lab stands and so on." Hampton opened a cupboard. "Not so much this glass work they left behind."

"You can toss anything that gets in your way", said George. "The previous occupants won't be back to complain."

"Went bankrupt?" asked Hampton.

"Something like that", agreed George.

"I think it will work", said Hampton. "What do you think, Jennifer?"

"I agree, since it's free. Thanks George" she said as she kissed him on the cheek.

"Wow," said George, "You're a lucky man, Hampton."

"You don't know the half of it, George", said Jennifer.

George thought, 'I may not know the half of it but I can guess quite a bit of it.'

"So, what will you be working on here?" asked George.

Hampton looked at Jennifer. Jennifer took over. "It involves lasers, optics, and electronics," said Jennifer. "Do you know anything about Physics?"

"I know that I don't remember much about it from high school. Too many formulas and much too much Math."

Jennifer smiled and said, "Then I'm afraid it would be hard to explain what we want to do. In simple form, we are going to split the laser output from an Argon-Ion laser, refract it multiple times, and then recombine the beams and observe the results."

George passed his hand horizontally above his head. "Woosh", he said. "Way over my head. If that's the simple form, I'm glad you spared me the complete version." Turning to Hampton, he said "You said the Colonel was helping you with special materials. I'm curious as to what those might be."

Again, Jennifer intervened quickly when Hampton was struggling on how to answer George. "Colonel Youkoumian prefers to keep his participation in the project confidential and we've agreed to that."

"No problem", said George. He locked up, they all went downstairs, and he handed over the keys to Hampton. Jennifer and Hampton walked southwestward toward the university campus through Independence Mall. George stood for a few moments watching them go.

There was definitely something going on, not only between those two, but with Youkoumian as well, he thought. He tossed the spare set of keys in his hand. They couldn't be there all the time. And what would be more normal than the property manager stopping by to keep tabs on the space. Seeing what they were doing would probably be enlightening, but once they established themselves, he might learn even more with a visit when they were absent.

Chapter 21

After leaving Front Street, both Jennifer and Hampton were quiet as they threaded their way through the crowds of tourists in the Old City area. Reaching Independence Mall, they passed the outline of the foundations of George Washington's house which included the slave quarters associated with the first presidential residence. A little further along they saw the Liberty Bell pavilion with lines of families waiting to get in to see the famous symbol.

Jennifer decided to let Hampton know about her deductions and conclusions about the space George had just shown them. "I'm now more than a little suspicious of George."

"Why?" said Hampton. "Suspicious of what? I thought it was pretty nice of him to help us out with space to work in."

"Sure, if you think he's nice to put us in what recently was a Meth Lab."

Hampton was rather startled by this statement. "How do you know it was a Meth Lab?"

"That sweet smell is pretty distinctive. It's the tang of ether. Didn't you ever have crystal blue at the universities you worked at?"

"Uh, no, somehow I missed that chance."

Jennifer looked at him with an irritated frown. "Believe me, as it's cooking it smells sweet and permeates everything.

For some reason he wants us to be in that space, and not just out of the goodness of his heart. He's probably using us as a cover up of some kind." Jennifer had begun to worry about getting involved with George. What effect might he have on her chances of getting diamonds? She wanted that process to be as simple as possible and George looked to her like a complication she didn't need. Still, what could she do about him? Hampton was right. They needed space

Hampton was skeptical. "He's certainly pretty prosperous looking, but he never sounded to me like someone who was involved with drugs."

"He may not be directly involved with the production or even the sales. Maybe he's just trying to cover up that he let some Meth dealers use space that he's responsible for. I would assume the company he works for would be quite upset at that." Jennifer smiled at that thought. "Despite what he's doing, for us or to us, that might give us some leverage on him. He probably would think twice about talking about what we're doing if he knows we could blow the whistle on him."

Hampton shook his head. "I always took him at face value … a nice single guy with nice clothes and some extra money."

Jennifer shook her head. "You're just too naïve. He gives me the impression of always being on the make. He's a little too suave when he talks to women. That Gillian thought the same thing about him. We'll have to be careful around him. We have to be sure not to reveal too much of what we're doing."

Hampton could understand that. He didn't relish the idea of talking about inter-dimensional travel with anyone, even people who were doing favors for them. Hampton was still puzzled by her remarks about George and the Meth Lab. He wondered how she got her experience with smelling Meth. Despite what she said, he didn't think crystal Meth or any other hard core drug was a usual part of the University experience. Why was she so certain about the situation? Was it possible that she had actual experience cooking crystal blue in a lab? She certainly was smart enough, but would she risk a great career, terrific potential salary, and her entire future with fooling around with drugs? Hampton was certain she wouldn't do that. He dismissed those speculations. Despite these questions in his own mind, he was, as usual, clearly impressed with her experience, analysis, and definite conclusions about what they should do.

Jennifer said, "Now that we have a place and that we should be able to handle George, all we have to do is get tools and equipment over to the loft and we can start work on the prototype."

Hampton thought about it. "I suppose we can borrow some of the unused equipment from Ritt Labs."

"As long as we don't have to tell anyone", said Jennifer.

"Yes, it might be a little awkward to have to sign out stuff", said Hampton. What materials do you think we are going to need?"

"To start with," Jennifer said, "we need a working Argon-Ion laser of about 150 milliwatts, some framework to hold diamonds and provide optical paths for the laser light, and a power supply big enough to make the whole thing go."

Hampton grimaced. "Nothing that can't be moved, but since neither of us has a car, we'll probably wind taking a lot of trips on buses. Fortunately SEPTA has a pretty comprehensive bus system so you can get almost anywhere if you're willing to put up with some long delays waiting for scheduled vehicles."

Jennifer said, "When we get close to a working prototype, we can approach Youkoumian for the diamonds we need."

"How many are we going to need?"

Jennifer had it worked out. "Not many, only about 250 2 carat diamonds."

Hampton whistled, "Wow, he's going to lend us 500 carats worth of diamonds. I can't even imagine that much money in one place."

"That's chicken feed for most jewelers", said Jennifer. "They routinely mail each other greater amounts than that without insurance or even special precautions. Despite what people think, the USPS routinely only misdelivers less than one package in every million. And the CSPS is even better."

"CSPS?" asked Hampton.

"Confederate States Postal Service".

"So, he's going to trust us with that many diamonds?" said Hampton.

"Why not?" said Jennifer. "He knows how to find us if he needs to. Running away with a piddling 500 carats is nothing, and certainly nothing I would consider doing. And he thinks you're so trustworthy he probably would give you the keys to his store. He's pretty secure in whatever he decides to do. He knows we won't screw him over."

"So the next step is to get this piddling amount of diamonds?" asked Hampton.

"No," said Gillian. "The next step is to get the prototype complete to the point where we need the diamonds to make it work. When we have it ready, he's already agreed to let us have them on loan. It's hardly worth considering."

"So when we have the demo device ready, all we'll have to do is walk over to his place on Sansom Street and pick up the diamonds?"

"Yes, I think that would be the next step."

They continued their discussion on their walk through Independence Mall, not noticing two dark suited swarthy men conversing on a bench to the side. They were not expecting to see anyone they knew, and hence did not notice that one of the men was Youkoumian.

Chapter 22

It rather pleased Youkoumian to meet with his superior, al-Tunji, in Independence Mall. He considered it secure cover. The mild late spring weather had brought out many tourists including noisy families with children walking about the area. It was highly unlikely that anyone would take notice of two dark suited men talking on a bench distant from most activity. Since he also was not expecting to see anyone he knew, it was highly unlikely that Youkoumian would notice anyone passing. He certainly did not see Hampton and Jennifer as they passed 100 yards away while he consulted with his boss, al-Tunji.

Al-Tunji had arrived first. He was a tall, slim, well-dressed man with a darker complexion. When the native Syrians were contesting the French League of Nations mandate for Syria and Lebanon in 1920, al-Tunji's great-great-grandfather had been one of the leaders of the resistance. The French military called him "Le Faucon" for his facial resemblance to that bird of prey and for his predilection for swooping surprise attacks. The current al-Tunji greatly resembled his ancestor in both respects.

As expected by Youkoumian, his superior was strongly skeptical of the idea of a visitor from another dimension. Al-Tunji was highly incredulous about the likelihood of multiple dimensions and potential travel among them. "This sounds like the western fables of the tales of the Arabian nights", he said. "How can you be sure that this female Physics student is not just making everything up?"

Youkoumian said, "I too was suspicious about her proposal. However, the level of detail she furnished on the Middle East situation in her dimension was convincing and intriguing. The idea that there is a caliphate in Damascus equal to the western states in both economic and scientific areas is something that could be of vital help to our struggle here. And she has offered to construct a prototype machine which would absolutely prove the existence of multiple dimensions. It would require the loan of 250 of our diamonds to make it."

"Perhaps that is her motive for this fantastic tale …. a way to disappear with a fortune belonging to us."

Youkoumian shook his head. "It is possible, but highly unlikely. She is working in one of the most prestigious universities in this country. After receiving an advanced degree, her career prospects promise wealth considerably beyond the value of 250 diamonds. She would be quite unwise to exchange those rewards for a sum considerably smaller."

Al-Tunji was still wary of losing diamonds. However, he, like Youkoumian, was intrigued with the possibility of an actual Islamic caliphate. If it existed. The idea that there was a Caliphate that could compete on equal terms with Western expertise and was based on Shari'ah law was tantalizing. At last Moslems would have the political structure they deserved, that had been missing since the golden age of pure Islam, when much of the Middle East and North Africa had been conquered by true believers.

The potential for aid from such a Caliphate for his own group was extremely attractive to al-Tunji. However, he was deeply concerned about the necessity to preserve the funds of his group as constituted in the diamonds. Money was the life blood these days of any movement. Hard to get and harder to keep. The loss of even a small fraction of their assets would be disastrous.

Youkoumian repeated Jennifer's idea of proving the existence of the Caliphate by demonstrating a prototype apparatus which would show that communication between dimensions would be possible. He emphasized that none of the 250 diamonds would be harmed and that he would be in a position to oversee their safety in the demo.

After considerable discussion about pros and cons, al-Tunji and Youkumian arrived at a short-term compromise. Al-Tunji authorized the jeweler to provide the diamonds for the prototype machine which would demonstrate the proof anyone would need. Al-Tunji emphasized the need to be careful with all aspects of the project and to be extremely vigilant, especially with the diamonds. As he put it, "If it's necessary, you will kill to preserve our diamonds."

The jeweler reassured his boss that he was fully prepared to do just that.

"It is ridiculously easy to get guns here. I have several to protect the store and can get more if necessary."

Al-Tunji considered this. "I think it would be wise if you also had some additional man power to take care of contingencies. I will arrange for two of our couriers to remain here for a time as needed. They can use the H1-B visas we have and they will have Egyptian passports which will match."

Youkoumian agreed with this. Some years ago, he had arranged for H1-B visas ostensibly for foreign workers for his jewelry business. They were used for any of the group's couriers traveling between the Middle East and Philadelphia. The couriers interchanged passports among themselves to match the visas which allowed flexibility in courier assignments. American custom agents could not detect any differences between their appearance and the passport photos. All bearded Middle Eastern males looked much alike to them.

Al-Tunji was satisfied that the matter would be under control. "You are certain that this whole project with the diamonds will only take a short time?"

Youkoumian replied, "I was assured by the graduate student that the prototype will be completed in no more than a few weeks."

"Very well, proceed with utmost care and do not hesitate to have the couriers use extreme measures if necessary."

Youkomian assured his superior that he would do just that. Youkoumian thought that it was highly likely there would be no need to encourage the couriers to use force to protect the diamonds. He thought the opposite might well be true … it might be hard for him to keep them under control and avoid unwanted attention from local authorities.

The group maintained a safe house in Philadelphia's Queen Village for any members who might need to stay overnight. Al-Tunji was going to make use of it that night before returning to the middle east the next morning. Together they walked the short distance from the Mall to the location of the house. Al-Tunji was always secretly amused by the name of the street on which it was located. Christian Street.

The group's safe house was a modest two story row house in the Queen Village neighborhood. The house was sufficiently close to Jewelers' Row that any of the group staying there would be conveniently at hand when needed at the store. Youkoumian showed his boss how to turn on the laptop and internet access in the house. He also got the brief case containing the hand guns.

Youkoumian began to plan for the arrival of the couriers. In order to facilitate their movement around the city they might need to rent a car for transportation. Youkoumian certainly did not want to rent it using his own identity documents in case problems arose. The courier's H1-B visas and passports should be adequate for them to have no trouble. And he could deny knowledge of their activities if problems arose and the authorities took an interest in them.

He did not want to draw attention to his Youkoumian persona. There had, in fact, once been a Youkoumian, an Armenian, who had bought diamonds in the Netherlands and Russia, and sold wedding and engagement rings for over thirty-five years to many in the Philadelphia metropolitan area. Hassan continued this business. His customers, some from second and third generations to patronize the store, assumed he too was Armenian, and in fact called him Mr. Youkoumian. His fellow merchants on Sansom street also addressed him as Mr. Youkoumian and stereotyped him as a hard bargaining but quite likable Armenian. Youkoumian was in fact a valued member of a middle east organization which found it extremely useful to own a jewelry store in the US. Youkoumian provided banking facilities for those who were combating the Crusaders.

Carrying the briefcase, he started on the short walk to his store on Sansom Street, and felt he was completely ready for the arrival of the couriers which were to be his assistants in the project.

Chapter 23

A few days later, Jennifer walked from her apartment in the University Housing at Cira Centre South to the Front Street loft in the morning and found Hampton hard at work.

"Wow, it's beginning to take shape. You've made a lot of progress."

Hampton passed his hand across his forehead. "Well, here's the power supply mounted in this electronics rack. And it's connected to the laser assembly here on the lab bench. As you specified, the beam from the laser emerges into an external path which is split into two by these half-silvered mirrors. One beam enters this opaque sphere of insulating material. The sphere has an internal diameter of 10 cm and the top half opens with a hinge to display the inside." He opened the top lid to show her the inside.

"You can see the interior has mounts for the diamonds when we get them. After that beam is refracted by the diamonds within the sphere it will re-emerge from it and recombine over here with the other half of the original beam."

"Great," Jennifer said, kissing him, "you are the best. Now you will have to mount the diamonds one every 30 square centimeters on the inside surface making sure that the beam coming from the source laser enters the chamber and is re-fracted between all of them in the sequence I gave you."

"And that will send the whole contraption into another dimension?"

"No, just whatever is enclosed by the path of the beams in the interior volume of the sphere."

Hampton looked at the framework skeptically. "The sphere seems like a small space to make an effective demon-stration. I know you explained this before but could you go over it again? If you can't even see into the sphere, how will this convince Youkoumian that it transfers anything? How will this demonstrate the existence of multiple dimensions?"

"Relax. We're going to show Youkoumian an actual two way transference between the two dimensions. The sphere has to be opaque because external light would interfere with the process. But the results will be observable before and after the transfer. I'm going to write a note requesting a gold coin minted recently in the Caliphate of Damascus. I'll put the note into this demo chamber and send it off. We'll then show Youkoumian that the chamber is empty. Then a little later we will get the coin back from my dimension and open the device again to show him that it was transferred. That should impress him."

"Why a coin from the Damascus Caliphate? And why a gold coin?"

"Because there's nothing like it in this dimension so he can be assured we're not faking it with a substitute. Also, he was somehow fascinated with the idea of a real Caliphate in the Middle East. I told him a lot of interesting details about it, and he couldn't seem to get enough of them."

"I guess that makes sense … an Armenian might well be interested in differences in the Middle East between this di-mension and yours."

"He was more than just interested, he was completely absorbed in whatever I could tell him." She didn't mention to Hampton that she thought Youkoumian might be Arabic.

Hampton considered that. Then he thought of another aspect of the process. "So how do you get a note to a specific location in your dimension?"

"If we had time and the right electronics and mechanical adjusters we could build controls for an arbitrary sequential refraction in the diamonds that could adjust the destination of the focus of the device to any location. Lacking that, the sequence I specified, which you will make mechanically with rigid fittings, will connect exactly up to labs in the University of Virginia in my dimension. It will be hard wired in."

"And how do they know where in our dimension to send their coin?"

"I'll just specify the GPS co-ordinates of where we want it. The adjustable devices and monitors on the equipment in my dimension's home labs will let them send it anywhere they select."

As usual, Jennifer had a ready answer for every question Hampton had. He felt guilty at his feelings. He was becoming a little irritated about how self-assured she was and how much more she knew than he did. Almost as if he didn't matter that much. And in all honesty, he had to admit that he didn't matter that much. Almost anyone with reasonable mechanical ability could do what he did. He wondered if she hadn't chosen him because he was easy to convince and perhaps too ready to admit his lack of knowledge and follow her lead.

Despite his lack of understanding of how everything would work, Hampton was willing to believe that Jennifer's reassurances would turn out accurate in the long run. Based on the level of Physics that Hampton was familiar with, he could not contradict anything that she'd told him so far. Still, the whole episode appeared surreal to him. It was hard enough to accept that she was attracted to him. Trying to understand what she was saying on dimensions was just too much.

"You seem pretty confident that the people in your dimension will be able to find a gold coin from Damascus and will be eager to send it here," remarked Hampton.

"It's been six months since I made the transfer. My professors are probably sick with guilt about not being able to reach me. Believe me, they will fall all over themselves doing what we ask." Jennifer said confidently.

Hampton was still skeptical. "And they'll be able to get a gold coin from the Middle East without long delays?"

"They won't have to send to the Middle East. Any bank in North America in my dimension will have money from the Caliphate of Damascus for exchange purposes. It's one of the few currencies in my dimension based on gold, and the only one with actual gold coins in circulation. Naturally that gives them a huge advantage in trade and their money is much sought after. Almost all banks have some since a lot of international trading is denominated in Caliphate Dinars. Basically, they are one of my world's reserve currencies."

"Naturally? What's a reserve currency and why is it natural?" asked Hampton.

"Baby, don't worry about that. If you'd ever had an economics course you'd understand why money backed by tangible assets is far better than fiat money such as your dimension prints."

Hampton didn't even know what she meant by fiat money. She was right, thought Hampton, there is an awful lot about how the world works that I don't understand. But she is so sure of herself and so confident that it seems reasonable to accept her explanations.

"OK, then," he said. "I guess it's time to call Youkoumian and arrange to get the diamonds."

"I agree." And she proceeded to do so.

Chapter 24

Youkoumian was not happy that morning. The couriers designated by al-Tunji to stay in Philadelphia and assist him had arrived and been directed to the safe house in Queen Village where they left their bags. They then proceeded, as instructed, to the Sansom Street store where the interior guard immediately declined to allow them entrance. Youkoumian was summoned and could understand the guard's reluctance. He stepped out and instructed them to go to the alley behind the store. He proceeded through his store, opened a rear door, and escorted them to a little used storeroom with a few chairs.

On the other hand, Youkoumian was unsure about their discretion in taking action to serve the cause. It had become quite clear to him over the years that he served his organization most effectively when he did not adopt extreme attitudes or postures to anything he found here in America. Such actions could only draw unwanted attention to himself and hurt his basic function in taking the steps which advanced the cause. He was already a little worried that their initial attempt to enter might draw unwanted attention.

He instructed them. "From now on, when directed to meet me here, you will never come to the main entrance. You will always come to the alley door at the specified time and I will unlock it for you. Is this understood?" They nodded their agreement in a fashion that Youkoumian considered surly.

"Al-Tunji has described what is required of you while you are here," said Youkoumian. They agreed as a matter of course. Both of them were swarthy and suggested Middle Eastern ethnicity. Youkoumian thought that their appearance might be a bigger handicap to their operating effectively in the U.S. than anything they could do to help protect the diamonds.

Youkoumian continued "For the moment, we wish you to ensure the safety of the diamonds which we will be lending to the people from the University of Pennsylvania."

They had no response to this.

Youkoumian said "We will be distributing a substantial amount of diamonds to these people. For the moment, the assignment is to follow and keep track of them without disturbing anyone or making your presence known. If we require any direct action, I will inform you specifically. So, you will do nothing until I tell you."

Bored, they acknowledged the instructions.

Youkoumian produced the hand guns he had acquired from the safe house: 9mm Glock Gen4 models each having three 17 round magazines. Total weight of gun, magazine, and ammunition … less than 2 pounds total.

They were beautiful little engines of death and at last inspired the couriers to interest and even enthusiasm. It was clear that the assistants al-Tunji had provided were appreciative of such well-engineered weapons. The couriers immediately occupied themselves with examining the magazines, cartridges, and sighting through the barrels of the semi-automatic weapons eagerly commenting in Arabic with each other about such fine instruments.

None of this behavior helped to make Youkoumian happier about the necessity of having to deal with these thugs.

"To avoid any possible unnecessary accidents, I am directing you to not load the magazines with cartridges and to not load the magazines into the weapons until you are explicitly told to do so by me. There will be time enough to accomplish these chores if they should become necessary. Is this clear?"

They nodded, indicating that it was.

Finally, Youkoumian said "Despite my orders not to prepare your weapons before I say so, you must understand that, if necessary, they will be used in any fashion required to protect our diamonds. There is to be no hesitation in that situation. If necessary, you will shoot to kill."

The couriers exchanged a look. This final admonition did not fit well with his earlier commands not to attract attention. However, it did have the effect of interesting them even more, and one even smiled a little as they indicated they would obey directions.

Youkoumian was not happy about having his courier assistants in his office at the jewelry store. They were a jarring contrast to both his staff and customers. They fit in neither group. Anyone looking at them would think "thugs". He resolved to find some other way to get their reports rather than having them come through the store.

Youkoumian was rather doubtful about the possibility of his assistants performing their duties without being noticed. But, if they were, it would probably not have any consequences, at least for him. He believed he was well insulated from the possible fallout from any gunmen who might be working for him. He was determined that any suspicion that focused on them would not also include him. He intended to isolate himself from them as much as possible.

He escorted the couriers through the rear door with instructions to return to the safe house and await further instructions. As they exited his store, he was satisfied that he had taken all needful steps to try to control them.

The two couriers looked at each other as they returned to the safe house. They were not impressed. To them, it appeared that playing at being the owner of a prosperous store and imitating an Armenian had seriously corrupted the man known as Youkoumian. He was not much like the men they reported to back in the Middle East. In many respects, he was much like the Americans they casually encountered in western cities and on planes and in airports. Like them, he almost reeked of smug success. Even worse, although secretly proclaiming his faith, he did not appear to have much concern about Islam or the struggle it was in. He appeared soft and wishy washy. This confirmed the warning they had received before they left.

Al-Tunji had expressed definite concerns about this man who ran the jewelry store. Although he did not discuss details with the couriers, he suggested that perhaps Youkoumian had been so long in the west that he was no longer completely dedicated to their cause.

Privately, al-Tunji thought that this sudden proposal concerning alternate dimensions and involving diamonds was completely bizarre. Could this preposterous story be some kind of cover for a plan so that Youkoumian could use the diamonds for his own purposes? Could he be planning to steal from their group?

Chapter 25

With the prototype essentially finished except for the diamonds, Jennifer was getting more and more excited. The prospect of holding even a small fraction of the diamonds she needed was enough to send thrills of anticipation through her. She was getting closer and closer to her goal.

Jennifer called Youkoumian to request a time at which she and Hampton could receive the initial complement of jewels. To her surprise, he was ready to transfer the diamonds at once. They agreed on a time later that afternoon. He then phoned his new assistants at the safe house and told them to report to the alley door immediately. When they arrived, he escorted them to the rear store room.

Youkoumiann told them, "You will shortly begin your duties by maintaining surveillance of two young Americans, a male and female, who will shortly exit the store. I will entrust them with a quantity of diamonds and you will follow them without being noticed to determine where they take them. Is this understood?"

They indicated that they understood.

"Good", said Youkoumian. "You will now wait here. Just before these Americans leave, I will notify you to leave by the rear door and proceed to the main entrance so that you can follow them."

Jennifer and Hampton walked from the Front Street location to Jewelers' Row to collect the initial 250 diamonds from Youkoumian. He, as usual, was welcoming and affable as he escorted them to his office.

"May I offer you some coffee?" he asked pleasantly.

Jennifer shook her head. She was much too excited to savor coffee or make small talk with Youkoumian. "No, thank you, Colonel. We're now so close to completing the device that I'm looking forward to demonstrating it for you and convincing you that it can be done. The sooner the better, since I'll be that much closer to getting back to my home dimension." Of course, she knew what she meant was the closer she would be to having the 10,000 carats of diamonds in her hands.

Youkoumian still had his doubts about this entire affair, but he also felt, that, if it was real, the potential gains for his organization would be enormous. And there appeared to be no real risk involved. He felt secure in lending these young people a sizable quantity of diamonds. He had already had one of his store assistants find out exactly where both Jennifer and Hampton lived.

"As you wish," he said. He reached into the right-hand pedestal of his desk and withdrew a ordinary quart size opaque freezer bag with a zip lock top. "Here," he said, placing it in front of Jennifer, "we have 250 2 carat diamonds, as specified."

"Excellent, we're grateful." said Jennifer.

"Do you want us to sign a receipt or anything?" asked Hampton.

"Between trusted friends, such details are not necessary. I am completely convinced that you are honorable people who will eventually return the diamonds unharmed. However,

I would appreciate knowing the address of where you are working on the device and where the diamonds will be."

"Of course," said Jennifer, "That's no problem." She wrote down the Front Street address for him. "It's on the second floor."

Youkoumian said, "Thank you Jennifer. I am much anticipating seeing the mechanism in action."

Jennifer said, "Very good. You can expect to hear from us in a few days with a time when we can show you how the prototype works."

"I will look forward to it", said Youkoumian. "Please excuse me for a moment."

Before he ushered Hampton and Jennifer out, he went to the rear storeroom, collected the couriers, and instructed them to circle around onto Sansom Street and discreetly follow the two young people who would shortly exit the store. He gave the couriers the Front Street address which Jennifer had provided and told them this should be the ultimate destination of both the young people and the diamonds. If it was not, they should call him immediately and continue to follow until the subjects did enter an address. He emphasized the need to not draw attention to themselves. He then returned to his office and courteously escorted Hampton and Jennifer to the front door.

Once on the street, Hampton and Jennifer reoriented themselves to walk eastward toward the loft location on Front Street. As they walked eastward on Sansom, they did not look backward and see Youkoumians thugs slowly following them.

This procession wended through Independence Mall and eventually turned north on Front Street. Hampton and Jennifer quickly entered the loft above the old warehouse. The couriers were in essence alone on the street and slowly continued north, then turned about and slowly walked south again. The couriers apparently argued between themselves for a while but eventually left the scene.

On the second floor of their building on Front Street, Jennifer immediately opened up Youkoumian's freezer bag and spread out the diamonds with satisfaction. "Beautiful", said Jennifer. "We're getting there. How long do you think it will take you to mount them in the device, sweetie?"

Hampton rather liked being called her sweetie. "I would say about two days if I can work without interruptions."

"Great, if I can help by doing anything just tell me" said Jennifer.

Hampton picked up his mounting tools and Jennifer's specification for diamond placement. "OK, if you could adjust the blinds on the front windows, I should have just enough light to see what to do."

"Sure", said Jennifer, who went to the front windows and looked out. "Shit!" she said.

"What's wrong?" asked Hampton.

"I just saw George outside on the opposite side of Front Street."

Hampton was puzzled, "Why is that bad?"

"Do you think it's just a coincidence that he's down here on the same day we got the diamonds?" Jennifer was definitely irritated. "Somehow he found out about them."

"He could be down here looking at properties he's managing. It *could* be coincidence," said Hampton.

"Then why did he turn around and walk away North as soon as he saw me looking out the window? Not what you'd call friendly behavior. If he's into Meth, he'd definitely be into picking up some easy money in diamonds."

Hampton said, "So what should we do?" Hampton thought about it. "Maybe George by himself could be a coincidence. He is the property manager, maybe he's just here to check it out."

"And you think it's just coincidence that he turns up almost in the same moment we pick up diamonds from Youkoumian," Jennifer said tartly.

"I don't see how anyone could know anything about that."

" He's got to be after the diamonds. You're sure you didn't tell him what we're doing?"

"The last time I saw George was when he showed us this place. I couldn't have told him anything because I didn't know we were picking up diamonds today until an hour ago." Jennifer was not convinced. The closer she got to handling the larger lot of diamonds the more nervous she was becoming. She was determined not to let George upset her careful planning. There didn't appear to be any obvious course of action at this point. She could only shake her head and worry. "Somehow, he figured something out," she muttered.

She looked out the window again. "Shit," she said, "Now that Gillian is out there and she's walking south down the street. They must both be in this together. And they must both be after the diamonds."

Hampton didn't see how that was a logical conclusion, but he knew Jennifer was better at reading people and analyzing situations than he was. It did seem that seeing both George and Gillian on the same block on the same day they picked up diamonds was beyond coincidence. Were they working together on something? They hadn't seemed to know each other at the last meeting of the 71st. Neither he nor Jennifer knew much about either George or Gillian beyond the fact they had showed up for that meeting of the 71st VA. Since diamonds had never been under discussion, how could George and Gillian possibly have known about the diamonds they had just received?

Hampton was not at all comfortable at being responsible for an expensive batch of jewels and wished that they were done with them. It seemed to him that the sooner he completed the prototype and they demonstrated for Youkoumian, the better. After that, he could build the full-sized version, Jennifer and he could go to her dimension, and Youkoumian would have all his diamonds back.

He sort of surprised himself with this line of thinking. Apparently, he was already convinced of the truth of everything she said. That train of thought suddenly impressed on him that he apparently believed her story completely. She thought the device he built would work as she said it would. And apparently so did he.

It startled him that he was thinking about going to another dimension with her. He wondered what changed things he might encounter. It might well be like immigrating to another country with the same language. Perhaps a few subtle differences but all in all similar. Still, what would probably be a one-way trip was a prospect which brought up some apprehensions. One way trips were pretty scary in themselves. Obviously, he was beginning to firmly believe her story.

He looked at Jennifer. "Clearly, neither Gillian nor George are about to burst in here and steal the diamonds immediately. I think the best thing we can do is finish this prototype for the demo as soon as possible, get the remaining diamonds from Youkoumian, and get to your dimension."

Jennifer agreed. But she was still upset about George and Gillian being in the neighborhood.

Chapter 26

As it happened, there was a rather non-threatening reason why Jennifer saw both George and Gillian on Front Street. The two had had a cocktail date together earlier that day.

Yesterday, Gillian had been rather frustrated at her inability to develop any more information about the Hampton, Jennifer, Youkoumian "project". She did think about it in quotes. She had learned a little the last time she met with George. Perhaps it was time for another drink with him to see if he had any more details. Gillian was convinced, with good evidence, that she could charm almost anything out of any young male. And she didn't need to pretend to be a "girly-girl" to do it. She called his cell and asked him to meet her at Devon again today. Perhaps he would begin to think of it as "their place." Males were so easily influenced by such simple things. She could tell that he was pleased that she had asked him for another date. Like most men, he quite liked women to show they were interested in him. In truth, she *was* interested in him. But she was more interested in getting information about the "project".

That afternoon, at Devon, as usual, she was late.

"Hi," George greeted her. "I ordered your sweet vermouth on the rocks already."

Gillian suppressed a shudder as she sat down on the stool next to him. She stared at the glass containing the sweet vermouth. Sometimes ploys came back to bite you in the ass, she thought. She had ordered the sweet vermouth on their first date just to get his reaction and play off the movie "Groundhog Day" to see what he might be like. She would rather have had her favorite drink, a mojito, this afternoon, but she smiled bravely and said with enthusiasm, "That's great! I'm surprised you remembered."

George liked her response. "You know the old song," he said "... easy to remember and so hard to forget."

Gillian had never heard of that song, and was ready to barf at the saccharine sentiment of the verse, but managed to transfer it to a great smile for George. He was suitably charmed. Now, she thought, how do I start pumping him about "the project"?

But George showed himself to be more interested in her than the project.

"I know you mentioned that you live in SOWSO, but you never told me where you work or what you do." Said George.

She certainly was not going to tell him she was an agent for ATF. Among her talents was the ability to make up a story easily when required to do so.

"I work at an insurance company headquartered in the Comcast Tower. Not at all exciting. I'm just an administrative assistant to one of the vice presidents."

George said, "That's pretty impressive, working for a vice president."

Gillian smiled ruefully. "It might be thought so, but there are 132 of them scattered over five floors. Almost anyone who can spell the words *is* one."

George smiled also and said. "Still, being an administrative assistant is distinctive."

"Not exactly. In the insurance game, it's pretty much a euphemism for secretary."

"So not so exciting, I guess."

"The most exciting thing I've done this week was to go to the Gallery to buy an anniversary present for my boss's wife."

They both laughed at that.

Gillian looked at him. "But you must have much more interesting things to say about Center City real estate."

"If I was a realtor, that might be true, but alas, I'm in property management."

Gillian knew nothing about that and was interested. "Which company do you work for?"

George, thinking fast, said "It's a local company called First Buildings Inc."

"And just what does a property manager do?" she asked.

George grimaced. "It's kind of like being a glorified janitor. You have to arrange to take care of problems in a lot of different buildings, not just one. The only good thing about it is that I don't have to push out the big dumpsters on garbage days."

"Oh dear, that doesn't sound like much fun."

"It isn't." George looked at her ruefully. "We don't have much interesting to say about our jobs, do we?"

Gillian found his honesty surprisingly refreshing. It rather reinforced the interest she was occasionally feeling for him since meeting him at the re-enactors meeting. "It sort of looks like the most interesting thing we have both done recently is the meeting of the 71st VA."

George sipped his drink. "Yes, the intriguing interaction between Hampton, Jennifer, and the Colonel. An unlikely trio for a joint project, I think." He thought about mentioning that he had arranged for Hampton and Jennifer to have a secret location in which to work. But there didn't seem to be any need to reveal that at this time.

Gillian thought about it. "They seem to be quite secretive about their project. I hinted that I'd like to see it, but Jennifer clammed up right away. Do you think they would care if anyone knows what they're working on? I can barely spell Physics, let alone understand any information about it"

George had to agree to that assessment. "I'm sort of in the same position. I have no idea what they're doing or how significant it is. But they definitely are closed mouth about it."

Gillian turned that into a remark on his motives. "I can well understand why you would be intrigued by the project. Jennifer is gorgeous."

George raised his head in mock outrage. "But not half so sweet as you, my dear."

Gillian looked him over carefully and thought he was somewhat sincere. He was attracted to her, he made that clearly obvious. But most likely the attraction arose because she was the only woman close to him at the present time. Still, she thought of him as being somewhat honest. At least as honest as might be possible for someone with a Y chromosome. It was clear that he did like being with her. And there was little phony pretense. She decided to test him a little. "I think I can understand your interest in her."

"You do? You don't think it's just curiosity about three such different people in close association?"

Gillian took a sip of her sweet vermouth, suppressed making a face, and said "There's that, but I think I detect other motives for your interest as well."

This rather startled George. Why would an administrative assistant suspect him of other reasons for being interested? Could she somehow have figured out where and for whom he worked? Did he still have a cover? "And what do you think mine are?"

Gillian cocked an eye at him. "If I had to guess, I would say your interest in their project is related directly to Jennifer."

"Well she is extremely good looking. But so are you. And I might add, more so. And you're not only more attractive, you're more interesting to talk to"

"Thank you. That's courtly of you. But I think your interest in her is related to procreation."

George was startled and showed it. "I admit that she's quite attractive, but I certainly haven't thought about producing children with her, or anybody else for that matter."

Gillian smiled at him and said, "You may not have considered it explicitly, but it's one of the three Ps that drive male behavior."

George looked at her skeptically. "The three Ps." It was a question.

Gillian explained it for him. "In 1990, an anthropologist researcher named Dr. David Gilmore published a cultural study "Manhood in the Making", which proposed that in all societies, three activities define the male's role: Procreation, Provision, and Protection. So even if you are not consciously seeking to produce children, procreation, that is, sex with potentially fertile women, is one of the most persuasive driving factors for younger males. At least in Gilmore's theory."

George was totally taken aback by this. "So basically, you're saying my testosterone level has control of everything I do."

Gillian smiled at him. He was pretty sharp at picking up on the implications of things. "I think it's certainly a big factor."

"Yes, but if it controls me, wouldn't I be tearing off your clothes right now?" He deliberately shaded into risqué to try to throw her off her composure.

Gillian had another small sip and smiled at him again. "I think you'd like to, but your socialized inhibitions limit you to means that are more acceptable to the social mores of our context. You control yourself by limiting your tactics to maneuvers and language that could result in getting me into bed."

George instead was completely thrown off *his* composure. He had never talked with a young woman who was so forthright. And unflappable. He wasn't sure whether she was patronizing him or perhaps just being refreshingly frank. He found himself thinking that he'd almost rather talk with her than go to bed with her. Almost.

"Well, I can understand where you're coming from with that, but I'm disappointed that you think I'm totally motivated by glandular activity."

She put her hand on his arm. "I don't think that totally controls what you do." But of course, she knew that, if not totally controlling him, it was a major factor influencing him. She also clearly knew that touching him would have an effect on how he viewed her.

George rather liked her hand on his arm for several seconds. He had to admit that she had some insight into male behavior and reactions. And she also obviously knew all the tricks of flirting. She certainly knew how to affect masculine thinking. But there was a taste of realism and directness behind what she said and did. Of course, he was not willing to acknowledge this immediately to her.

"Ok, I get it. I hope you didn't think I was coming on too strong to you."

Gillian reassured him. "You weren't. I had been a little jealous that you might be more interested in Jennifer than me." Her smile alone was enough to have an effect on his attitude. It didn't turn him into jello, but it started him along that path. It was pretty clear to Gillian that she had a clear advantage with George. He was obviously drawn to her, and not only could he not control it completely, he didn't try to do so.

He did surprise her with a comment. "So, if the 3 Ps define a man's role, what defines a woman's role? Did this guy Gilmore come up with some thoughts on that?"

His remark impressed her. He was clearly capable of assimilating new information quickly and discussing it. "As far as I know, he hasn't. But you and I both know that men are the biggest factors in defining a women's role."

George thought about it. "Yes, I suppose you're right. Aside from the obvious factors of child bearing and nurturing, I suppose men do the most in controlling women and their roles. Probably an off shoot of that Protection motivator. You can protect a woman most effectively by totally controlling everything she's exposed to and what she does. Sort of like in Islam."

Gillian was impressed. This guy was not only open to new ideas, he was quick in applying them. Much different than the other guys she'd had dates with. She cocked her head at him. "That's perceptive. Let's have another drink and talk about it. Only this time make mine a mojito." Their date ended, and to Gillian's surprise it *was* like a date, interesting in that both parties learned new things about the other. They left Devon and went their own ways. George toward the East, and Gillian west across 18th Street into Rittenhouse square ostensibly to walk south toward SOWSO.

Despite some budding feelings about George, Gillian was determined to find out more about him, especially where he lived. She wondered whether that was because of the feelings or because of her need for more information on the "project".

Looking back from the square, she was able to see that George turned East onto Locust. It was simple to cross back over 18th Street and tail George.

He didn't appear concerned about anyone following him. This rather surprised Gillian. If he had something to hide, one might expect him to be more circumspect.

For his part, George had never been in a situation for the FBI when he might expect someone to tail him. It was inconceivable. Even if they knew he was FBI, they would not dare to try to follow him to try to find out information about his activities. What would they gain? It made no sense. So, George was blissfully oblivious to anyone who might be following him.

Even with this easy target, Gillian was careful about tailing him. She followed him as he worked his way east, eventually following him across Independence Mall until he made the series of turns that brought him up to an old Front Street loft building. He paused across the street from it but did not attempt to enter. Instead he continued North on Front Street and disappeared down another side street. Gillian made a mental note of the loft building address.

From her position across the street from it she could observe the front windows of the loft. She noted Jennifer looking out as George walked north and then saw Hampton pass by the window. Well, well, she thought, this is interesting. She had thought tailing George would produce more information on him, such as where he lived. Instead, it looked like she'd hit the jack pot and found out where the "project" was. His familiarity in this area proved that he was intimately involved in whatever Hampton, Jennifer, and Youkoumian were involved in. And he wasn't telling her anything about that. Probably significant. She turned around and headed South on Front Street. Jennifer, taking another peek out the window, noticed her as she left.

Later, back at her apartment, Gillian looked up the Front Street address on the internet. Bingo. A location on that block showed up as the takedown site of a Meth operation within the last year. Could this be real? Could the squeaky-clean university people and the well-dressed property manager be involved with drugs? Puzzling, in that they showed none of the signs of people who were involved with such things. If they were assuming covers, they were well done. Gillian decided to consult her boss, Gloria, on the advisability of getting some first-hand observations of the Front Street loft.

Chapter 27

After leaving Front Street, Youkoumian's new "assistants" found their way back to the Jewelry store on Sansom. They called first, telling him that the diamonds were apparently being kept at the address he had given them. They also wanted to talk to him about surveillance details. Youkoumian told them to again come to the rear door, where he gave them entrance again.

In the rear supply room, they confirmed that the Front Street address was likely the place where the diamonds would be kept. This was reassuring to Youkoumian. Hampton and Jennifer were doing nothing suspicious with the diamonds.

However, his "assistants" were not happy at the prospect of trying to observe the location for extended periods of time. They emphasized that they there was no cover at all on the street. No businesses, no stores, little pedestrian movement, and almost no car traffic. They suggested that they required a car to provide a place from which they could observe without drawing unwanted attention. And, as one put it, it would help them get around this city. They were not used to walking everywhere.

Youkoumian was not particularly happy at this show of initiative. When these men confronted problems back in Syria, someone usually died. Youkoumian did not feel personally threatened by them but he had been established long enough in center city Philadelphia to know that instances of violence were usually pursued relentlessly to the ultimate detriment of the perpetrators. Violence in the city's ghettos often remained unsolved, but those who ran the city took great care to ensure that most people felt secure in the center.

He reluctantly conceded their point, but established a tone which he hoped would leave no doubt in their minds who was in charge. "You have established where they took the diamonds, so it may be necessary for you to maintain continuous watch over that location. Since it would be impractical for you to stand outside for long periods. It will probably be necessary for you to rent a car so that you can observe without being conspicuous. Is this clear?"

This part of their instructions had the effect of making them a little happier. They obviously both liked the idea of having a car to use. A little more cheerfully, they said they understood.

Youkoumian furnished a prepaid credit card and indicated that they could use it to rent a suitable vehicle. They could use that for both transportation and cover in the vicinity of Front Street. He again shepherded them out the rear door. After they left, Youkoumian took the opportunity to report to his boss.

Finished with the watchers, he left the supply room and went to his office. There he reported his actions and current progress to al-Tunji via code phrases in an email.

His email was directed to an internet site which was manned by their organization and had the ostensible appearance of a diamond wholesaler. Because of his face to face conference with al-Tunji, the common code book for both sides had now been augmented by a number of jewelry related phrases that could conceivably be relevant to the situation he was now dealing with.

Thus, the phrase "Last shipment currently delivered to customer" would inform al-Tunji that the initial batch of diamonds was in the hands of the Physics people. "Gems being sorted" would tell him that work was progressing on the prototype. In similar fashion, Youkoumian related what steps he had taken with the couriers who were currently being used to watch the diamonds. He did express his misgivings about his new assistants.

When Youkoumians email was decoded, al-Tunji was not pleased. After all, Youkoumian had come from the same kind of people as the new assistants. Not so long ago, the objections Youkoumian was expressing about them could well have applied to him. It was only after living continuously in the West for several years that he had become somewhat more 'refined' as he expressed it. Basically, Youkoumian had adopted some of the attitudes of the West. As al-Tunji thought about it, Youkoumian had become corrupted.

The coded replies from al-Tunji dismissed Youkoumians apprehensions. It was absolutely necessary to have people on the scene capable of performing whatever actions would be necessary to insure that the organization would not lose any of the capital it had in the form of diamonds. Al-Tunji referred to the actions that the assistants had recently taken in various villages and towns in Syria and Iraq as "insurance" that no Gems would be lost.

Youkoumian was not happy at the prospect of working with his "assistants" for an extended period. But he was aware that trying to replace the current ones would probably serve no purpose since no one in the organization was less foreboding than the current ones. Youkoumian consoled himself with the idea that it would not go on for long. The email exchange ended with Youkoumian assuring al-Tunji that the diamonds would be protected up to and beyond the point of possible torture and killing. He asserted that, he, Youkoumian, was also ready to use his karn in the old style if necessary. At the end of the exchange, Youkoumian was quite confident that he could not be held accountable either by al-Tunji or local authorities in case anything went badly wrong.

Al-Tunji was somewhat disturbed by his conversation with Youkoumian. From his point of view, Youkoumian's misgivings about the couriers were really points in their favor. After all, if it came to a situation where the diamonds might be lost, any and all means should be used to preserve them. The fact that Youkoumian did not appreciate that might be an indicator that he had spent too much time amongst the kaffirs. Perhaps it was time to have him replaced with a new Youkoumian.

Upon reflection, Youkoumian felt that the project was progressing well. He was still not sure whether he believed the strange tale of the beautiful young female graduate student. But he felt that he was well protected in case everything failed. He knew where the diamonds were. He knew the people who had them in custody and where they lived. If all else failed, he had a dedicated pair of assistants who were quite capable of retrieving the diamonds under any circumstances and regardless of consequences. Even if his assistants' actions had criminal implications, they were not connected to Youkoumian except through the H1-B Visas. And he could deny any involvement other than to temporarily employ some jewelry artisans. It would not be his fault if two such otherwise exemplary young men went off the tracks and were caught in criminal actions. He would protest that he had always thought them complete gentlemen and never suspected them of any such behavior.

Satisfied that he was quite secure no matter what happened, he allowed his imagination to speculate on the rewards he might expect if everything was as real as the young graduate student had claimed. Clearly his organization would need a liaison to interact with the Damascus Caliphate. His Arabic had become a little rusty after his long sojourn in Philadelphia, but he was sure a few weeks exposure would sharpen his skills. The advantages of spending some considerable amounts of time in another dimension were not lost on him. His wife had always vehemently objected to his taking additional wives, but what happened in another dimension could not be held against him, could it? At the least, it was quite likely that there might be young nubile females in the Caliphate who would find a fighter from another dimension suitably attractive.

For their part, the couriers returned to the safe house also satisfied that they could control the situation. They had not been informed why organization diamonds had been put into the possession of kaffirs. But they had no doubts about their capabilities for retrieving the gems if they were required. Since they had no assigned duties to watch the Front Street location at night, they often returned to the safe house and spent their evenings watching the internet.

Many of the government sponsored ISPs in the Middle East were somewhat puritanical in what they allowed their customers to watch. For the couriers, this meant that the amount and variety of pornography available in the U.S. greatly exceeded what could be watched in their home country. The men from al-Tunji took full advantage of the situation.

Later, tiring of the parade of female bodies, they happened upon a web site discussing the claim that jihadist martyrs were motivated by the supposed reward of 72 voluptuous houris if they died performing acts against the infidels. The web site claimed that the actual text in the Koran promised 72 raisins, not virgins, as a reward for those killed. This amused the couriers from two perspectives. First, they thought it laughable that anyone would be persuaded to trade his life for a mere 72 raisins in paradise. Second, they were amused that anyone would think that those working for their cause would be eager to trade their lives, even if they succeeded in killing many as a result. They agreed between themselves that they would much prefer just to kill many infidels without blowing themselves up. As was the tradition in this group, cutting throats to the neck bones was their preferred method of execution.

Chapter 28

Aban at the airport had successfully noted the re-arrival of the Arabic holders of the H1B visas he was tracking. Unfortunately, he was not able to find a cab quickly enough to follow them into Philadelphia and make certain of exactly where they were staying.

Again, he thought it not appropriate to pursue his investigation of the H1-B visas directly into Youkoumian's jewelry store. He was still looking to accumulate as much information as he could before possibly alerting the owner by confronting him directly. Using this approach, he first again tried to locate the whereabouts of the two Arabic speakers by checking hotels and other places of residence for the names recorded from their H1-B visas. He had no luck, but was not discouraged. Since there had been no record of the visa holders leaving the country after this recent arrival, he was reasonably certain that they were still in the U.S.and in Philadelphia.

His next approach then assumed that an extended stay might well require them to acquire local transportation. It did not take him long, using discreet references to DHS and the assistance of computer experts in the home office in Washington, to find a record of a car currently rented to one of the men. The address given in the rental agreement turned out to be a non-existent number on Church Street so there was still no direct way to find them. However, the phony address was still in center city Philadelphia, so Aban felt there was quite a good chance that the car was being driven in that area.

Aban made use of his new contacts within the 6th district police station and requested that the cruising Radio Motor Patrols, RMPs, be alerted to note the license number of the rental car and that he should be notified if it did appear anywhere. Within less than a day, a patrol unit of the 6th gave a parking ticket to the rental car parked on 7rd street south of Bainbridge. This was not far from Youkoumians store on Sansom. That tied in rather nicely. Aban felt that there was a good chance that it was being used by the men he wanted to locate.

He arranged to rent his own vehicle and began a watch on the rental car in which he was interested. It was still parked at the 7th Street location. Again his efforts quickly paid off as he watched two swarthy, bearded young men leave a row house on Christian Street and walk to the car. He wondered if there was any significance in two men with passports from Muslim Countries using a House on Christian Street. He followed them in his car as they drove to Front Street where they seemed to begin their own surveillance by waiting in the car and watching buildings on the opposite side.

Aban took advantage of the time by taking some telephotos of the men as they occasionally exited the car, apparently for food or perhaps simply to stretch their legs. This also allowed him to observe that the subjects were carrying handguns in the pockets of their jackets. This also seemed to fit, since anyone here illegally might well feel more secure with access to a weapon. After some hours of observations, Aban was convinced that they were staking out the cross street location that apparently was of great interest to them. Since it appeared he would be able to locate the car either around 7th Street or Front Street, he took the opportunity to return to the 6th precinct and inquire about any recent events on Front Street that might be of interest to the bearded men. He was quickly rewarded with the information that 6th precinct detectives had recently participated with the DEA and FBI in apprehending the operators of a Meth Lab in an unused loft of a warehouse there.

Aban was now full of more questions than he had before he started. Could it be possible that Middle Eastern nationals had involved themselves in meth production in the US? Could jihadists be acquiring or laundering money by doing this? What did it all have to do with Youkoumians? What was the connection? He set out to find it.

Aban was still pursuing paper trails from the Arabic men who had entered Philadelphia recently. He submitted, to CIA analysis, the copies of the visas and photographs of the two men who had arrived from the Middle East. The results came back within 36 hours. One of the passport photographs was associated with a young man known to have been eliminated last year in a drone strike in Syria by the CIA. Aban thought that this was a rather interesting development. Either the analysis of the drone strike was incorrect, or the individual who had entered recently was using a bogus passport. Of the two possibilities, Aban leaned toward the idea that the current passport holder in Philadelphia was an impersonator. And so, probably, was his colleague. Why they would choose to impersonate known jihadists was not immediately apparent.

In line with this information, Aban took steps to continue to follow the holders of the two H1-B passports in Philadelphia. On successive days, he had no problem in picking up the men below South Street as they left their lodging. Following them to Front Street, he was able to park on an adjacent street and discreetly observe them as they appeared to be focused on the Front Street address of an older warehouse loft style building. This appeared to have some significance for them. It remained to be seen why they should be interested given their ostensible connection through the H1-Bs to Youkoumians jewelry store. What possible connection could there be between a jewelry store and the Front Street location? And why were they observing it instead of being inside and participating in whatever was going on. The connections remained to be worked out. However Aban did succeed in getting several photos of the men. He took these back to the hotel in which he was staying.

Comparing the photos to those on the H1-Bs he wondered how they had been allowed through passport control. He could clearly see differences between the men on the H1-B photographs and the current holders. His eye was tuned to them because of his trips back to the Middle East. However, after some thought, he could accept that a passport control officer in Philadelphia, who probably seldom saw an individual from the Middle East, might not be able to notice subtle differences between the men in the photos. Basically, it took some degree of exposure to be able to tell that.

In any case, now he would be able to submit the pictures he had just taken to the CIA face recognition software which could potentially positively identify them in the catalog of known operators in middle eastern anti-western organizations. He wasted no time in doing this.

He got results by the next day. Both men were known to be in the CIA data base as soldiers in one or more of the jihadist organizations recruiting and performing operations in the Middle East. Interestingly enough, they were identified as belonging to several organizations. Apparently their membership was quite fluid. But they did have extensive experience in what Aban privately considered atrocities which resulted in murder and torture of civilians in Syria, Libya, and Yemen.

Aban wondered about how such people justified their actions in the name of their religion. Aban was not perfect, but he considered himself a Muslim and was proud to acknowledge it to anyone who might ask. But the idea of torture and killing of helpless civilians seemed to him completely foreign to the basic message of Islam. Still, it didn't matter what he thought, or even what the men who used the H1-Bs thought. The important point was that these were extremely brutal men capable of almost anything. They were definitely a clear danger while in the U.S. It would be necessary to liaison with appropriate organizations, both local and national, about them.

Aban set about this by letting the Philadelphia 6th Precinct detective squad know about the presence of illegal aliens in their area. The detectives were not immediately alarmed since they routinely went through alert periods when possible terrorists were thought to be in their territory. The men using the H1-Bs had not yet committed any known crimes as far as they knew, so there was no reason to try to apprehend them. They would however alert the RMPs about the situation so there would be no confusion if action became necessary. Usually such reports tended to be overblown and the alert would wither from lack of sustaining reports. In essence, most such events went away on their own.

Aban, however, had the feeling that this was a significant set of circumstances and decided he would alert others who might be affected. He decided to contact the SAC in charge of the Philadelphia branch of the FBI, even though, at present, there was no requirement for any action on their part. Finally, since he knew for certain that the men in question had hand guns, he would also alert the Philadelphia branch of the ATF.

Chapter 29

Despite Jennifer's worries about George and Gillian, there was considerable progress on the prototype in the next few days. Worries escalated when Jennifer, who was beginning to keep a regular watch on the outside, noticed two swarthy types apparently loitering in a car across the street and down the block from their location. They were almost in the exact position which George had occupied a few days before, and in the direction Gillian had disappeared. Could they be involved with George somehow? Perhaps some foot soldiers enlisted to keep watch on them?

"Now it looks like we have additional watchers", she said to Hampton.

He put down his tools and walked over toward the window she was observing from.

"Not directly," she hissed, "Stay out of the line of sight from outside."

"OK, OK." muttered Hampton. He discreetly edged to the side of the window and managed to peer past the molding. "It's the green car down the street, right?"

"Since there's nothing else down there, of course that's it," she said acerbically.

"It does look like two guys just sitting in the front seat."

"They weren't there an hour ago. Could they be working for George and Gillian?"

Hampton looked at her with a puzzled expression. "Why would you think that? I can't see them too well, but they don't look like property management types to me. Why would George hire guys to watch us?"

"Hello, Meth Lab, diamonds, possible criminal connections," she said sarcastically, "it could all fit together."

Hampton pondered that. To him it seemed quite a stretch, but she did have legitimate concerns. Why had George and Gillian walked past their loft and why were these strange guys outside? What other reason could they have to be on this sparsely traveled street? Another thing to worry about.

In retrospect, he appreciated the earlier time when he just had to struggle with her explanations of dimensions and the equipment necessary to transit between them. Trying to understand this additional complication of people who seemed to be watching them was way above his pay grade.

Still, what did they have to worry about? Duh, the diamonds of course. Youkoumian had entrusted them with a large quantity of diamonds and Hampton was beginning to get uncomfortable about it. While he didn't think George or Gillian would ever come storming up the stairs with guns demanding the gems, he didn't understand these new men apparently keeping them under surveillance from a car. He looked at Jennifer. "What do you think we should do about it?"

Jennifer thought quickly. "I don't think we can do anything until we get the rest of the diamonds from Youkoumian. Assuming George and Gillian know about them, too, somehow, they probably won't make any move until we get everything." Jennifer knew she wasn't going to rock the boat until the full quantity of diamonds was available.

Hampton reflected that the whole situation seemed to be getting more and more complicated. Jennifer by herself was hard enough to keep up with, but the ramifications of her dimension ideas seemed to be multiplying constantly. Everything seemed to follow logically in small steps but the subsequent situations were getting more and more bizarre. Hampton had never possibly imagined that he could be working on diamonds in a loft that was being scrutinized by strange men sitting in a car with unknown intentions.

He realized he had slowly been drawn further and further into Jennifer's world. Or maybe her dimension. It began to seem to him that while in the beginning her ideas on dimensions might be harmlessly eccentric, recent developments seemed to be leading in ominous directions. And why was he following these ideas? Clearly because she was the most attractive woman he'd ever met and held him in a fascination that he couldn't resist.

He briefly considered that she had bewitched him. But that was ridiculous. It was scientifically impossible. It was much more straightforward than witchcraft. There were tangible reasons why he was attracted to her. She was overwhelmingly beautiful, and that was probably the biggest factor. But it didn't stop there. She was the smartest woman he had ever been with, had the most confident approach to the world, and was indeed the most unusual and interesting person, male or female, that he had ever met. Given that, it would probably be considered strange if he wasn't completely enchanted by her.

Did he regret getting involved with her? He was certainly having misgivings now, but he knew those were not enough to make him want to walk away. He wondered if he would ever reach a point where he was motivated to give up everything he had with her. Right now, he couldn't imagine what circumstances would get him to that point.

At any rate, it seemed to Hampton that he was now so far into the situation that he was clearly past the point of no return. He could see no possible way of extricating himself and Jennifer from this affair easily. Especially given the fact she was adamant about pursuing her dimension travel machine to a conclusion. And of course, he didn't want to get away from her. Somehow, he would like to keep her and be done with all the dimensions and diamonds, and so on. Clearly, his only option now was to produce the equipment Jennifer wanted and hope the circumstances could be resolved without catastrophe. Potentially the equipment would work, and she, and hopefully he, would be transported to another dimension, as outlandish as that thought might be. Optionally, possibly the equipment would not work, Jennifer was not from another dimension, and the failure would cause her serious mental stress. He refused to consider a third possibility … that George, Gillian, or the men outside observing the loft would take steps to acquire the diamonds with serious consequences for himself and Jennifer.

Jennifer peeked out of the front window without showing herself. "Now they appear to be arguing with each other." She could see arms moving in the cabin of the green car.

The thugs *were* arguing. They were both hungry. There was no proper Syrian food in this Crusader city. However, they had talked to a Greek cabdriver on Christian Street the previous day. The cabdriver had some basic words of Arabic and the thugs had some English. They had been looking for Greek food, since their group had learned that Greek restaurants had the type of food closest to Syrian. Recognizing the cabdriver as Greek, they had asked him where they could get food. He had communicated to them that there was an Italian Street Market on 9th Street south of Christian. At least it was close to where they were staying. The thugs were arguing about taking their chances on finding eatable food there.

Apparently, the driver was the more daring of the two. He ended the argument by starting the green car and doing a u turn. They made their way to Second Street and then proceeded south on Front toward Christian Street. Surprisingly, they found a parking space on Christian near 9th Street. Proceeding on foot and turning left on 9th Street they found a site they could recognize ... what looked like a thriving street market of shops, street stalls, and customers. Several places appeared to sell bread, but it was the soft white doughy bread in long loaves that they associated with Turkish Bread. They didn't want Turkish bread. They wanted khubz, Arabic flat bread cooked in a low circular tray in hot ovens. Preferably with za'atar seasoning. As might be imagined there was none to be found on South 9th Street in an Italian Market. But they did find some food which suited them ... a street vendor with a sidewalk grill was preparing and selling kabobs. They tentatively tried a sample and found it to be lamb ... what they knew as Kufla Kabob. They each had two. While they were not as good as those sold in the Tel Abyad market in Racca, they were acceptable to hungry men. Satisfied, they walked back to Christian Street and followed it east to their safe house.

Chapter 30

Gillian was rather frustrated. She'd made some progress in getting additional information about "the project" but wanted more. She had easily trailed George in an attempt to try and find where he lived. She hadn't got that but had wound up with a location for the Jennifer and Hampton project. She'd seen all of them in the neighborhood but so far was unable to determine anything about what they were doing at the Front Street address. George was probably not going to tell her anything explicitly, despite the fact that he was obviously attracted to her.

Should she work harder at trying to find out exactly what George's role was with Hampton and Jennifer? Despite her facility for dealing with males, she felt it was unlikely that further probes on that line with George would produce anything significant. In her experience, it didn't take much flirting on her part to have a young man blurt out information relating to any topic under discussion. What she had done so far should have been more than enough. The poor dears were often so anxious to impress her that they couldn't resist speaking of anything they knew, thinking it would interest her. She was sure George knew some things but so far at least he appeared to be strong willed enough to not divulge them.

What should she do next? The only thing she could think of was that perhaps it was time to enter the loft when no one was there and see what Hampton and Jennifer were working on. The problem with that was, without explanations of what she saw, it's possible she might not be able to figure out what was going on. She decided a consultation with Gloria would be appropriate.

Gloria as usual was pleased to see her and listened carefully to what Gillian had learned.

"It sounds like you are making progress, Gillian. Three unlikely people secretively meeting in an obscure location that was, and perhaps still is, a Meth Lab. It's amazing how you keep finding these situations on your own."

"Yes, that's progress to some extent, but I still have no idea of what they're doing in that loft."

Gloria smiled and said "When you hear hoof beats, think horses not zebras. Isn't it most likely that it still has something to do with Meth?"

Gillian thought about that, agreed, and said "You're right, but how do I confirm that?"

Gloria cocked her head and said "We both know what you'd need to do. If you could get a look at the place while they're not there, you'd undoubtedly be able to recognize the paraphernalia of a working Meth operation."

Gillian looked carefully at her Boss and replied, "OK, I think I understand you."

As Gillian returned to her office, she was sure she understood what Gloria was suggesting. Clearly Gloria could not advise Gillian to illegally enter a site without a warrant and look for evidence. On the other hand, both she and Gloria knew that Gillian had no qualms about doing just that when circumstances were right. It was not standard practice, and nobody would suggest doing it when trying to obtain hard evidence for a trial. But as an expedient when trying to develop information, it was sometimes the quickest way to proceed and confirm that they were heading in the correct direction. Gillian had done this twice during her tenure at the Philadelphia office of the ATF. She was quite accomplished at it and knew she could get the information without consequences. As with many law enforcement officers, Gillian had rather flexible principles about what constituted acceptable investigation, and what was plainly illegal. The principles usually worked and that was the important thing.

Gillian thought about her approach to the Front Street loft. It appeared that the loft was usually in use by Hampton and Jennifer during daylight hours. So, she would have to do her reconnaissance at night. No problem for her. Her heroines as a little girl had always been those females who operated mainly in clandestine roles ... bat girl, cat woman, Lara Croft. She recognized the juvenile appeal of behaving like her juvenile heroines but that did not diminish either her pleasure or capabilities in imitating them. Gillian could recognize the sources of her satisfaction and not be embarrassed by them.

Reviewing, she thought she would do best to wear dark colored clothing, bring along a camera to record what she observed, have a good flashlight with extra batteries, and most importantly, bring along her lock pics. While not all Federal agents were expert in picking locks, Gillian had used her own funds to get the instruction and tools required to swiftly enter most locked doors. She had already used her skills on more than one occasion to enter a location that would have otherwise have stymied an ATF investigation. As is true with most situations, the more she used her skill, the better and faster she became at it.

Chapter 31

At the FBI office, Dan, the Special Agent in Charge, showed up at the doorway to George's space.

"George, how's it going?"

'Great', thought George, 'what got him out of his corner office to wander down here?' Repressing that thought, he managed a greeting for his boss. "Dan, Hi."

Dan moseyed into George's office, seemed to scan the book shelves, looked out the window, and finally plopped himself down in the chair next to George's desk.

"So, didja watch the game last night?"

George grimaced internally. "No, didn't see that one", he said, hoping that would forestall an extended conversation about sports.

"Two in a row," crowed Dan. "The Phillies are on a streak!" he exulted.

Sure, thought George, but they're still below .500. He managed to come up with "That's great!" Which he privately felt was a pretty feeble response. Still, it didn't faze Dan.

"They still got a chance to win their division," said Dan. "They just need to get past an unlucky stretch."

George privately thought that what the Phillies needed to win their division was for all the other clubs in it to go out of business. But he restrained himself with the comment "Could still happen!"

Dan thought about it for a few seconds, then abruptly came up with "So how are we doing with the gunpowder guys?"

George filled his boss in on the Front Street loft. He finished with, "But I still don't know exactly what they are working on over there. Every time I've dropped by for a casual visit, they appear to be reluctant to talk about it."

"And you haven't questioned them about it?"

George justified himself. "Sure I have, but they always put out the line that the whole project is confidential and they're not ready to talk about it yet. Worse, I've admitted I don't know anything about Physics so they might tend to get suspicious if I started to interrogate them hard about it. Why would I be so interested?"

Dan nodded, "So you need more than a casual visit." Dan thought about it. "You still have an extra key. They can't be there all of the time. The logical answer is for you to visit when they're not there and see what you can see."

George screwed up his face, "That's kind of an illegal way to collect evidence, isn't it?"

Dan said, "You're not going to be collecting evidence. We're just looking for information on what is going on. Nothing wrong with us observing a site we're in charge of."

"But I probably would not be able to understand what they are doing."

"No problem, get some pictures and we'll get some expert answers from the lazy ass tech guys in the Operational Technology Section down in Quantico. Serve 'em right if they had to do some real thinking on their own for a change."

George thought about it and produced a slow smile. "You know, that's a pretty good idea, Dan."

Dan smirked at George as he left the office. "Of course it is. Sometimes you got to listen to your SAC."

George watched him leave. He had to admit it. Sometimes Dan could cut to the heart of the matter while he, George, was still agonizing over puzzling details. He thought that probably had some bearing on why Dan was in charge.

George wasn't sure whether he wanted to be the SAC for one of the FBI field offices. Sometimes it seemed that Dan had reached his current position more because of his affability instead of any smarts. One thing, he thought, if it requires faking an interest in sports, I'll never make it.

With Dan gone, he began to think about examining the Front Street loft. Whenever he passed by the location, Hampton and Jennifer seemed to be busy doing things. Obviously, his best chance would be to go there late at night when they were unlikely to be working on their project. He started to itemize equipment he might need ... flashlight, camera, gloves, what else? Dark clothing would probably be a good idea. He resolved to make the visit tonight.

Chapter 32

As might be expected in Philadelphia at 11:30 PM almost anywhere, Front Street was quiet. Gillian, while not exactly outfitted in Ninja togs, wore dark colored clothing and walked close to the buildings which abutted the sidewalk. She was inconspicuous.

A pause of 90 seconds at the doorway to the loft and the swift use of her lock picks gave her access to the stairs. Once on the second floor, there was enough light from the elevated street lights that she didn't need the pencil flash, which was part of her kit, to open the locked door at the top of the stairs.

Her attention was immediately drawn to the apparatus on the center lab table. An electronics rack contained a power supply with cables to a unit securely mounted on the bench. Since this unit contained optics and had a manufacturer's plate with the company's name and the words "150 mW Argon-Ion Laser" on it, she felt pretty safe in assuming it was a laser. Nice deduction, she ironically told herself.

It was placed at one end of a collection of lenses, half silvered mirrors, and full mirrors that seemed like lanes of little signposts proceeding to an opaque sphere with its top half opened. She risked a quick flash of her penlight into the interior of the sphere and noticed a number of fairly large brilliant cut diamonds in an array on the inside surface of the sphere. She found it interesting that she immediately recognized the distinctive shape of brilliant cut diamonds, as probably any woman would. Her first reaction was that brilliant cut diamonds were clearly an example of a patriarchal male culture trying to impress females with flashy trade goods, just as they bought Manhattan for $24 worth of beads. She recognized this and then thought, oh my god, I automatically respond to the trade goods and recognize them. Talk about male control.

Trying to suppress that thought, she did a quick survey of the rest of the room. Nothing stood out. Still she had learned at least two interesting facts. Hampton, Jennifer, Youkoumian, and probably George were all involved basically with diamonds. And two, there was no evidence of any chemical apparatus, no lab stands, no glasswork, nothing like any Chemistry Lab she had taken in high school. Pretty clearly, the secret project didn't involve Meth stuff. At least not at this location.

So why was George involved? If Meth was not involved why should he be so interested in the project? It didn't seem like he had much in common with Jennifer, Hampton, or the Colonel.

So what could the participants be doing with diamonds? Youkoumian made sense since he was a jeweler. But how could the other three contribute anything. Unless they were all a conspiracy to somehow smuggle or illegally sell diamonds either in this country or otherwise. But that didn't make much sense either. Why would the owner of what was probably a prosperous jewelry store be doing illegal things with gems? Was it possible that Youkoumian needed money and was thinking of disposing of diamonds and then claiming losses for insurance purposes? Then why were the other three involved … how would they help?

Puzzled with the results of her foray and the questions that brought up, she turned off her pen light, made her way down the stairs, and locked the door behind her with her picks.. She paused for a moment scanning the street, and then started back toward the center of Philadelphia. She was satisfied that she was not observed. However, she was wrong.

On the other side of Front Street, behind where some construction materials had been stored, George rose and discreetly watched her depart. He clearly recognized Gillian, even in her dark colored clothing. He had been watching since Gillian paused at the door and then went inside. He realized she could have picked the lock. Unless Hampton or Jennifer had given her a key. The latter seemed more likely to him, since he did not think lock picking was a required skill for most secretaries, even if they were called administrative assistants.

Regardless of that, he made his way across the street, unlocked the outside door with his key, and made his own way up to the second-floor loft. Like Gillian, his attention was drawn to the equipment on the center lab table. He wasted no time trying to figure it out but immediately began taking pictures of it from various positions. He, like Gillian, also noted the diamonds in the open opaque sphere. Unlike Gillian, he did not recognize them as brilliant cut diamonds. He did make sure, however, to take pictures of the interior.

Finished, he too made his way down the stair, relocked the entrance door, and began to make his way to his apartment in Society Hill. While the Lab setup was interesting, and the presence of diamonds seemed to define why Youkoumian was part of the project, George was most interested in the thought that Gillian was probably in close association with it. After all, how else could she get in so easily, or even know where the project was?

The idea that Gillian might be part of some shady scheme was a downer. He was starting to enjoy being around her, and not just for her attractiveness. How could she possibly be involved in whatever Hampton, Jennifer, and Youkoumian were doing? He could not think of a reason, but he was mightily disappointed that there might be one.

Chapter 33

Having made appointments with the FBI and ATF for liaison conferences, Aban decided it might be a good time to see what Youkoumian's store was like. He travelled down to Jewelers' Row and was admitted to Youkoumian's store as a potential customer, a Mr. Hansen. For obvious reasons, he did not identify himself as belonging to DHS. Instead, he made believe he was shopping for a ring for his wife for their anniversary. While the staff person attending to him went to get different selections, Aban had time to size up the store. There did not seem to be either any Armenians or Arabic speakers in the front show room. Certainly not anyone who resembled the men he had observed on Front Street. Perhaps there was a rear workshop where some were employed.

He asked his staff person whether he could see the workrooms where jewelry was created. He was told that Mr. Youkoumian would need to be consulted on that and the staff person went to find him. When they returned, Aban was surprised that he was being introduced to a Mr. Youkoumian who was clearly not Armenian and also clearly of Syrian descent. Aban himself could tell that "Mr. Youkoumian" knew that he, "Mr. Hansen", was also of Syrian descent. Both men were clearly on guard and wondered what the other was up to, but neither seemed to feel calling out the situation for what it actually was would help their position.

When requested, Youkoumian courteously showed Aban the jewelry work rooms. There were no Armenians or any people of obvious middle east origins in them. They engaged in polite niceties concerning the facilities as Youkoumian escorted "Mr. Hanson" back into the care of the staff sales person. After Youkoumian went back to his office, Aban examined a few more pieces and then decided he would need to return with his wife to make a final selection. The staff person was disappointed not to make a sale, but assured Aban they would be more than ready to help when he and his wife returned.

Aban was considered one of the rising stars of Homeland Security's Division of Intelligence and Analysis. His value to the government was almost incalculable considering he was fluent in reading, writing, and speaking Arabic. He and other members of his family still had relatives and contacts in various areas of the Middle East. He himself had traveled there on many occasions and he was often taken to be an American when he visited. Despite this, he did not incur any insults or hostile behavior when there. Most people everywhere were simply trying to do the best they could with their lives and were not interested in generating conflict. In the department, Aban was thought to have a good grasp of the situation in many of the countries involved and often was consulted for his take on various situations. As Aban expressed himself, he was almost like a beneficiary of reverse prejudice. There was such a need for his expertise, and such a desire to show "diversity", that it was almost impossible for him *not* to be a star in the agency.

As he left, Aban felt he had learned a lot.

For one thing, the person who ostensibly owned Youkoumian's was not a Youkoumian or even an Armenian. In turn, that raised questions. Why did it benefit the owner to masquerade as an Armenian? For continuation of name recognition and residual good will it might perhaps be advantageous to do that. Perhaps, since "Youkoumian" was from Syria, American customers would be better disposed to an "Armenian" who probably shared at least some parts of their Christian background. That made sense from pure business reasons.

But why go to the trouble of sponsoring H1-B visas? Clearly having an Armenian owner led naturally to the idea that those with the visas were "Armenian" workers occasionally being in the store, and hence as inoffensive as the owner. Having H1-B visas would greatly simplify comings and goings for the people who had them. This in turn suggested that the people using the visas, in regularly entering and exiting the country, could quite likely be transporters of something. And the things they were most likely to transport back and forth to a jewelry store were money and gems. Aban felt that was the likely reason that there were such visas sponsored by this jewelry store.

A second thing Aban felt he had discovered was that the Arabic speakers from the H1-B visas were not regular workers at the jewelry store. The point of getting them H1-B visas was to allow them to enter and exit the U.S. easily, not to do work in the store. Repeated entry and exit would be a good way of transferring money and gems. Aban was convinced, that, since Youkoumian himself was almost certainly Syrian, any such transfers were probably an integral part of an Islamic organization. Odds were, that if it was secretive, it was hostile to the West.

For his part, Youkoumian was a little disturbed by the sudden appearance of this man with the un-Arabic name of Hanson. Clearly the man was of middle eastern descent, and probably had antecedents from one of the tribes in Syria. So it was unlikely that his name was Hanson. Yet, considering his clothes and speech, he projected as any American might. Further, he apparently was married but instead of a gold band, he wore a plain silver ring. This was definitely a tell, since, under Islamic custom, gold was reserved for the adornment of females. Males were expected to use other precious metals, usually silver. This was a further indicator that the man was presumably Muslim. Why should he use a patently false name and still observe Islamic customs? If some organization was beginning to suspect that he was operating a money laundry for his organization perhaps they might send a Muslim to investigate him. And it was possible that the Jordanians could well be interested, if not for themselves, possibly to help the U.S. There were plenty of Syrians living in Jordan. It perhaps signaled the possibility of a threat to himself. But he was at a loss to identify where the threat was coming from, Jordan or the U.S.. Yet another factor to consider in this complicated project.

Chapter 34

A day later, with the demo machine nearing completion, Jennifer and Hampton took a break to walk down Second Street for a coffee. Walking past Christ Church, they went into the Old City Coffee shop and got a table inside looking out through the large windows at Church Street. They were assured by their server that the coffees they ordered were not only freshly brewed but that the beans used had been roasted on site only a few minutes ago, which was a specialty of this coffee house. When they arrived, Jennifer reluctantly endorsed the result as acceptable even by Costa Rican standards. As they waited, Hampton noticed Gillian walking past on the opposite side of the street. He casually remarked "That looks like Gillian over there."

Jennifer immediately said "Where?" She quickly looked in the direction Hampton was looking, and immediately put up her hand to shield her face. "Shit!"

"What's wrong?"

"Stop looking over there and turn to face into the store." Hampton did as he was told. Jennifer was totally pissed off. "What the fuck is she doing down here? Have you been talking to her?" Jennifer looked like she was ready to kill him on the spot.

Hampton was completely taken aback. "No, of course not. I haven't seen her since the meeting of the 71st VA."

"Then there's absolutely no reason for her to be down in this area. Shit, shit, shit! And we saw her hanging around Front Street a few days ago. What the hell is she up to?"

Hampton recognized this as a rhetorical demand and wisely didn't try to come up with an answer for Jennifer.

"It's too much of a coincidence that she should be down here. She has to have found out about the diamonds. Maybe that was why she was on Front Street."

Hampton agreed that what she was doing over in this area was a concern. "If she's hanging around where we are working, I think the best thing we could do is finish the prototype and get ready to demo it for Youkoumian."

But the whole issue was compounded as Hampton and Jennifer started to walk back to Front Street. As they went down the Church Street alley toward Second Street, they noticed Gillian passing the alley entrance on Second Street. Jennifer looked at Hampton. "Now will you believe me?"

Hampton reluctantly conceded. "It does seem more than coincidence that she should be prowling around in this area at the same time as we are. There obviously is something going on."

Jennifer was getting more and more nervous about these developments with George and Gillian. To her, they were red flags indicating something was going wrong with her plan. She felt she couldn't bear for her careful actions to fall through because of George and Gillian. She could cheerfully shoot either or both of them if her plans were frustrated. But the something going on was not what Jennifer anticipated. There was a simpler reason for Gillian to be on Church Street. In one of her passes by the Front Street address, she had taken note of the rental green car license plate. It was relatively easy for her to trace this back to the rental agency and get the false address which the couriers had provided. As she walked around the area, it was frustrating to find that the address did not exist, but that was often the case for investigations. Careful planning and attention to detail, but with no information produced for all the investigative effort. With resignation, she left the area to return to the ATF offices.

To avoid Gillian, Jennifer got herself and Hampton started North on American Street hoping to avoid seeing her. With a few detours she got them back to the Front Street loft where they climbed the stairs and both sighed in relief to be in what they now considered to be safe territory.

Jennifer sat on a high lab bench and proclaimed "This is getting ridiculous. We have to finish this off. The sooner we can demo for the Colonel, the sooner we can get the 5000 diamonds we need."

Hampton remarked, "Even when we get the diamonds, it'll take some time to construct a full sized unit. It won't be that easy."

"Yes, of course," said Jennifer, "but I know you can get it done." She rather dismissed any consideration of future complications. In her mind, the important thing was having the diamonds in hand, not the construction of a device to travel between dimensions. Hampton was less sure that completing the demo would end their concerns.

As he started into making the remaining connections to the demo unit, he mused, "Maybe we should consider finding a different location for the final unit." mused Hampton. "Perhaps if we moved to a location not known to George and Gillian we would not have these worries about threats from them or any men they may have hired."

Jennifer was quite taken with that idea. "Excellent! I would feel much more secure if we rented some space that nobody else but we knew about."

"That might be expensive,' said Hampton.

Jennifer dismissed his concerns. "Don't worry, I have enough in my Doctoral fellowship to cover it. It's not like I'll be needing it when we go to my dimension." It was easy for her to dismiss his concerns, since her objective was not the fanciful dimension traversing machine she had invented, but rather the jewels themselves. She was getting so close! She wondered if she could contain herself until they demoed the prototype machine and Youkoumian came across with the 5000 diamonds.

She made a rather enticing sight with her delicious looking legs dangling down from the high lab bench, but Hampton suppressed his urges and concentrated on final connections and adjustments.

Chapter 35

Aban had finally gotten an appointment with the SAC for the Philadelphia FBI. It was understandable that joint meetings between the DHS and the FBI were not high priority for the FBI. Since it was established in 1908, the Bureau had worked hard to promote its public image as the protectors of the U.S.and Americans "...against all enemies, foreign and domestic". To some extent, this carefully crafted historical narrative had been diminished by the establishment of DHS as a cabinet level institution, with over 170,000 employees, and, perhaps the most annoying factor of all, a budget which dwarfed that of the FBI. No wonder the feebs were miffed.

However Dan Carolli was not about to show anything of this to Aban Hassad as he welcomed him into the SAC's corner office.

"Come on in, come on in," said Dan. "It's a pleasure to meet you. Here, let's sit over here in these chairs so we don't have a desk between us." Dan made a point of getting Aban into the chair in which he would not have sunlight in his eyes. "So, is it OK if I call you Aban, or would you prefer Mr. Hassad?"

Aban was slightly amused at all of this camaraderie. He recognized Dan's type ... there were quite a few just like him at

Homeland Security. It seemed to be a type attracted to "public service". More heartiness than competence. With a smile, he replied "Aban is fine" as he sat down.

"Ok, Ok, great. Just call me Dan. Can I get the girl to get you coffee or anything?"

Aban wondered if got away with calling his secretary "the girl" to her face. In today's hyper-sensitive PC environments, probably he managed to avoid doing that. Otherwise he might well be chastised and demoted. So somehow he was disciplined or clever enough to only use it when he felt secure from political correctness. This argued for a considerable amount of acumen in quickly deciding how to express things, either as his natural feelings came out or politically correctly. Aban was somewhat impressed. "No, I'm fine, Dan" Aban replied as he settled down in the comfortable office chair.

"Ok, great," said Dan as he settled himself down. "So you're from New York. How about those Mets, eh?"

Aban agreed that the Mets were indeed a fine baseball team this season.

"Don't get too cocky, though, Aban, the Phillies are gonna start a winning streak and catch up and make it a race."

Aban politely agreed it was possible, even though he was aware that the single win the Phillies had managed last night was more than overbalanced by their prior streak of four losses. Without trying to disguise the fact that he was changing the subject, Aban changed the subject.

"Basically, I'm here to alert you to some potential problems which might arise from some Arabic speaking men who have entered Philadelphia recently. I believe these people are here illegally using H1-B visas which were not issued to them. They are using a rented car and have been observed to be carrying weapons."

Dan, who had no idea what an H1-B visa was, nodded knowingly. "Ok, sounds bad."

Aban also nodded, "Interestingly enough, the sponsor of these H1-Bs is a store in your Jewelers' Row, Youkoumians. We find it a little strange that this store needs to use H1-Bs to import these men to conduct their normal jewelry business. Although it would probably be possible to take these men in on weapons charges, I think we could all learn more if we continued to just observe them. I have all the collected information in this folder and if circumstances arise, I hope we can co-operate to stop these people before something bad happens."

"What do you mean, something bad?" asked Dan.

"Both of these men have been identified by Middle East sources as being active jihadists. Basically, they maim, torture, and kill anyone who doesn't do what they want. It's conceivable that they have something planned that could be of major harm to Philadelphia."

"You mean they might be here for a terror attack?" asked Dan.

"It's possible," replied Aban. "Although nothing has been currently identified."

"And what's your estimate of likelihood?"

"I think it's about 50%" said Aban

"Wow," said Dan with an expression of surprise. He thought about it for a while. "So let me recap this to make sure I understand it completely. You've got evidence that two Arabic speaking jihadists are in the U.S.and are directly connected with a local jewelry store, Youkoumians."

"That's correct."

Dan said, "You know, one of my agents has been investigating that store on a low priority basis already. The owner heads up a local Civil War re-enactor's group and my agent was getting suspicious about their black powder supply. What caught his attention was that they are a group with a Confederate regiment designation in a northern state."

Aban blinked. "That's definitely anomalous."

"I think you two should discuss this directly. I'll walk you down to his office and you two can exchange information." said Dan.

"That will be greatly appreciated," said Aban.

Both men stood and Dan escorted Aban to George's office, introduced them, and left.

On his way back to his own office, Dan went over the situation in his own mind. He had seen alerts of this kind before. There were almost never any instances of an alert like this moving forward successfully. On a few occasions the attack was foiled by U.S. agents. Usually, nothing came of the alerts, there was no further information, and they were quietly allowed to die. Thinking about it, he was sure George was the guy in the Philadelphia office with the most experience of Youkoumian's. Perhaps he had been right all along in his hunch that the reenactor's group was a front for being able to get gunpowder. Possibly for a terrorist attack.

Back in George's office, Aban explained his interest in Youkoumian's and what he had found out in the last few days. George was rather impressed with the information the DHS agent had found out in such a short time. However, he didn't feel resentful. Realistically he knew DHS had far more resources to collect and analyze NSA and CIA reports than he did. These had certainly helped start Aban out on the path to Youkoumian by flagging the H1-B visas. But George was honest enough to recognize and appreciate Aban's skills in collecting information, analyzing it, and interfacing with organizations. He was impressed.

As George explained what he had found out about the situation, Aban, for his part, was also impressed. George's persistence and being alert to anomalies were definite marks in George's favor. Both men now exchanged the information they had each discovered.

For Aban, the fact that the Front Street location was not a working Meth site eliminated many possibilities. Additionally, finding out about Hampton and Jennifer added new complications. This new factor of a project involving Youkoumian, Hampton, and Jennifer was definitely surprising information. What complicated the situation was the factor of the diamonds. Aban could understand the diamonds being used in transferring funds. What he couldn't see was how a "project" involving people from the Physics department of the University of Pennsylvania could be helpful in using or transporting the gems.

George learned that Youkoumian was probably a Syrian and had connections with known jihadists. Did this mean that Hampton and Jennifer were also linked up with terror groups through Youkoumian? George still wondered how Gillian connected to the situation. Since he was still uncertain, he did not include his suspicions about her in talking with Aban. Of course, the real reason he didn't mention her was that he was strongly attracted to her and did not want to cause trouble for her. He couldn't believe that she was doing something bad.

After Aban left, in his office, George thought he was now much closer to understanding what was going on with the Hampton, Jennifer, Youkoumian project. If Youkoumian was a Syrian instead of an Armenian, and linked to members of jihadist groups, it would support what seemed to be the fact that he was importing Arabic speakers. The most likely use for these periodic visitors was transporting gems and money between the Middle East and Philadelphia. That made sense.

What didn't make sense is why he was apparently sponsoring a lab setup in the Front Street loft which involved diamonds. How did that help his transport logistical problems? If anything, it seemed to introduce an additional level of complexity. Still, he needed to get the report from the Quantico Physicists on the pictures he had taken. Maybe that setup was intended to somehow disguise the diamonds so they were less detectible when going through controls. The damn scientists were always coming up with strange things and almost anything was possible. He would have to await the results from the research nerds.

Surprisingly, he got the analysis on the Front Street location from the research facility at Quantico that afternoon. The nerds assured him the purpose of the setup had nothing to do with Meth. But they didn't provide any clues as to what its real purposes were. Apparently, it looked like "… a typical classical Michelson-Morley experiment designed to detect interference between two parts of a beam of light." However, there did not seem to be a detector at the point where the beams recombined. The lab guys suggested that that part of the apparatus was still incomplete. Finally, the researchers could offer no explanation for directing half of the beam into a hollow sphere with diamonds mounted on the interior. As far as they knew, there was no known physical effect of refracting light in diamonds.

George had no idea what a classical Michelson-Morley experiment was, or why the geeks in Quantico thought it helpful to point that out. He thought the only useful part of the report was the elimination of Meth as an objective for the Front Street Project. Whatever was going on, it did not seem to be involved with either Meth or gunpowder.

Chapter 36

Aban also managed to make an appointment with someone in the Philadelphia branch of the ATF …. Gloria Wentworth. Gloria was quite pleased to see this slender, darkly handsome young man as he entered her office. The attitude of the ATF toward DHS was altogether more relaxed than that of the FBI. The fact that DHS was so much bigger and had so much more prestige was of little importance. Gloria herself was running out her time until retirement and hence had no reason to quarrel with the young man sitting across from her.

"So how can I help you, Mr. Hassan?"

"Please, call me Aban."

"Certainly."

"I'm just here as a precaution to give you some relevant information about some potentially dangerous people who have entered Philadelphia recently," said Aban. He went on to explain his activities in tracking the H1-B visa holders and provided her with a folder with the information he had found so far. "I'm here at ATF because I have personally observed these illegal entrants with hand guns which are probably illegal. I wanted you to have as much information as possible in case something untoward occurs."

"You mean in case the shit hits the fan," said Gloria. She surprised even herself with this comment. As she got closer to leaving, she was getting saltier and saltier. At least it didn't shock this young man.

Aban was almost laughing, "Yes, that's a good summary of why I thought you might find the information interesting."

"Holy cow," said Gloria as she leafed through the folder. "This involves Youkoumian's jewelry store."

"Yes, it does. Are you familiar with the place?"

"I have an agent who is working on a related issue that touches on his store. According to this, you're sure he's not Armenian."

"Yes, I think that's pretty certain."

"And you think he's Arabic, probably Syrian."

"Yes, that's a high probability" said Aban.

"This definitely changes our take on the situation. I'm going to have you talk to her directly."

Gloria checked to be sure that Gillian was in her office and then walked Aban down there and introduced them. As they walked there, she looked at him and noticed again how handsome he was. Maybe he might be the one to charm Gillian into a relationship. Then, she also noticed he had a silver ring on one of his fingers. She hoped it wasn't what she thought. "That's a beautiful ring, Aban."

"Thank you," he said, "It's the same idea as Christian gold wedding bands, but Muslim men are traditionally expected to not wear Gold. Hence the custom is for male rings to be based on silver."

Goria introduced Aban to Gillian as an investigator from DHS. Gillian made him welcome and asked him to sit, Gloria immediately noticed that she was attracted to the good looking agent. And he was also attracted to Gillian. As she left, Gloria thought 'Too bad, all the handsome ones are already taken.'

Once Aban and Gillian were settled in her office, Gillian scanned the folder. "This is quite an eye opener. It provides a lot of information on questions I have in my own investigation around Youkoumian," she said. She explained to him her interest in Youkoumian as colonel of a Confederate Re-enactors group which might have ready access to gunpowder.

Gillian said, "My information has been that Youkoumian was Armenian and long accepted as such in this city. Since you are certain he is Syrian, it makes a lot of aspects clearer. My suspicions have been centered on a project he has going with some people from the Physics department at the University of Pennsylvania. I've surreptitiously visited their site and, while I don't understand their setup, it does involve diamonds which they presumably got from Youkoumian's store."

Aban was struck with the fact that both George and Gillian were investigating Youkoumian's apparently without being aware of each other's interest. At least neither mentioned the other. Additionally, neither had any qualms about looking for evidence without a warrant. At least neither had mentioned getting official permission to examine the Front Street location. And neither had mentioned the other as having an investigative interest in the site or referred to the other. That was intriguing to Aban. For the moment, he kept that information to himself. He decided to just listen. He wanted to hear her reasons for investigating Youkoumian. It would seem that her initial interest arose from the gunpowder that would be available to a re-enactor's group. The fact that explosives might be readily available to them significantly raised his estimation of the probability of a terror attack. Still, such an overt action would be a significant change of behavior in what he observed to be going on in the jewelry store on Sansom Street.

He explained to her about Homeland Security's researches into the ongoing travels of Middle Eastern men using H1-B visas obtained via the jewelry store. To his surprise, she immediately picked up on the significance and pointed out that regular visitors who are able to easily enter and depart the U.S. could be exceedingly useful to a radical Islamist organization. She described it as a big red flag.

Gillian outlined for him what she knew about the project on Front Street. To her surprise, he already knew that location. He mentioned that the Philadelphia 6th precinct detectives already knew of the location as the site of a Meth raid and subsequent arrests. He identified it as a place of interest to the people holding the H1-B visas. Gillian contributed her observations on the location. "I can vouch for the fact that there currently is no Meth processing going on there. Aban refrained from asking her how she knew this, but suspected that she. like George, had visited the site without seeking court approval. By putting together the parts that they each knew, they felt they could understand Youkoumian's motivation to support the operations on Front Street. The use of H1-B visas for ostensible employees of the jewelry store was probably oriented around the movement of gems and cash back and forth between Philadelphia and the Middle East. So Youkoumian's support of Hampton's and Jennifer's project might have something to do with improving that process, or making it easier, or more secure. As yet, they could not come up with any ideas on how that might be accomplished.

Gillian did not discuss her suspicions of George's involvement with Youkoumian. Although she didn't mention it, Gillian was still uncertain about George's connection to the Front

Street location. If he wasn't involved in Meth, and Front Street was not about Meth, why was he connected? Was it just about the diamonds and the elaborate experimental setup? If not, why was he so interested in Hampton and Jennifer? In any case, Gillian did not feel comfortable at mentioning George's possible involvement. She thought about that, and concluded that she was starting to have feelings about George. She honestly admitted this to herself. She liked him and did not want to see him in trouble.

Chapter 37

Back at the Front Street location, Hampton was finishing with the fussy work of mounting diamonds in the small opaque hemisphere and adjusting laser beam paths in the prototype device on the lab bench. He checked what he had done against her specifications. It looked to him like he had completely followed everything correctly. Hesitantly, he looked at her. "We're ready to turn on the laser and let it rip. Shall we?"

Jennifer said, "Sure, do it, make sure it's all ready to show Youkoumian."

Hamptonn was reluctant to start it because he still did not know whether her specifications would produce a gateway to her dimension, assuming it did exist. In fact, he wasn't convinced of that either.

Sighing, Hampton made sure they both had protective glasses on and toggled the laser. It took almost five minutes to warm up, but then a blue-green beam instantly appeared proceeding out from the laser assembly. The beam could be seen splitting into two parts by impinging on the half-silvered mirrors. One part disappeared into the 10 cm diameter opaque sphere which contained the mounted diamonds. The sphere also was visible glowing in an encouraging fashion. A beam could be seen coming out of the sphere and it seemed to combine with the original half of the laser beam. Nothing happened.

Hampton said, "Nothing's happening."

"Don't worry," said Jennifer, "it looks perfect." For Jennifer's purposes, the machine was in fact working perfectly. The lights and laser were impressive and she knew they would attract the attention of Youkoumian. She was getting twinges of excitement at getting one step closer to getting the 10,000 carats.

"Nothing's going to happen until we put a message in the chamber and it's transported back to my dimension. Once that's done, impressive things will happen. I'm going to wait until we have Youkoumian here before we do that so that he will see all of the steps of the process and understand that we are not just telling him a tale. He can see everything we do to communicate with another dimension without any tricks. You did it perfectly, babe." She kissed him. "You can turn it off, sweetie"

Hampton appreciated the kiss, but didn't think the apparatus was that impressive. He turned off the laser. The power supply had heated up considerably since it required 15 kilowatts to make the laser work. He was worried something might go wrong when Youkoumian was here, but, as usual, she was in charge and acted like she was fully in control of everything. She certainly was in control of him. He thought about it and came to the conclusion that that was OK. Despite the omnipresent male assumption that a male should be running everything, Hampton was quite comfortable with Jennifer running things. Did that mean he was a wuss? Even if it did, he decided it was worth it. Apparently, he was not particularly macho, except when he was in bed with her. She seemed to accept his running things there quite well.

"So," he said, "why don't we send a message to your professors in your dimension now and ensure we've made contact before we get Youkoumian over here?"

Jennifer said, "Because it will be more dramatic if we do everything as he watches and sees what in fact goes on. What's your problem, don't you think it's going to work as I say it will?"

That was exactly what Hampton was worried about, but it was not something he could admit to her. He didn't understand the whole process or the Physics she said it was based upon. The whole thing smacked of magic to him. What if it didn't work as she said it would? It would be embarrassing for both of them to have a failure in front of Youkomian. But if it didn't work as she said, it might have serious emotional consequences for Jennifer. Hampton didn't know much about the psychology of people who had an "idee fixe" but he thought that being confronted with a situation that contradicts the obsession would not be good for the believer or those associated with her.

Hampton manned up and said "Of course I think it will work. I'm just thinking about ways to avoid embarrassing glitches."

"That's OK, sweetie," said Jennifer. "But I've got it all covered. Just believe in me and everything will turn out fine." Hampton was not so sure. In his experience, lab experiments often developed glitches which needed some corrections. He still thought they would be better off testing the sending of a message, but was quite willing to go along with her direction. As usual.

Chapter 38

After his visits to both the FBI and ATF, Aban thought it would be beneficial to have a three-way meeting involving everyone with some knowledge and interest in Youkoumians. Since neither George nor Gillian seemed to be aware of the other's activities, such a meeting might improve everyone's comprehension about the situation. After several calls, Gloria, head of Gillian's ATF section, volunteered her conference room and the meeting was set up for a day later at the ATF Philadelphia office.

It was rather a surprise for George to enter the conference room and see Gillian already sitting at the table wearing her ATF identity placard. It was no less a surprise for Gillian to see George's FBI placard, but she recovered faster.

"Nice to see you again, George," she said satirically. "First Buildings Inc. seems to be treating you well."

George managed to recover fairly fast himself. "I guess I could say the same about your insurance company. I hope your vice president isn't docking you for not being there this afternoon."

Aban was amused as he observed this exchange and said. "It looks like you two already know each other."

"We do, but apparently not completely," said Gillian with a smile.

"Yes," said George, "Apparently, both of us are pretty good at keeping things secret."

Aban could see that it was a kind of private joke between them and proceeded to begin the discussion. Everyone contributed where they were in their investigations. Gillian and George were each obviously interested in the other's activities, but neither mentioned the suspicions each had had about the other. George was amused that Gillian had managed to find the Front Street location by the simple expedient of tailing him. For her part, Gillian was amused that, since both had been at Front Street several nights ago, George probably saw her illegally enter the place but didn't mention her presence to Aban. Another good example of his discretion.

Aban tried to summarize their joint findings. "So, what we have is a jewelry store purportedly owned by an "Armenian" who is almost certainly an Arabic Syrian. The owner is the head of a group of Civil War reenactors which have the unusual distinction of having a confederate regimental designation while being in a northern state. This group has access to gunpowder for their rifled muskets. The store sponsors H1-B visas for Arabic speakers with known Jihadist connections who use them to commute between the Middle East and Philadelphia for unknown purposes. Most recently, the owner of the jewelry store started a project with a Physics grad student and a lab tech, both from the University of Pennsylvania. This project apparently consists of a ..." he read from his notes, "... 'classical Michelson-Morley experiment' ... whatever that is. The unusual part of it is that it involves diamonds, presumably supplied by the store owner. But no one can even hazard a guess about its purpose. Does that about sum up what we jointly know?"

Gillian said, "A concise and accurate summary." George agreed that it was.

Gillian added, "Another thing we don't know for certain is the suggestion that the H1-B Jihadists are functioning as runners for transporting jewels and cash between Philadelphia and the Middle East. If Youkoumian is in fact expediting that, simply confronting him with questions will not get us any new information. We need actual confirmation from hard evidence."

George said, "For my part, I don't see any other way to proceed unless we get more information directly from Youkoumian or whatever his real name is. To me, that means a search warrant, particularly for his computers."

Aban agreed, "We all seem to be on the same page. I'm going to have my boss ask your superiors for you to be temporarily assigned to a task force consisting of the three of us to investigate this problem. While that happens, I'm going to ask a federal judge for appropriate search warrants for Youkoumian's store and computers, as well as the house where the H1-B visa holders are staying. Finally, while we don't need a warrant, we should do a thorough search of the loft on Front Street. We'll need tech experts to check out any computers and electronic devices we can find."

George and Gillian nodded at that.

"George, since you provided that Front Street location I think it would be well if you led the team that checks it over. Presumably the FBI can supply the investigators necessary to go over the place."

George said "Yes, we have CSI agents with the required expertise to work over almost anything. If your bosses talk directly to Dan Corelli, I'm sure he will agree to come forward with the necessary resources for the search.

Aban continued, "Since I've spent some time observing the Queen Village house, I'll take care of the team investigating that. And we can get local CSI people from the Philadelphia office of Citizenship and Immigration Services. Homeland Security." He turned to Gillian. "If it's all right with you, Gillian, I think you should be in charge of the people that check out Youkoumian's store. I suspect that's where we'll get most of our information. Also, it would be well if the ATF supplied the investigators to examine things at the store."

Gilllian said, "OK with me. I'm sure my boss Gloria will be glad to supply people to check everything out. When do you think we might do this?"

Aban checked his watch. "Since it's now close to six o'clock and there's no real urgency, I intend to do everything carefully and start getting the warrants tomorrow. By slowing down slightly, we should be able to eliminate glaring mistakes. Hopefully we'll have the warrants by tomorrow afternoon and we can start early two days from now."

Everyone agreed and collected their notes while preparing to leave.

As he left the ATF offices, George looked at Gillian with a twinkle in his eye. "Devon?"

Gillian said in response, "Devon!"

Gloria, at her office doorway, was waiting for Gillian's take on the meeting. But her immediate interest was in Gillian's relationship with George. "He's cute," said Gloria, "even though he's FBI. I hope he's unattached."

Gillian reddened slightly. "He is," she admitted. "That's George. He's the one I was cultivating to get information about the gunpowder group."

"Ah ha," said Gloria, "so you already know he's unattached! You go, Girl!"

Gillian said as she shook her head slightly, "Gloria, you are such a Mom, sometimes."

Gloria said with a smile, "More like a Grandmom, dear. I'd just like you to find someone for yourself. And he looks well dressed, prosperous, and sincere."

"You can tell sincerity just from a 15 second look at a guy?"

"Believe me, Dear, after 40 years you can read them like a book. I heard you both say something about Devon, so you can tell me about the meeting tomorrow and scoot along now." Gloria made scooting motions with both hands. "But I will demand full details on you and your young man tomorrow!"

Gillian laughed and scooted along.

Chapter 39

At Devon, George arrived first, as usual. He was feeling especially good. He was extremely pleased that Gillian was not involved in any skullduggery associated with Youkoumians. He was still bemused with the fact that she had convinced him of her casual interest in the 71st VA. while pretending to be working at an insurance company. He was looking forward to teasing her about her made up background. And he realized that he would be getting an equal amount of repartee about his own cover story. He thought he would thoroughly enjoy the remainder of the evening.

"Hi." Gillian said as she took the stool he was saving next to himself. "How's the property management business?"

George almost laughed at that. "I think it's definitely on the decline. Probably something like the insurance business."

"We're both pretty good at improvising and maintaining a cover, aren't we?" said Gillian.

"You definitely had me fooled," said George. "I completely believed everything you told me, including that sweet vermouth on the rocks."

"Oh God, I don't know why I came up with that. I sometimes have these odd impulses."

"Impulses, that's something I like in a woman. Tell me more." George's smile leered a little at her in an obvious fashion.

Gillian shook her head. "Just when I think you are acting like a normal human, you go all Y chromosome at me."

"Hey, it's not my fault. I'm just influenced by the three P's"

"Oh God, I should never have told you about that, either. Now you can use it to excuse everything you do. I hope you didn't order me a sweet vermouth on the rocks."

"No, after our last get together, I rather got the impression you would like something different. So, I decided to wait until you could decide for yourself."

"An excellent principle for all Ys, and observant of you." she said. Catching the bartenders eye, she ordered her favorite drink, a raspberry mojito.

"What exactly is in a mojito, anyway?" asked George.

"Almost anything you want", said Gillian. "But basically, they all usually have rum and mint in them."

George shook his head, "They seem to be popular with young women. I've had dates with several who preferred them."

"So, you consider our meetings at Devon dates?" asked Gillian.

"Yes, I do" George stated unequivocally. "You are definitely someone I would like to date. You're smart, have interesting ideas, and are totally attractive to boot."

"When you restrain your three P's, you just keep scoring points, don't you?" said Gillian. "Why hasn't some girl snapped you up already?"

George said "There are many possible answers to that, most of which you will find out for yourself in the fullness of time. Until you are fully aware of all my faults, I would like to stipulate that I would much prefer to be snapped up by a young woman, like yourself, rather than a girl. Meanwhile, tell me more about your duties as an administrative assistant."

"Only if you tell me more about being a property manager."

"Touche. I can't tell you how relieved I am to find you're not involved with whatever scams Youkoumian, Hampton, and Jennifer may be running."

"And why is that?"

George replied "Isn't it obvious that I like being with you?"

Gillian said, "Yes, it is. But the ultimate motivation for that observation is still in question."

George took a moment to look at her. "As far as it is possible, I believe I have harnessed my Procreation drives and directed them to genuine considerations about our possible future relationship."

Gillian looked at him for a long moment. "You know, I can believe you're sincere."

George said, "Great, let's go back to my apartment and tear each other's clothes off."

Gillian laughed out loud. "You are sometimes so Y chromosome that I have to laugh! It's amusing to have you come out with these outrageous male proposals."

George said, "The most refreshing thing I find about your reaction is that you don't reject me out of hand."

"All right, I admit I could be tempted," said Gillian. "As long as you don't become too Y."

George said to her, "I can promise you that I won't do that."

Gillian smiled back and said, "Good." She took a longer look at him. "I'm not sure how we got to this position."

"We've both definitely gone through a lot of pretending to be someone we're not," said George.

The two began to discuss their reasons for their joint initial interest in the 71st VA. They found that they had a lot in common in that both had been interested initially because of the anomalous nature of a re-enactor's group in Pennsylvania choosing a Virginia regiment for its name. Once that had got their attention, both had wondered about the status of the gunpowder that such groups were known to have. And when they finally went to meetings, they both found Colonel Youk-oumian, the self-styled Armenian, to be a jarring dissonance which raised their antennae.

"It just goes to show that, despite all the connections which we supposed might be there, despite all the false trials and leads we pursued, developments showed that both our instincts were correct, and there was something suspicious going on," said George.

"Speaking of developments with this whole affair, this agent from Homeland Security, Aban Hassad, seemed to get a lot more information than we were able to develop." Gillian said.

George remarked, "I don't feel bad about that. He had access to a whole boatload of meta-data gathering from DHS. They get reports from CIA and other U.S. intelligence agencies as well as info from spooks in other countries.

Gillian said, "Still, given that information, he managed to develop many more details than we did."

"He is definitely discouragingly competent," said George.

"And that doesn't make you jealous or envious?"

"Well, he has an organization behind him with enormous resources to devote to data analysis. Still even without considering those advantages, he has gotten impressive results in understanding the situation we're involved with."

"And you can accept that he's accomplished more than you in understanding our situation?"

"I don't see how denigrating what he has provided could possibly help me" said George. "He's good."

"I shouldn't admit this to you, but the more I listen to you, the more impressed I become." said Gillian.

"I'm already impressed with you and expect it to continue and increase."

Gillian said, "Now you're getting mushy."

"I thought women liked a little mush in their men."

"Different women like different things. I personally don't like extravagant expressions of interest."

"OK," said George, "duly noted."

Gillian smiled at him and said. "I wasn't accusing you of anything. What I do like is that you are consistent in speaking of 'women' instead of "ladies' or 'girls' or worst of all 'gals'."

"So where does that leave us?" asked George

Gillian said. "We obviously like to interact together. We should let that proceed and see where it takes us."

"Damn," said George, "I was hoping that I had completely overcome your reservations and that we could make immediate progress to a bed."

"You never give up, do you?" said Gillian.

"I'm a Y. I keep trying just in case," said George.

"Won't work in this instance," said Gillian. "AT least for right now. "But, I do admire your persistence." She smiled at him.

Chapter 40

Hampton and Jennifer had nothing else left to do. The proto-type device was neatly arrayed on a lab bench in the center of the second floor of the Front Street loft. The laser power supply made encouraging noises and the laser interlaced between the mirrors in precise beams. The only problem, as Hampton thought about it, was nothing seemed to change. But Jennifer was OK with its functioning and that meant the time had come.

Jennifer phoned Youkoumian and asked him to come down to the Old City Front Street loft to see the apparatus and witness the demonstration. He was not happy about the location and somewhat nervous about being in the area. Still, he was reassured that his courier assistants would be in the vicinity and engaged in active surveillance of the site. He felt reasonably secure.

The climb to the loft and the associated smells were not reassuring. However, the apparatus that Hampton had built occupied a center bench in the loft and looked impressively neat and scientific. This is what we need, he thought, more scientific effort to support our cause. He was ready to see the demonstration and was even predisposed to hope that it would be totally convincing and lead to much needed support from their brothers in another dimension.

Jennifer explained the basics of the apparatus. Not much registered with Youkoumian, but he was reassured by the certitude and confidence of her explanation.

"So here is the message I will be sending," said Jennifer. She showed him a small scrap of paper with numbers. "The numbers are the GPS coordinates of this location." Youkoumian was sufficiently familiar with western technology to understand that this was a precise way of specifying the return address. "And here I'm asking them for a recent gold piece minted in the Caliphate of Damascus." She placed the message in the small apparatus chamber, closed the hemispherical top and nodded to Hampton.

Hampton handed out the safety glasses to protect against any possible visual effects of the laser beam. When they were firmly in place, Hampton, without fanfare, activated the laser. After a warmup period, the laser beams instantly produced an impressive pattern of interlaced light. The small apparatus chamber produced an impressive interior glow but there was no other effect.

"Turn it off, Hampton." Hampton did so.

Jennifer then asked Youkoumian to open the small chamber. He said, "It won't shock me, will it?"

"No it's perfectly safe."

Youkoumian slowly and carefully opened the top so that everyone had a good view of what he was doing …. to reveal nothing. The chamber was empty. The scrap of paper had disappeared.

Youkoumian turned to Jennifer with a confused expression. "What happened to the paper?"

Hampton was more than confused. He could not imagine what had happened to it. Both were astonished as they saw no way for the paper to leave the chamber.

"As you can see," said Jennifer, "we have successfully transmitted it to another dimension. Now we only need to wait for my professors in my dimension to transmit the gold coin back here. That may take a little while, so I have coffee here for us while we wait."

Youkoumian was more than a little startled by the demonstration so far. It certainly looked as if the paper had been transmitted .... somewhere. It remained to be seen if there would be an actual appearance of the promised gold coin. But his hopes were rising that this was indeed happening and what he wanted to happen was now taking place.

Hampton was more than startled. He was flabbergasted. Is she easily communicating with another dimension? He would not have thought it possible, but so far, she had made it look easy, in keeping with her competence in everything she did. While they waited, Hampton had questions about it but refrained from expressing his doubts in front of Youkoumian. Jennifer, for her part, was as charming to the Colonel as only she could be when she made an effort. She engaged him in conversation about his Family and suburban home in an attempt to make him more comfortable. After a relatively short period of time, she announced that they could check the demo unit to see if the requested coin had arrived.

"Colonel Youkoumian, would you do the honors of checking the chamber? That way, you can be sure that the coin has been transmitted without intervention by Hampton or me."

Rather hesitantly, Youkoumian approached the device. Jennifer reassured him that it was perfectly safe with the laser power supply turned off. He lifted the hemispherical top to reveal .... a small gold coin.

Youkoumian slowly picked up the little object and turned it over in his fingers. "So shiny. It looks as if it had just been minted. Ahhh," he said. "Arabic characters. And the crescent and star on the back." Youkoumian could read the Arabic characters; they translated to the phrase, 'The Islamic State – a caliphate based on the doctrine of the Prophet.' Youkoumian quickly realized that it would be unusual for an Armenian to express familiarity with the Arabic, and so stopped himself from translating it. "This must be an Islamic calendar date," he speculated to the others.

Hampton moved in a little closer to observe the coin in Youkoumians fingers. It certainly looked authentic to him. Shiny, perhaps newly minted as Youkoumian had thought. How the heck had that got into the device? It looked like everything Jennifer had explained about dimensions was true. She really was from another world.

Youkoumian was still staring at the coin. "May I retain this coin for a short period?" he asked.

"Of course," said Jennifer, "it is yours to keep. It will make a good souvenir of our project. I'd just like to mention that you can see that, in the interior of the spherical container, the diamonds you lent us are still as perfect as before. Nothing has happened to them and Hampton can detach them and return them to you if you wish."

Still a little dazed, Youkoumian shook his head. "But you will need even more than those to construct a device capable of allowing a person to travel to your dimension. You might as well retain these as I begin to arrange for the larger number."

Jennifer thought to herself: Yes! He's buying it! I'm going to get the 5000 diamonds! Restraining her excitement, she said, as calmly as she could, "I was hoping you'd say that. Hampton can start on the larger apparatus immediately and, depending on when you can allow us to have the rest of the diamonds, I can get back to my dimension soon."

"Yes, yes," he said. "You may come to the Samson street store in two days and I will have everything ready. I am still amazed that it works so easily."

Jennifer was elated. "We'll be looking forward to it, Colonel."

Youkoumian said goodbye and returned to the street to drive back to his store.

In the loft, Jennifer was grinning at Hampton. "You have that sweet bewildered look that's so typical of you. You didn't expect it to work, did you?"

Hampton had to admit it. "I was doubtful," he said.

"But now you're totally convinced." Jennifer knew, despite what he might say, that Hampton still did not believe what had happened before his own eyes. But that didn't matter as long as he could perform the technical work correctly. He was a sweetie, she thought. And committed despite his misgivings. He got a kiss as his reward. She owned him.

Chapter 41

Youkoumian was still in somewhat of a daze as he drove back to his store. He was still having trouble believing that he had witnessed a transfer of a note from this dimension to another one. And then a transfer of a coin from the other dimension to this one. Was he getting close to additional help from an Islamic state for his cause and organization? He obviously needed to report to al-Tunji as soon as possible to let him know of the success.

Once he was secure in his store, he got out the code phrase book with the additions that had possible short sentences which he could use to express the situation to his superior. Once he had the email complete, he sent it. He got an acknowledgement of message received from the organization's web site, but did not expect an explicit reply from al-Tunji for some hours.

In the meantime, he securely wrapped the gold coin in a shipping package and asked one of his store employees to send it immediately, using international overnight express, to headquarters in the Middle East. He was certain al-Tunji would be impressed with the coin and wanted to get his approval for his actions in pursuing this rather strange project to what looked like a successful and promising finish.

In the meantime, he began preparations for delivering the remainder of the 5000 diamonds to Jennifer and Hampton. Instead of an ordinary gallon-sized zip-top freezer bag, he got one of the organization's special bags used for long distance transport. This was quite like a commercially available freezer bag but somewhat more robust. In addition, it had a special feature. The bottom seam of the bag contained a small electronic tracking device. This enabled the organization to use a hand-held device, about the size of a smart phone, to locate the bag and its contents on a GPS map display. They had never had any problem with couriers absconding with either funds or gems, but the tracking device was insurance in case the unthinkable ever happened.

Youkoumian would use his own store's diamonds for a portion of those needed, and he expected to receive borrowed diamonds from various sources within the U.S.in the next two days. Once they arrived, he would place everything in the bag and see that Jennifer and Hampton received it. He was ready.

In a shorter time than he expected, he had a reply email from al-Tunji. His superior congratulated him on the progress made so far. Al-Tunji approved of the dispatch of the gold coin to headquarters. He was anxious to see the evidence of dimensional transfer with his own eyes. Meanwhile, he instructed Youkoumian to continue to be extremely careful in the next steps of the process. In code, he stated "Take all steps necessary to protect diamonds."

Youkoumian knew this was an injunction to kill if necessary to preserve the gems. With the precautions he had taken, and the two assistants at his disposal, he felt he was completely covered with his boss. He had no qualms about killing anyone he had to in order to protect his group's assets.

Chapter 42

Two days later, Jennifer and Hampton were back at Youk-oumian's store on Sansom Street to receive the promised diamonds. The freezer bag containing them was placed in a shopping bag with Youkoumians store logo on it, and Hampton carried it with them as they left.

He couldn't help remarking to Jennifer as they walked back to Front Street, "I don't feel comfortable carrying around thousands of diamonds through the streets of Philadelphia. Too many bad things could happen."

Jennifer was far more sanguine. In fact, to Hampton, she appeared almost euphorically happy. He attributed that to the fact that she was getting closer and closer to getting back to her own dimension.

"Don't worry about it, sweetie," she said to him. "The probability of anything happening during the few minutes we walk back to Front Street is vanishingly small."

Hampton glumly reflected that vanishingly small still provided a non-zero possible outcome and anything like that would be completely bad.

Once back up to the loft, Jennifer could not wait to empty the bag on one of the benches.

"God, they're so beautiful," she said as she spread the diamonds out. She sifted them through her fingers and fondled them. Hampton was surprised at her actions. She was always so much in control, yet now she seemed to be giving in to uncontrollable emotions on finally obtaining the means to return to her dimension. This was quite unlike the Jennifer who always seemed so much in charge of both herself and any situation she might be in. Hampton was more than a little disconcerted by this version of Jennifer. Still, in some way, this more expressive Jennifer seemed even more attractive to him. Less intense and more personable, almost friendly. He decided he liked it.

He was even more disconcerted when she climbed up onto the lab bench top and lay prone on top of the diamonds. To be sure, it turned him on to see her get what seemed like pure lascivious pleasure out of being around the diamonds. But it seemed to Hampton that she was out of control. She began taking handfuls of the gems and letting them cascade over her clothes. She looked at him. Somehow her usually flint hard eyes had become smoky.

"You know what I want."

They both knew it was not possible for him to refuse.

Chapter 43

Afterward, the diamonds had to be recollected and safely stored in their freezer bag. In preparation for building a unit large enough to accommodate a person, Hampton began removing diamonds from the prototype unit and stored them in the bag as well. He left the freezer bag of diamonds on the lab bench Jennifer was still sitting on.

He began to think about what materials he would need to construct the larger unit. Clearly the biggest problem would be to construct a framework for the diamonds large enough to accommodate a person.

"Jennifer, how large does the big device need to be?"

Jennifer appeared to still be fascinated by the bag of diamonds. She replied absently, "Big enough to enclose a person obviously."

"And what about the interior shape? Should it be spherical like the prototype?"

"Sure, that will work."

"And the refracting path through the diamonds, will it be the same as the small unit or will that require adjustments in position?"

"The path will be the same just … uh… expanded outward enough to allow a person to be enclosed in it."

Hampton looked at her, "Don't you mean expanded enough for two people, you and me? You're still taking me, right?"

"Uh yes, correct."

"So, we need a spherical shell at least 1.5 meters in diameter, would you say?"

Jennifer was still staring at the diamond bag. "Uh, yeah, that will work."

Hampton was a little perturbed that she still seemed to be fascinated by the bag. "You seem to be still distracted by the diamonds. I think we ought to wait until tomorrow to work out the details together. It's getting dark out, we should come back tomorrow."

"OK, good idea."

Hampton picked up the bag and placed it in one of the cabinets in the loft.

Jennifer said, "Why don't we take them back with us? They would be quite safe in my apartment at Cira Center South."

Hampton objected to that idea. "I don't think it's a good idea to be walking through Philadelphia with a bag of diamonds, especially at this time of night. If we decide to build the bigger unit here, they might as well stay here. If we build it somewhere else, we should wait to move them until we find a place."

"You're sure they will be safe here?"

"They'll be safer here than being carried across Philadelphia."

Jennifer could hardly bear to be separated from the diamonds, but reluctantly, she agreed.

Hampton decided that, on their way back to his apartment, he would stop at one or more stores to begin getting some of the stuff he would need.

Hampton was quiet and seemingly lost in thought as they walked home. In contrast with her usual behavior, Jennifer linked her arm with his and snuggled close. He was reminded of a cat his family had had in Highland County when he was younger. The cat usually was absorbed in its own cat affairs and often disdained his family's attempts to show it affection. Yet occasionally, the cat would bump around someone's legs, climb up on their chair, and sit on their lap, giving and getting attention on its own terms. He wondered if Jennifer was part cat. It would suit her.

Chapter 44

Youkoumian received a phone call at his suburban home at 5 AM. He at first thought it might be connected with the store ... a burglary or perhaps a fire. It was even worse. It was al-Tunji, breaking all the rules of restricted contact with incredible news.

Al-Tunji was extremely cold but coherent. "You must retrieve our diamonds at once from your university partners. They are fakers and were only interested in getting possession of the gems."

Youkoumian was dumbfounded. "This cannot be. Why do you say this?"

"The coin you sent to us has been examined by our technical experts. It has been chemically coated with a thin layer of gold but it is in reality an ordinary 1 dinar copper coin from Syria. You have been swindled and you are to blame."

"But I saw a note asking for the coin disappear from the chamber and later, when I was the first to open the chamber, the coin had appeared from nowhere."

"Have you never seen a street magician perform in Racca? They are extremely skillful in making appearances seem to be what they are really not. Somewhere in the process, someone palmed the objects and made it seem as if they had disappeared and then came from nowhere."

"But the only other person handling them was the female student."

"That is even more reason to be suspicious. A female can be just as clever as a male in concealing coins and notes and would have the added advantage of her allure to distract you."

"But ..."

"Stop. We have no time to argue about this episode. The first thing you must do is contact the couriers and have them repossess the diamonds. When that is accomplished, it will be time to discuss the responsibility and consequences of this disaster. Instruct your assistants to get the gems back, and ... do not leave any witnesses to this embarrassing event."

Al-Tunji had hung up and Youkoumian stared at his cell phone in disbelief. This could not be happening. He had been careful and thought himself well protected against any turn of fortune. Still bewildered, he attempted to call the couriers to give them orders. Calls to both of their cell phones went immediately to voice mail, which indicated that their phones had their power turned off. Cursing, he now had no alternative except to get dressed and drive into center city Philadelphia and get the couriers onto the task of getting the diamonds back. He proceeded to get dressed.

It took over 45 annoying minutes to proceed from his suburban location to downtown Philadelphia center city. Once there, he had to pound on the safe house door to get the attention of his assistants. Once they were awake and alert, he proceeded to instruct them with the urgency to get the diamonds back from the young people who had them in their custody at the Front Street location. To emphasize the importance of what he was saying, he told the couriers to load their weapons and insure their success in repossessing the gems by any means necessary. Before he left, he made sure his assistants knew how to operate the GPS tracking display. It still showed the diamonds as being in the Front Street location. Youkoumian left to go to his store on Sansom Street.

The couriers themselves were in a bad mood from being awakened so early in the morning. They grumbled to each other as they loaded the Glock magazines and prepared to make their way across center city to the loft where the diamonds were. They decided extra magazines were not necessary since in their observations of the young Americans in the loft, they had never seen any evidence of weapons. They were quite confident that they could easily retrieve the diamonds. As they left, both their iPads notified them of the arrival of email. Both were coded messages from al-Tunji. Both ordered them to retrieve the group's property without delay. Once that was done there were further instructions concerning Youkoumian.

The couriers left the house, got in their green car, and decided that using I95 would be the fastest way to get up to Front Street. It was a mistake.

As sometimes happens in Philadelphia, an overturned 18-wheeler had completely blocked I95 North Bound as it skirted the East side of the city. The couriers were stuck on the limited access highway.

Chapter 45

That morning Jennifer was particularly eager to get started back to the Front Street loft. The longer she was away from the diamonds, the more anxious she became. She wasn't even willing for them to take time to get something for breakfast at Sandy's diner. Hampton protested that he was hungry, but she would have none of that. She didn't care. And she insisted on taking SEPTA to the loft instead of walking across Center City. Since the bus was close to being on schedule, it was faster than walking

So, Hampton and Jennifer returned to the Front Street loft from his apartment. They climbed the stairs as usual and Jennifer immediately checked on the freezer bag of diamonds. It was still in the cabinet where they had placed it yesterday. That made her feel much better. She felt something of the exultation she had experienced yesterday when they had first opened the bag. It was going to work!

Hampton thought his first order of business should be to disassemble the small table top prototype and get the components they had borrowed from Rittenhouse Labs returned. Then he could begin to prepare larger arrangements that could accommodate the passage of persons to another dimension.

He began this process. However, in passing back from the cabinet toward where Hampton was studying the table top, Jennifer passed one of the front windows and noticed movement on the street below. She cautiously looked out the window and saw the green car pull up and park on the opposite side. The two swarthy looking men they had seen before emerged from the car looking annoyed. They checked their coat pockets and had guns in hand as they crossed the street and proceeded toward the entry door for the stairs up to their loft.

"Oh my God, Hampton, George's thugs just parked on the street and are coming this way with guns!"

Hampton believed her immediately. He didn't waste time looking out the window to check her observation. He immediately thought their best course of action was to block the second-floor door leading into the loft.

"Help me move this work bench up against the door."

Between the two of them they managed to get the bench firmly planted holding the door from opening inward.

"Hampton, what are we going to do?" she wailed.

Hampton, took her arm and guided her across the room to one of the rear windows. "We're getting out of here," he said, opening the window. He looked out. It was a short drop from the windowsill down to a slanted roof that sloped toward the back alley. They could hear the thugs noisily climbing the stairs. He grabbed the freezer bag of diamonds, gave it to Jennifer, and helped her perch on the windowsill. The thugs began hammering on the door, demanding admission. "And we're doing it right now," he said giving her a little nudge to get her started down the roof.

The thugs were now banging and pushing on the door but the lab bench prevented them from making any progress inside.

Hampton and Jennifer managed to slide down the slope to where he could drop into the alley and catch her as she hung off the roof. They heard a shot from inside the loft, and Jennifer screamed.

Once on the ground, they quickly made their way to another alley and then out to Second Street where they headed south. There was no indication that the thugs were following them.

They slowed slightly to catch their breath.

"My God, Hampton, they fired shots at us!" cried Jennifer.

"Strictly speaking," said Hampton, "it was just one shot. Fortunately, neither of us was hit. They don't appear to be good marksmen."

Jennifer was totally terrified, "But they could have killed us! What are we going to do?"

Hampton was fairly calm about the whole problem. "I think the best thing we could do is go over to Youkoumians store on Samson Street and give him his diamonds back. Once he has them, those thieves should have no further interest in us."

"Oh God," Jennifer said, "It took so much to get these diamonds. I hate to give that up." She had calmed down a little from her original panic but was still almost in tears at the thought of losing the diamonds. She clutched the freezer bag closely.

Hampton was pragmatic about it. "We won't have the diamonds, but we'll be alive with a chance to borrow diamonds again. If we try to hang on to them, we may well get killed and lose the diamonds anyway. It seems to me to be a win-win."

Teary eyed, Jennifer reluctantly had to agree and they started south on Second Street and then west on Arch Street to make their way to the jewelry store on Sansom Street.

Chapter 46

As they walked rapidly west on Arch Street, Hampton became vaguely aware of horns honking and people shouting behind them, east on Arch Street. Looking back, he could see a green car crossing 3rd Street against traffic and causing quite a disturbance as it threaded its way through cars who were going through with a green light.

He grabbed Jennifer's hand and started to run. "It looks like the guys in the green car somehow found out where we disappeared to. They're following back there. Don't turn, we've got to keep going. Fast."

Jennifer looked even more scared but managed to keep up with him. They reached the entrance to Christ Church Burial Ground. Hampton pulled her into the entrance with him. "What are we doing?" she cried.

Ignoring the protestations of the person collecting admission fees at the gate, Hampton said "I think we might have a chance to shake them off in here." Together, they raced down the path and passed Benjamin Franklin's grave, with its cover slab almost covered in pennies.

Risking a quick glance behind them, he saw the two men from the green car muscle past the admissions collector. One of the men chasing them paused and leveled a hand gun pointing at them. The shot was extremely loud in the park-like setting of the burial ground. Jennifer screamed again and tourists everywhere immediately hit the ground. Hampton heard the ricochet off one of the adjacent grave markers, and immediately turned left with Jennifer to dodge among them.

Many of the markers were elaborate monuments, some rising above their heads. Hampton thought if they kept low as they ran, they might be able to shake off the thugs. In a zig-zag path, bent over, they managed to reach the southern boundary of the burial ground, a head high brick wall. Looking back, Hampton saw no visible presence of the guys who were chasing them. He told her to give him the diamond bag which he stuffed inside his shirt. Without hesitation, he then lifted Jennifer up beside the wall and pushed on her butt until she managed to use her arms to clamber up on top. He joined her on the top, jumped down on the other side, and then caught her around the waist and helped her down as well. Turning, they both ran across 5th street and entered Independence Mall. Slowing down on the foot paths in the Mall, Hampton hoped they would blend in with the rest of the tourists. If they weren't running, perhaps the thugs would not be able to pick them out.

"Hampton, I've got to rest," she said as she collapsed on to a mall bench.

Hampton joined her and said, "I think we both can use a break." He looked in all directions around the Mall. "I don't see any trace of them around here."

"Do you still think we need to give the diamonds back to Youkoumian?" she begged. "Can't we just take them back to your apartment? We talked about finding some new place to build the full-size device, anyway."

Hampton was convinced the right thing to do was to get the diamonds back to their rightful owner, Youkoumian.

He also thought it would be the safest thing, since once he and Jennifer no longer had the jewels, the guys chasing them should no longer have any interest in them as individuals.

"I don't want to take the chance that they might find us at my place or yours," he said. "Those guys don't seem to have any hesitation about using guns. Once we get the diamonds to Youkoumian we should be safely out of the picture."

"I suppose you're right," Jennifer said reluctantly. Looking over at the 6th street side of the Mall, she moaned "Oh God, oh God, there's that green car."

Hampton immediately urged her up. "OK, let's walk slowly South, just like normal tourists. We won't stand out that way."

Although every instinct they had was to run away as fast as they could, Hampton restrained their way south to a saunter. They passed the President's House exhibit which showcased the foundations of the house which both Washington and Adams had used when the capitol was located in Philadelphia. They crossed Market Street and shortly were shielded from 6th street by the long Liberty Bell Pavilion. They slowly came up to the entrance to the Liberty Bell exhibit.

Hampton said, "We don't need tickets. Let's just go in. Maybe if we disappear into a building that will shake them off." Jennifer agreed.

They did that, casually entering the pavilion with a line of other tourists. They walked apprehensively around the subsidiary displays and were approaching the Bell itself when shouts sounded behind them. Looking back, Hampton saw the Park rangers trying to restrain the men from the green car who were pursuing Jennifer and Hampton with no consideration for others. Clearly the thugs didn't think they needed permission to get in and get the diamonds. Shouts and whistles echoed in the pavilion. The men who were pursuing them ignored everything and Hampton saw one of them stop and level a hand gun at them. Hampton immediately grabbed Jennifer and took her to the floor.

The resultant shot apparently hit the bell itself. A soft melodious tone emanated through the chambers amid the gunshot echoes. Everyone else in the pavilion also dropped to the floor and the two gunmen and the Rangers were the only ones left standing. One of the Rangers bravely tried to stop the gunman and was shot for his courage. Apparently frustrated, the second gunman also fired his weapon. This generated a general movement of everybody toward the south exit.

Hampton wasted no time. He rose to a crouch, dragged Jennifer up, and headed to the south exit. Running, they exited the Pavilion near 6th and Chestnut, only two blocks from Jewelers' Row.

Chapter 47

Somewhat earlier that morning, George, Gillian, and Aban had met at the ATF conference room lent by Gloria Wentworth. Aban announced that his bosses at DHS had approved the joint task force, contacted both Dan Carolli, and Gloria Wentworth, and obtained approval all around for the joint operation. The meeting included a number of CSI experts from each of their organizations. Aban had obtained warrants for Youkoumians store and the house on Christian Street. They would not need a warrant for the loft on Front Street since it was still under the auspices of the FBI. Aban, Gillian, and George were all wearing shoulder holsters which carried their handguns., as were the CSI agents. Everyone had a ballistic vest and placard which identified themselves and their organization.

Aban repeated their assignments. He himself would take the Christian Street house, since it housed the two men using the H1-B's, who were known to have firearms, and who would be the most likely to resist. George would take the Front Street loft, and Gillian would take her ATF CSI people to Youkoumians jewelry store. It only remained now for the three of them to lead their teams to those locations and start work.

George arrived at the Front Street loft with two CSI experts from the FBI. Strangely, the door to the stairs up to the loft was hanging askew. It had obviously been subjected to some great force. This did not bode well, but George had no clue about what had happened or what was going on. He drew his gun and cautiously sidled up the stairs. The door at the top had also been forced open and a blocking work bench behind it was pushed back enough to allow someone entrance. Even more ominous, there was a bullet hole in the door. He edged past the door and the lab bench and was followed by his search experts.

There was nobody in the loft. The equipment setup he had seen on his first night time visit was still in place. The Argon-Ion Laser, power supply, and equipment rack were still in the same positions. The Lab bench still had mirrors and filters proceeding in precise lines toward the opaque sphere and beyond. However, the opaque sphere no longer contained any diamonds in its interior. Obviously, a significant development. There had been several hundred rather large diamonds mounted in the sphere when George had last seen it. Since the diamonds were gone, it probably indicated someone was several hundreds of thousands of dollars richer. The bullet hole in the door testified that the transfer of ownership was probably not done by mutual consent between whoever was the real owner and whoever had the diamonds now.

A window in the rear wall was open. George edged over to it, careful not to expose himself to a possible gun shot from someone still outside. He noted scratch marks in the slanted roof which led down from the window. Perhaps this indicated an avenue of escape for either Hampton and Jennifer, or for those who might be trying to appropriate the diamonds. Nothing was immediately apparent.

There seemed to be no computer and little else of interest left in the loft. However, to cover all bases, George asked his CSI experts to examine everything. While they did that, George called Aban's cell and reported what he had found and not found.

Chapter 48

Aban and his CSI team had reached the safe house on Christian Street where Youkoumians H1-B visa holders had been staying. The green car was not around, which suggested that the visa holders were not present either. Still, Aban, mindful of the reputation of the men, took all possible precautions. Each of the team had her or his weapon out. One was dispatched to the rear door in case the suspects were still in the house and decided to try to evade the team. Aban and the remainder attempted to enter the place. Anticlimactically, the door was found to be unlocked and the team was able to enter without effort.

Careful progress through the house showed that it was clear. The H1-B men were not there and there appeared to be no computers, papers or anything else of documentary interest in the place. The most significant thing found was two 17 round Glock gun clips on the kitchen table. There was no sign of the Glock automatics themselves, so it was a pretty safe assumption that the men had the arms and almost certainly other magazines with them. Aban asked the CSI persons to carefully bag the spares as potentially future useful evidence. He copied the serial numbers on the magazines to the analysis section of DHS in Washington. Since he was in charge of running a major operation with joint participation of Justice Department agencies, he got an almost immediate response. The magazines were in the DHS data base as having been purchased by a store owner named Youkoumian in Philadelphia.

As an aside. Aban's team did find numerous pornographic magazines in the safe house. They could be divided into two categories, magazines portraying moslem women engaging in sexual acts as willing participants in their own degradation and magazines portraying young men willingly participating in homosexual acts. Aban found these not exceptional and well within the bounds of pornography that was currently popular in the middle east when accessible. He made no judgements on it. He felt no need to comment explicitly on this.

When George called Aban, they discussed their joint lack of success. George reported the bullet hole in the door at Front Street and Aban discussed the Glock implements he had found and the proof that Youkoumian had supplied them. Both men found the evidence for firearm use something to worry about. It seemed a pretty good bet that the men they were looking for were heavily armed and quite willing to use their guns.

George and Aban agreed that they were making progress on getting information on Youkoumian. They both thought they and their teams should move on to Youkoumians store where Gillian was probably already engaged in searching the place.

Chapter 49

Gillian had indeed been admitted to the store. Showing her ATF badge, she was accompanied by the search team from ATF. She found Youkoumian in the front showroom and showed him the search warrant that Aban had arranged. He immediately started to go to his office but she restrained him. She asked the computer experts in her team to go to the office and to prevent anyone from tinkering with any computers there. She also asked agents to supervise any computers in the show room, as well as those in the workroom. George and Aban soon arrived at the store and joined her as she confronted Youkoumian.

Walking rapidly, Hampton and Jennifer had reached 8th and Sansom. As they neared Youkoumians store between 8th and 9th, they could see the interior through the showroom windows. Gillian and George appeared to be in deep conversation with the owner.

"Oh, my God," said Jennifer. "That Gillian and George are both in there talking with Youkoumian. We can't go in there, there's something going on with her, George, and Youkoumian. They're all part of it together."

Hampton wasn't sure about that but could think of no rational reason for Gillian and George to be associating with the owner at his store. Could Gillian and Youkoumian be associated with George's thugs as well? Jennifer grabbed his arm and he decided it would be best to go with her until they could learn more about the situation. They rounded the block onto 9th and continued north toward Chestnut Street.

At Chestnut Street, they turned left and continued west. Hampton saw no indications that the men with guns were anywhere near. Since the traffic on Chestnut Street was one way east, they did not need to worry about the green car coming up behind them.

At 10th and Chestnut, Hampton steered them into a Starbuck's, thinking they needed to talk about what was going on. He got a Chai for Jennifer and a small black for himself and they found a table away from the windows so they would not be easily spotted from the street.

After they sat down, Jennifer said, "You still have the diamonds, right?"

"Yes, they're still right here under my shirt. I'm just not sure what we should do now. I was certain we would be all right if we could just give Youkoumian back his diamonds."

Jennifer said, "There's something going on. I think George, Gillian, and Youkoumian are all in this together for the diamonds."

"But Youkoumian had the diamonds to start with," said Hampton.

"It has to be some sort of an insurance scam," said Jennifer. "He probably wants to claim that we stole the diamonds, get reimbursed for them, and then have George and Gillian and their thugs recover the diamonds from our dead bodies."

Hampton was not convinced, but had to admit that it could fit what was happening. He thought about it. "So, what do you think we should we do now?"

Jennifer was ready, having had time to develop a plan while Hampton had gotten the coffee and Chai. She had two primary problems. How to avoid being killed by the thugs chasing them, and how to get away from Hampton with the diamonds. The primary objective of her plan was to keep the diamonds in their possession until she was safe, without going to any police. "We need to get out of town as soon as we can, to avoid the guys in the green car. Then we can see about getting the attention of police. I don't think we can go to the police right away. You saw what happened to that Park Ranger who tried to stop the thugs at the pavilion."

Hampton nodded.

"We should go to 30ᵗʰ Street station. Once we get on a commuter train to the suburbs, the guys in the green car won't know what train we took or, even if they can figure that out, they'll never know the station where we get off." Jennifer also knew that she could probably ditch Hampton, either in 30ᵗʰ Street station or at some intermediate stop. She did feel a little bad about doing that. She liked Hampton. But she liked the diamonds more.

Hampton was skeptical but had agreed to her suggestions since he had no better ideas. They exited the Starbucks, happened to look north along 10ᵗʰ street at cars coming one way south and saw the green car. Since Chestnut Street was one way east, they started west so the green car would not be able to immediately tail them. They walked to make time but not be conspicuous.

"How the hell do they keep finding us?" said Jennifer.

Hampton thought about it. "Maybe they're observant enough to drive around looking for a man and women wearing shirts of the same colors we have on." Hampton had a distinctive blue and white vertically striped long sleeved shirt. Jennifer was similarly recognizable from a distance in her form fitting short sleeved shirt that presented a bright orange design with sequins.

"Then maybe we need to change shirts," said Jennifer. They were just passing the old Wanamaker's department store, which was now a Macy's.

Hampton suggested "We could go in here and get new shirts. And if they do see us go in and follow us, we have the added advantage of many different exits to leave by." Jennifer agreed.

They entered the store and both found different less conspicuous shirts to wear. They left their old ones in dressing booths and proceeded through the store. They passed through the grand entrance hall of the former Wanamaker's Department Store with its majestic stair case to upper floors. Customers were standing nearby listening to the glorious tones of the old Wanamaker pipe organ. Usually played only at Christmas time, apparently today was a special occasion. As might be expected, Jennifer and Hampton were much more concerned with getting out of the place alive rather than stopping to listen to the beautiful chorale.

Chapter 50

Back at the store, the CSI computer tech in Gillian's party asked her, George, Aban, and Youkoumian to come into the store's office. He wanted them to see a device on Youkoumians desk. It was apparently some kind of hand held tracking device currently running and displaying a location in center city.

The techie said "It looks like it's displaying a street map of downtown Philadelphia and this icon has been moving west along Chestnut Street. Probably a tracker of some kind. From the slow progress of the tracker, it looks like it's associated with pedestrians."

Youkoumian was dismayed that the diamonds were still moving west and his face showed that. He knew he was in trouble with the police, but he would be in worse trouble if al-Tunji decided that he was responsible for losing 10,000 carats of the group's diamonds.

Gillian picked up on his expression and said, "Mr. Youkoumian, do you want to let us know who you are tracking with this setup?"

Youkoumian had seen enough TV crime shows to make an appropriate response. "I will say nothing until I consult with my attorney."

While Aban, George, and Gillian were speculating about the significance of the tracking display, Aban got a phone call from the 6th district police. Clicking off, he turned to George and Gillian.

"It appears that the men holding the H1-B visas are engaging in some sort of shooting spree in Old City. 6th District has reports of gunshots fired at Christ Church burial ground. Apparently two men came out of a green car, fired at a man and woman running south through the cemetery, and then got back in their car. I'm pretty certain the green car is the same one the H1-B men have rented. They also have reports of a shot fired in the Independence Mall Liberty Bell pavilion at a young man and women by two men who later got back into a green car as well. Both the young man and woman were wearing jeans. The man has a blue and white vertically striped long sleeve shirt and the woman is wearing an orangey shirt with some kind of design on it in sequins."

George said, "Since there was no one left at the Front Street loft, it seems a safe bet that the young man and woman being chased by the green car guys are Hampton and Jennifer."

Gillian said, "I think you are correct. The question is, why are they being chased? And why are they being shot at? Since those men are here under H1-B visas sponsored by your jewelry store, do you have any answers for that, Mr. Youkoumian?"

"As I told you, I have nothing to say until I can consult with my attorney."

"I think you will have to do better than that, Mr. Youkoumian," said Gillian. "Hampton and Jennifer are known to be working on a project in association with you. They are known to have had a sizable quantity of diamonds at the Front Street location. The diamonds could only have been supplied by you. I think a Federal District Attorney would find that sufficient evidence to link you to the felonies being perpetrated by your ostensible employees with the H1-B visas. If they succeed in killing someone with their reckless discharge of guns, you would definitely be an accessory to murder and face the death penalty."

Youkoumian blanched. Literally. He had thought himself well protected against developments like this. How had this happened? Now what could he do?

Gillian said, "If you know anything about why the holders of H1-B visas requested by you are recklessly discharging firearms and pursuing these young people through the streets of Philadelphia, it would be best for you to inform us now, before someone is killed. After that, nothing you can say will help us. Or you."

Aban took another call on his cell phone. After hanging up, he said, "That was 6th precinct detectives again. Apparently one of the Park Rangers in the Liberty Bell pavilion was hit by a shot. His condition is serious but he's still alive for now, and being taken to an ER."

Gillian said, "Time is running out Mr.Youkoumian. If that ranger dies, you will probably become an accomplice to murder. You can only help yourself now if you give us the information we need to avoid such catastrophes."

Youkoumian face showed his fear. He caved. "All right. Those young people from the University have obtained diamonds from me through fraudulent means. I asked the young men working for me to recover the diamonds. But of course, I never authorized the use of deadly force to do this. They are acting on their own in this respect."

Aban said, "So you have supplied the men you sent to get the diamonds with a device that tracks the couple?"

"They do have a device like this one. It is also tracking a radio source concealed in the bag which carried the diamonds."

George said, "So we can expect to find the gun men you sent out somewhere in the vicinity of the broadcast device in the bag of diamonds. And presumably the bag of diamonds is being carried by Hampton and Jennifer."

Youkoumian agreed this was probably the case.

All turned to look at the tracking display just in time to see the icon location indicator fade and disappear on Chestnut Street just west of 13th.

Everyone turned to look at the computer expert who had drawn their attention to the device.

In response to their questioning looks he said, "It could be a battery failure in the tracking device." He thought about it a little. "They could also have entered a building big enough and thick enough to not permit the signals to penetrate walls."

George said "It disappeared on the middle of Chestnut between 13th and Juniper. They could have gone into the old Wanamaker Department Store building. Macy's."

The computer tech responded, "That building is certainly massive enough to present an obstacle to radio transmission from its interior."

Gillian said "I wonder why they would go into Macy's?"

"After having been shot at twice, they have got to be aware that the guys in the green car are chasing them, "said George. "Maybe they figured to go into a building to avoid the car."

Gillian said, "That's a reasonable supposition."

Aban said, "I'm going to alert 6th district police that the shooters in the green car are probably in the vicinity of Macy's. Also, the couple that they're shooting at are probably also in or around Macy's and should be detained to protect them. Hopefully they'll be able to pick out a young couple wearing those distinctive shirts." He proceeded to make the call to 6th district detectives.

Afterwards, he reported on how the Philadelphia police were doing. "They Still have no sightings of either the green car or the young couple."

Chapter 51

Unfortunately, as Hampton and Jennifer exited Macy's they were no longer wearing the distinctive shirts. They walked a short distance west from Macy's Market Street entrance and almost immediately entered the imposing bulk of the Philadelphia City Hall at Market and Broad Street. Like Macy's this structure was solid enough to block radio transmission from its interior.

During the short time they were on the street the tracking device revealed their presence to the men in the green car which immediately began to circle the imposing structure said to be modeled after the Paris city hall, the Hotel de Ville. A statue of William Penn topped the highest cupola of Philadelphia's City Hall and for much of its history had been the tallest structure in the city through an unspoken agreement of those who controlled things. In recent years, this gentleman's agreement had been unceremoniously dispensed with to enable building modern cost effective structures of 500 feet or more. From a city that looked somewhat like Paris without the Eiffel Tower, Philadelphia transitioned into a replica that could pass for one of the boroughs of New York. Indeed, the streets of Center City were quite popular with TV and film maker's seeking New York City street scenes. It was far cheaper to shoot film in Philadelphia Center City than Manhattan.

Hampton and Jennifer's brief reappearance on the tracker was not noticed by the participants at Youkoumians. Aban, George, and Gillian were intensely interested in what their technical search experts were revealing about Youkoumian and his store.

Among the interesting things found in the office safe were multiple passports with pictures of a younger but still recognizable Youkoumian. These passports had been issued by Syria, Egypt, and Yemen and identified the man who was acting like he owned the store as Hassan al-Sidaan.

Aban was quite pleased with the search results. Aban immediately copied the name al-Sidaan and the passport numbers to the DHS intelligence section in Washington.. He expected to get feedback almost immediately.

Gillian commented "Aban, this definitely confirms your observations that he's not Armenian. Although it's hard to tell what nationality he really is."

George agreed. "But these documents do show that he has ties to the middle east, including Syria. The multiple passports tend to indicate some sort of need to conceal his identity. And they also fit in with connections with the H1-B visas.

The results of Aban's Washington query came back in a cell phone call. After listening, Aban ended the call and relayed the information to Gillian and George.

Hassan al-Sidaan had entered the U.S. on an Egyptian tourist visa in 2008. There was no record of that passport ever leaving the country and the identity of al-Sidaan had never reappeared in the U.S. since the time of his entry. In effect, he entered and then disappeared from official notice.

Additionally, in the safe, the techs found code books, receipts for weapons, and title and tax statements for the safe house on Christian Street.

"These definitely tie him in with the H1-B Visa holders that are shooting up the town," said Gillian. "He won't be able to deny responsibility."

Aban was pleased that they had found documents which supported his observation that the ostensible owner of the store was not Armenian. Hopefully, when the men in the green car were seized, the ID numbers on their guns would match those in the gun receipts found in the safe. That, with the passports, should be enough to hold Hassan al-Siddan indefinitely under the Patriot act.

Chapter 52

Hampton and Jennifer entered City Hall through the East Portal. They walked through the massive building, passing stair cases to upper floors and many offices with imposing heavy walnut doors housing city bureaus. In the center of the Hall, they reached a rather pleasant inner courtyard. Both felt relatively safe here and they sat down on one of the existing stone benches in the courtyard and each took a deep breath. After a short rest, they were ready to proceed westward again to reach 30th Street Station.

The first thing Hampton and Jennifer saw as they exited the west side of Philadelphia City Hall at Dilworth Park on 15th street was the back of the green car slowly proceeding south. This re-contact with the thugs in the green car was enough to convince Hampton to turn back into City Hall to find another exit. He and Jennifer took the main first floor corridor a quarter of the way around the building to a south exit which came out at Broad Street. They cautiously peered out the doors.

They saw no sign of the green car and tentatively started south on Broad toward Walnut Street. They passed the rather stately façade of the Union League building, a striking example of 2nd Empire architecture. The Union League was founded in 1862 as a patriotic club to support the policies of Abraham Lincoln. It continues today as a private club consisting of the makers and shakers who run Philadelphia. Hampton found it somewhat ironic that he, as a southern re-enactor, was passing what had been the headquarters of the strongest supporters of Lincoln.

Hampton and Jennifer continued down Broad Street, passing Moravian Street. Hampton's objective was to get as far south as Walnut Street. From there he and Jennifer could then take Walnut Street westward toward the Schuylkill River and the bridges they could use to get to 30th Street station.

Chapter 53

On Walnut Street, Jennifer complained that she was exhausted. Hampton was convinced that the men in the green car would probably find them while just walking, so he thought it would be a good idea to take a bus. They boarded a bus at 15th and Walnut to give themselves a break.

On a bus, they would not be immediately exposed to scrutiny from cars on the street. Hopefully, there would be some alleviation from whatever was giving the men in the green car clues to where they were. Out of habit, Hampton ushered Jennifer onto a number 12 bus which would take them generally westward on Walnut Street toward 30th street station. Jennifer was too tired to complain and was content to use her bus pass to get on and get a place where she could sit and relax slightly. The bus proceeded slowly westward on Walnut street, stopping at all numbered streets and generally slowed by the normal afternoon center city Philadelphia traffic. Hampton, trying to look in all directions from the bus, could not detect any signs of the men in the green car. Perhaps changing their shirts had thrown the pursuers off.

As usual, those riding the bus in center city were composed almost entirely of three distinct groups: African Americans for whom the bus was useful in allowing them mobility around the city without having to own a car; students of both secondary schools and the many colleges in Philadelphia who enjoyed discounts on bus passes; and senior citizens who rode essentially free in most cases. Few others had the patience or inclination to use this mode of transportation in center city, which was useful and affordable to many, but often not timely or convenient.

The bus Hampton and Jennifer were on proceeded slowly westward on Walnut. It came to a jarring halt crossing 18th Street. The green car had cut in front of the bus and forced it to stop. Hampton immediately got Jennifer on her feet, went to the rear door well, and used his considerable upper body strength to force the rear door open just as the men from the green car boarded the bus at the front. Hampton and Jennifer ran around the back of the bus and entered the northeast corner of Rittenhouse square. The square itself was filled with strolling pedestrians with many benches available for those who preferred to sit and watch the parade. Hampton and Jennifer timed their pace to fit in with existing pedestrian flow. This was convenient since Jenifer was in no shape to do any running.

There were sufficient trees and other landscaping that Hampton could see no signs of the gunmen behind them. In the central plaza of the northeast to southwest diagonal walk, they passed the decorative pergola which sometimes had police on duty in it. Not today, however. And Hampton was not inclined to attempt to explain their problem to a police officer even if one was available. Since the Park Ranger in Independence Mall had been shot, Hampton's instinct was to keep moving and not try to involve law enforcement personnel.

Chapter 54

Back at the store on Jewelers' Row, the participants were following the pulsing icon on the tracker. It proceeded west on Walnut street. The CSI tech who was their expert on tracking devices could not tell whether it was being carried by pedestrians or was in a vehicle. The pace of the icon could fit either interpretation. At this time of day, walkers routinely travelled as fast as cars in center city.

As they watched, the icon departed from Walnut Street and proceeded slowly down the diagonal walk of Rittenhouse Square. Gillian remarked, "Going down the pedestrian walkway is a pretty good assurance that it's being carried by someone walking. Probably still Hampton and Jennifer."

Aban immediately reported this to the Philadelphia police who were attempting to find both Hampton and Jennifer, as well as the men in the green car. He terminated his call and reported.

"Still no sign of a young couple wearing the clothing we reported. Also, no sign of the shooters in the green car. The gunmen are the most immediate consideration of the detectives since the shooting of the park ranger at the Liberty Bell," said Aban. "They're going to try and concentrate their RMPs around Rittenhouse Square."

"Perhaps Hampton and Jennifer are trying to reach his apartment which is somewhere around Fitler Square," said George. "And Jennifer has an apartment in Evo at the Cira Centre South, just across the river. We should probably ask them to send cars to both places."

"Good idea", said Aban, and he proceeded to forward the request.

"We should probably head in that direction as well," said Gillian. We probably won't find out any more here that will help. And we might be able to spot them for the cops who are looking for them."

"Another good idea," said Aban. "You two start off and I'll make sure al-Siddan here gets to the 6th district holding lockup."

Thanks to the courtesy of 6th district detectives, George and Gillian got a swift ride in a Philadelphia RMP toward where they thought Jennifer, Hampton, and the diamonds were. They took the tracker found in al-Sidaan's store. As they rode, they saw the pulsing icon proceed west on Locust Street to where the railroad crossing allowed access to the Schuylkill River Parkway.

Gillian said, "It looks like they're trying get to the Parkway next to the river on the other side of the rail-line. Perhaps to get to Jennifer's apartment in Cira Centre South." They asked the officers manning the RMP to take them in that direction and they proceeded west on Spruce Street.

Chapter 55

Leaving Rittenhouse Square, Hampton thought proceeding west on Locust Street would be a good option. The car traffic on Locust was west to east, and since he and Jennifer were moving east to west the green car could not come up behind them. They could proceed west on Locust until they hit the CSX railroad right of way at the Locust Street crossing which would give them access to the Schuylkill River Pathway which ran between the river and the railroad tracks. Once on that, they could work their way north toward a bridge which would allow them to cross the river to 30th Street Station and the suburban commuter trains. Once in the station, they should be able to board a train on a commuter rail line and disappear into the western suburbs of Philadelphia and thus escape the green car and the guys chasing them. Unfortunately, for this plan, Jennifer had a problem.

"Hampton," she moaned, "I've got to pee. We need to find a bathroom, soon."

Since there is a scarcity of public restroom facilities in Philadelphia, Hampton thought that the best solution for this problem would be his apartment which was not far away. There was also something in his apartment which he thought he could use shortly.

Once in the apartment, Jennifer hurried to relieve herself. Hampton took the opportunity to pick up another gallon sized freezer-like bag which he had prepared the evening before. He now had two such bags under his new shirt, but Jennifer did not notice.

The two left his place and tried to continue westward on Locust. When they reached 24th Street, they saw the familiar sight of the green car proceeding south toward them on 24th Street. Jennifer immediately panicked. Hampton was scared himself, but retained sufficient aplomb to grab her arm and they both ran westward on Locust Street.

Unfortunately for them, the tracks of the CSX Railroad system separated them from the Pathway and the pedestrian railroad crosswalk at Locust was firmly barred by substantial gates and fences to protect anyone who might be tempted to cross the railway tracks by climbing over parked rail cars which blocked access.

Hampton was not dismayed. He was aware of an alternate way to get to the pathway. He and Jennifer would need to divert southwards through the Schuylkill River Park, past the Dog Run, probably the swankiest in Philadelphia, and use the pedestrian overpass which had been installed there to allow people to get to the Pathway when rail cars blocked the Locust Street access.

Unfortunately, there was nothing, other than signs, prohibiting auto traffic in the park. The green car came down 24th street to Spruce and turned right onto the pedestrian walkways. As Jennifer and Hampton walked through the Park, they could see the green car on the pedestrian path east of them and this immediately caused them to run past the Dog Run, to the ramp up to the overpass.

Fortunately, the ramp was not large enough to allow passage to an auto. The overpass ramp passed basketball courts where young men, both black and white, were playing on what looked like integrated teams. Interestingly enough there were numerous spectators on the overpass looking out over the dog park and being entertained by watching the dogs below. Hampton was glad of this because he thought it would provide additional cover for their movements. From the height of the overpass he could see no sign of the green car disappearing south toward South Street. But neither he nor Gillian was inclined to loiter to look for it.

They hurried as fast as they could walk, up the ramp, and across the overpass. Departing the overpass where it ended at the Parkway, both Hampton and Jennifer were glad to rest at a convenient bench where the Parkway continued north along the Schuylkill River. The Pathway also extended south on a structure called the boardwalk which had been specially designed and built extending into the river. At this point, the space between riverbank and railroad tracks was not extensive enough to support a path. To allow walkers, runners, and cyclists to move north and south along the river, the boardwalk had been built. It wasn't in truth a "board" walk of seaside type. It was a substantial cement structure with large concrete piers and a concrete pathway wide enough to allow ample room for those who used it as an exercise facility. It was even wide enough to take cars.

But it seemed that there was to be no rest for Hampton and Jennifer. The south end of the boardwalk ended in a ramp path which led up to South Street and a bridge over the river to the west bank. Hampton heard a familiar cacophony of shouts and horns coming from that end. Standing on the bench seat, he could see that the now familiar green car had managed to turn onto the boardwalk ramp and was now proceeding north, scattering bicyclists, runners, and just plain walkers, in fact, all parkway users, amid shouts and protests and the blasts of its horn.

Jumping down from the bench, Hampton told Jennifer that they had to run again. "Oh no," she said, "I'm exhausted, I can't go any more."

Hampton said, "We either run or we'll have to face those thugs with guns." He grabbed Jennifer's upper arm and got her moving north toward other bridges that provided crossings across the river to the west side. They passed under the Walnut Street bridge and turned a sharp corner in the path under the Chestnut Street bridge where a long pedestrian rampway led up to Market street and its bridge. Hampton could hear the green car getting closer, but he knew it would not be able to follow them up the pedestrian rampway. There was not suffi-cient width to allow a car to proceed up it. With luck, they would be able to shake the thugs here, continue up the ramp, and proceed a short distance on Market Street to 30th Street station where they could get on a commuter train and get lost in the suburbs.

Sure enough, when they were 2/3 of the way up the ramp, the green car tried to turn the sharp corner under the Chestnut Street bridge and was unable to complete it. The thugs got out with guns in hand, but they were too far away for accurate shooting. The last thing Hampton saw as they made it onto Market Street was the thugs starting to go up the ramp on foot.

Gillian and George, in the Philadelphia RMP, tracked the movement of the pulsing icon on to the riverside pathway. They initially thought Hampton and Jennifer were moving to-ward Cira Centre South and her apartment, but that was ruled out when the icon moved past the Walnut Street bridge. They asked the RMP Officers to drive them to Market Street.

Chapter 56

Once on the Market Street Bridge, Hampton and Jennifer crossed four lanes of traffic on Market Street, dodging cars and trucks amid the yells of angry drivers. They crossed Schuylkill Avenue which covered over the expressway underneath it. They headed for the southeast corner entrance to the 30th Street Station, where Hampton turned to look back. The thugs were closer and coming fast.

Gillian and George had reached the Market Street bridge in time to see a young couple go into the station through the southeast corner entrance. They guessed that they were Jennifer and Hampton. There was no sign of the green car. Surprisingly, the icon still tracked and displayed inside the station, even though the station was a massive structure quite similar to Pennsylvania Station in New York City. Gillian asked their RMP to drop them off at the south-east corner and reported everything to their 6th district police liaison.

Inside the station, Hampton and Jennifer dodged customers as they ran through the food court, passing a Saxby's Coffee, a Jersey Mike's Subs, a Subway, and several other food and drink stands selling eatables for travelers. They ran past the Stairways leading down to gates 6 and 4 which provided access to the boarding platforms under the station and which allowed passengers to board Amtrak trains going north and south. They made it into the main waiting area which they had to cross to get to the northwest corner ramp leading to the suburban commuter trains. As they were passing the central information counter in the center of the waiting area they heard a shot, heard a ricochet, and Hampton fell down on the opposite side of the counter. Throughout the station, people went to the floor.

"Oh God, Hampton, you're hit. Your foot is bleeding like mad," Jennifer said as she knelt beside him below the level of the counter. "Does it hurt?"

Hampton tried to stop the bleeding using a handkerchief as a pad. "It does smart a little," he admitted.

"You can't move with that," she said with conviction. And not a little satisfaction. After all the trials of the day, it looked to her that her luck was turning. She could get the diamonds all to herself! Without any objections from Hampton!

She did not think Hampton would want to keep some or all of the jewels for himself, but she was willing to bet that he would disapprove of her confiscating them.

And indeed, Hampton did not think he would be able to stand on his injured foot, let alone walk with it. Or carry any diamond bags.

Jennifer was inwardly exultant that she would soon have achieved her goal.

"Quick, give me the diamond bag and I'll go get on a train out of the city. They won't hurt you if you don't have the diamonds."

Hampton sincerely hoped that would be the case. And he didn't want her hurt either.

"OK", he said, passing her a bag from inside his shirt, "Go as fast as you can to the commuter tracks and get on the first train you can. When you're safe in a suburb, give me a call and we'll get back together."

She grabbed the bag and immediately started for the suburban train entrance. Hampton sadly watched her run toward the northwest corner. She said nothing and never looked back. He bid a silent, final farewell to her.

Chapter 57

Hampton held his improvised handkerchief pad bandage on his foot and waited for the thugs to come around the counter and do something to him. To his surprise, the first person he saw coming around to where he was lying was George, followed quickly by Gillian. He was completely dumfounded by George's placard hanging around his neck which identified him as FBI and Gillian's card which proclaimed her an ATF agent.

"So, buddy, for this re-enactment, you managed to get yourself shot for real. How bad does it hurt?" George was not in the least sympathetic to the blood flowing from Hampton's shoe.

Gillian was more concerned. "It's got to hurt like the devil,' she said. "We need to get him an ambulance." She immediately started to make arrangements on her cell phone. "Hampton, I suspect the best place for you to be taken is the ER of the Hospital of the University of Pennsylvania. It's also the closest one to here."

Hampton nodded his approval while still trying to slow the bleeding. In effect, he had insurance coverage there.

Despite the pain in his foot, Hampton managed to state the obvious. "So, you both have been government investigators all the time you were at the 71st VA. Why were you investigating them ... or us, I should say?"

George smiled and said "We both were interested in a re-en-actors group with access to black powder which anomalously had a Confederate unit designation in a Northern state. Once we got to the first meeting, Youkoumian, you, and Jennifer stood out as unusual people. And things just proceeded from there."

"I was certainly glad to see you and your badges as you came around the booth. I expected to see the thugs which were trying to catch us."

"They managed to get out of the station before the Phila-delphia police could collar them," said George.

"I'm still trying to grasp the idea that you guys are gov-ernment agents," sighed Hampton. "You know, Jennifer and I were convinced the thugs were working with you and Gillian to steal the diamonds. We also saw you at the Samson Street store talking with Youkoumian. It looked to us like you were all in it together, we thought for some insurance scam. And we thought you had hired the thugs."

"Me?" said George. "How could you think I would hire anyone like those guys?"

Hampton shook his head. "It was mostly the sequence of events. And Jennifer had ideas about everything. And she was convincing."

George said "I must admit Gillian and I were not the most forthcoming of government agents. At one time, we even suspected each other of working with Youkoumian and you and Jennifer."

Hampton shook his head, "You'll have to explain that one to me." He winced as his foot throbbed painfully. "The other thing is how did you find me here. You must have had something to do with scaring off the bad guys."

George smiled and said. "We've been tracking you via the jewel bag you got from Youkoumian".

"But I still have the jewels here in this bag."

"I know,' said George. "That's how we found you." He showed Hampton the hand-held tracking device, which showed a pulsing icon in the center of the waiting room of 30th Street station. "The bag holding the diamonds has a built-in tracker in its bottom seam."

Hampton thought about that. "But we got the diamonds and that bag from Youkoumian. So, he didn't trust us as much as he said."

"It's even worse than that, Hampton. The thugs were working for Youkoumian and they were tracking you and Jennifer using a device like this one."

Hampton thought about that. "That would explain why they always managed to show up wherever we were, even after we changed shirts."

George said, "And speaking of Jennifer, what happened to her? Why isn't she here with you?"

Hampton said sadly. "It's a long story, but she took off for the suburban trains. Carrying what she thinks is the bag of diamonds."

"And it's not?" asked Gillian.

"It's a bag of gravel from a construction site near my apartment."

George whistled. "Well, that's going to be a shock for her when she opens it up. Why did you give her that bag instead of the bag with the diamonds?"

The paramedics showed up before Hampton could explain.

Gillian said, "It's OK sweetie, you can let us know after your foot gets some attention." The EMTs put a clean bandage on Hampton's foot, started an IV with replacement fluid, and bundled him up in a rolling gurney. They were headed for the ER at the Hospital of the University of Pennsylvania.

Chapter 58

George looked at Gillian. "For a guy who was so into that girl, he doesn't seem that bothered by the fact that she ran off with what she thought was a fortune in diamonds and left him here all alone for the bad guys."

Gilllian said, "I think Hampton finally started to do some thinking with his head about Jennifer. That has to be a factor in why he let her go off with a fake bag of diamonds."

"From what I could observe about them as a couple, I thought he would do just about anything she wanted."

Gillian said, "I agree, the few times I saw them together, I thought his only question would be how high he should jump."

George smiled as well. "It should be interesting to hear what made Hampton keep the diamonds secretly."

"In the meantime, we are going to need to deliver the diamonds to Aban, and start writing up the charges against Youkoumian and his H1-B thugs."

Chapter 59

Many hours and a lot of paperwork later, George and Gillian, with Aban Hassad, found Hampton in the University of Pennsylvania hospital emergency room. They introduced him to Aban. Everyone, George, Gillian, and Aban, was interested in finding out more of what had been occurring between Hampton, Jennifer, and Youkoumian.

Aban said "Youkoumian claims that you and Jennifer fooled him with a bogus machine for traveling between dimensions."

Hampton was a little embarrassed about the whole episode. "Yes, she had a convincing story about arriving here by travelling from another dimension. And she persuaded me to put together a setup that would allow that travel to happen. As she explained it, it required coherent light to be slowed down by refracting through diamonds. We initially got 250 diamonds from Youkoumian and I mounted them to her specifications into an opaque sphere about 10 cm in diameter, roughly the size of a softball."

"But you work in a Physics Lab. Do you believe that there are additional dimensions and that you can move between them?"

Hampton said, "Well, she was the most outstanding graduate student in the Physics Department at the University of

Pennsylvania. She knew more and was smarter than any of the male grad students, and even some of the professors. They and the professors all thought she was brilliant ... another Einstein. I'm only a lab tech. As I said, she was convincing. And there's so much stuff going on in Physics today that almost anything could be possible."

Aban said. "OK, I can appreciate that. The information I have on her now indicates that her real name was Jennifer Lopez."

"Like the movie star", murmured Hampton.

George mused, "Just like her, including the rear end."

Gillian punched him in the shoulder. "You're such a Y at times," she said.

"Sorry," he said rubbing his shoulder. "As the scorpion said, sorry, it's my nature."

Aban continued. "According to the materials we found in her room, she came from Costa Rica, on a tourist visa. I had a scan made for the name Jennifer Lopez in local police reports. I found a woman of that name had been picked up last year by the New Jersey state police in a raid on a Meth operation. The lab was run almost entirely by Costa Ricans so it's possible she worked there for a while before she came to Philadelphia. Interestingly enough, she was never indicted and there's no record even of her being charged with anything."

Hampton said, "That would explain how she was able to recognize the Front Street location as a Meth Lab. She was familiar with the smell."

Aban smiled a little at that, but went on, "She also had false papers indicating she had graduated from a university in Costa Rica with the highest honors and recommendations. In reality, she's apparently never attended a college."

"That's remarkable," said Hampton. "Her IQ must be off the charts. To fake expertise in modern physics would require at a minimum a detailed acquaintance with terms and theories. She was so self-assured and convincing that everyone believed everything she said."

Aban looked over his papers. "Evidently she comes from an upscale Costa Rican family. Her father is an under-secretary in their Ministerio de Comercio Exterior, and her mother teaches math and physics at the Universidad Latinoamericana de Ciencia y Tecnología."

Aban looked up at the others "That probably explains how she got into the University of Pennsylvania. Either her mother or her mother's contacts could have helped her get the references and documents she needed to get into graduate school here."

Gillian nodded, "Also, her mother probably knows enough about Physics to coach her in support of her dimension story. That could explain why she was so convincing to everyone else. One wonders why someone with such advantages and abilities didn't stay in Costa Rica and rise as high as she wanted."

George remarked "Maybe she just didn't want to be the biggest frog in a small puddle."

Aban continued with his information. "We also found notes in her room indicating that she had researched jewelers in Philadelphia and she had discovered Youkoumian's involvement with the 71st VA.re-enactor's group. She also had notes that you, Hampton, were a part of that group. It looks like she had carefully planned her approach to you and Youkoumian in order to have access to many diamonds."

Hampton said ruefully. "That pretty much correlates with what I finally realized was going on."

Aban said," And that realization explains why you sent her off without the diamonds?"

"I think it started to dawn on me that she was more interested in the diamonds than anything else, including me. But
the thing that at last convinced me that she was not completely
honest was her statement that she originally made the transfer
from her dimension in the nude."

George said, "That's a picture to think about", and got
another punch in the shoulder.

Gillian said, "And what made you suspect that, Hampton."

Hampton said "When we first discussed her being from
another dimension, I asked if she could produce any physical evidence from her dimension. She said the transfer only
worked for living organisms. Ordinary materials would not
transfer. She claimed she made the transfer naked."

George manfully resisted a comment to preserve his sore
shoulders.

Hampton continued, "And later when we ran a demo for
Youkoumian on a scale model of the machine she specified, she
managed to make it appear that a note she had written was
transmitted to her dimension and that a gold coin was transmitted from her dimension to here. That was what convinced
Youkoumian, and I believed it too until I thought about it
for a while. And realized the contradiction with what she had
previously told me. At last I recognized that the demo we put
on was faked somehow. And that quite likely her whole story
was made up."

Aban remarked, "The information we were able to sift
from her graduate dorm apartment indicates that she put a
lot of effort and internet time into investigating diamond
merchants in Philadelphia. Apparently, she finally fixated on
Youkoumian's because of two things she discovered: he was
the head of the 71st VA., and you were also a member of that
group. That gave her a possible source of diamonds and your

connection to that group gave her a possible avenue to acquire them. She had all her notes about both of you in a single manila folder which suggests that she had decided that you provided a good path to obtaining diamonds from him. Hearing about her story and how she acted, I can well believe in her ability to weave a creative, believable tale."

Gillian remarked "I remember reading that scientists are the easiest marks to convince of illusions since they are conditioned to report truthfully about their results. Hence they can't believe that someone would try to fool them."

Hampton smiled a little, "Well I'm not a scientist, just a lab tech. But I was convinced when she ran the demo."

"As was Youkoumian", said George. "He's complaining bitterly about how he was tricked by you and Jennifer."

Aban, pursuing his questioning, said. "So, that was enough for you to give Jennifer a fake bag of diamonds?"

Ruefully, Hampton said, "I was convinced that the diamonds belonged to Youkoumian and that he ought to get them back. I knew if she had them no one would ever see them again."

"I don't think Youkoumian will ever see them again either," said George.

Hampton looked a question at the group.

Gillian took the initiative in explaining to Hampton. "Youkoumian was only his make-believe name. His actual name is Hassan al-Sidaan and he has passports from Syria, Egypt, and Yemen. So, we don't know his actual nationality. Documents found at his store indicate he was running it as a hawala for a jihadist group."

Confused by all these revelations, Hampton asked "And what is a hawala?"

Aban undertook to explain it. "It's an old, old system of exchanging money in the East outside of western banking.

Unlike western banks, it depends less on instruments of transfer and more on the integrity, reputation, and trust built up by interacting with others in the system. With Youkoumian, or al-Sidann as we should call him, it allowed his group to transfer funds from U.S. sources into diamonds which then traveled by courier to the middle East."

"So, what will happen to him?" asked Hampton.

Aban smiled slightly and said, "He faces many charges under the Patriot act. I think there is enough evidence that he will be in prison for quite some time."

"And the diamonds?" asked Hampton.

"The ones which came from his store are subject to confiscation by the federal government. The ones he borrowed from various legitimate sources will eventually be returned to their rightful owners. You know, Hampton, if you had given Jennifer the real bag of diamonds, we probably would have been able to track her and apprehend her."

"And what would you be able to charge her with, if you did catch her?" asked George.

"Good point", said Aban. "If she had had actual possession of the bag of diamonds we could probably have charged her with theft. She most likely was running a scam on Youkoumian, probably to steal the diamonds, but since she doesn't have them in her hands, I don't think anyone in legal would be interested in pursuing an attempt that failed. It would only distract from the case against him."

"So basically, she gets away free and clear", said Hampton.

"You're not sorry about that, Hampton, are you?" asked Gillian.

"No, I was into her, as they say. I liked her. And I still think she's the smartest person I've ever met."

Gillian gave Hampton a hug as he lay on the E.R. gurney. "Hampton, you are a sweetie."

Chapter 60

Several days later, George was called to his SAC's office. Dan waved him in. "Come on in, George, and take a seat. Take a gander at this folder." George accepted the folder, sat down, and opened it. It was a commendation letter for him from the Director's office. Basically, it commended George for participating in the joint task force led by Aban Hassad which successfully apprehended jihadists operating in the US. It was George's second commendation in his dossier. He looked up at Dan.

Dan smiled. "I got one too. For encouraging and supporting you in your investigation of the re-enactor group."

George smiled back. "Well, you certainly did that. But Aban produced almost all the information. I was mostly just along for the ride."

"As was I", said Dan. "When you're a SAC, you'll find yourself getting a lot of attaboys for the work your agents do. It's just the way things work."

"You think I'm going to be a SAC somewhere?" asked George.

"I'd bet on it," said Dan.

George sat for a few seconds enjoying the compliment and his letter of commendation.

Dan broke his mood with "So now that you're not tied up with the gunpowder guys, you can lend a hand to Gentry. He's still working on that corrupt city councilman. Help him develop a case on that."

George sighed and said, "That's almost as bad as working in insurance."

Dan smiled and remarked as George left "Hey don't knock it. Corrupt Philadelphia politicians keep this office in business."

Chapter 61

At approximately the same time, Gillian was in Gloria's office getting her own commendation from the director of ATF.

Gloria remarked, "As usual, I also got lot of credit for your participation and giving you the leeway to pursue your investigation into the re-enactor's group. I almost regret my retirement because you make me look good just by being you."

Gillian shook her head ruefully. "In reality, I had a completely wrong take on what was going on there. Initially I thought the people from the Physics department were doing something criminal. And then I thought the FBI guy, George, was into producing Meth with them. It took Aban Hassad's arrival to clarify what was going on."

Gloria was not dismayed at her protestation of not fully grasping the situation. "That's not uncommon in most investigations ... a lot of possibilities which you can gradually eliminate until you get to a closer version of reality."

Gillian was not convinced. Unfortunately, despite her abilities in analyzing situations, the evidence seemed to be tending in the direction that working in ATF was not a good deal for her. Perhaps she should have tried to get in the FBI earlier, as some special agents had suggested.

"The other thing that keeps bothering me is that I talked to Tom a few weeks ago, when we were together in the surveillance van at the sting store."

"Let me guess, Tom was pretty negative about ATF and couldn't wait to tell you how much he wants to get out."

Gillian looked directly at her group supervisor, "Yes, he does have a litany of what he called ATF SNAFUs and FUBARs .... Ruby Ridge, Branch Davidian, Fast and Furious, and then Operation Fearless, in Milwaukee, which he participated in."

Gloria nodded, "He does have a point. ATF has a continuing history of bad command decisions in upper levels. We're all aware of it. That's one of the reasons I've always been so proud of you. I know you have the smarts to bring some intelligence to higher supervisory positions. There are many field divisions in ATF in which you could be an outstanding group supervisor right now."

Gillian said, "Thank you, I'm glad you think that. But I'm not so sure any more that I want to go into management. I've always enjoyed analyzing situations and developing information about them. I'm not so sure I would be any good at supervising agents."

Gloria smiled at her and said, "I'm absolutely convinced that you would do an excellent job in whatever position you reach."

Gillian was pleased to hear this from her supervisor, but still had worries about where she was and what she should be doing. "I'm glad you think that, but I'm still uneasy about things."

Gloria leaned back. "Have you thought about what else you might want to do?"

"It has crossed my mind that Private Investigations might be more interesting and give me a chance to do more of the things I enjoy."

Gloria locked her hands behind her head. "I don't know why young people always seem to think they should somehow "enjoy" their work. It's work. Sometimes boring or unpleasant. That's why it's not called play and it's why they pay you do it."

Gillian said ruefully. "I do get that. I suppose I'm just longing for interesting stuff. That's why I sometimes think private investigation might be a better spot for me."

"90% of private investigations consist of getting evidence on a cheating husband for a divorcing wife. The other 10% is usually working with a private business trying to keep their employees from stealing money and product. It's certainly nothing like Nancy Drew, girl detective."

Gillian sighed, "Yes, I guess I can accept that on a rational basis. But I still keep hoping."

Gloria smiled and said to her, "Nothing wrong with doing that. But enough work-related stuff. How are you doing with your young man, George?"

Gillian could feel her face reddening slightly. "He's not my young man, he's just someone I enjoy spending time with."

"I can see you blushing, Gillian. You like him more than a little."

"OK, you're right. I do like him more than a little. He's cute, has all his hair, in good shape, fairly smart and quick, and he often makes me laugh."

Gloria said, "Sounds like a keeper to me. Set the hook and reel him in, girl."

Chapter 62

Aban Hassad had long since returned to New York. Of the participants in the Jewelers' Row raid, he alone did not receive a commendation. Instead he was promoted to head of the DHS section which was tracking suspected terrorists in New York City. He had rather suspected that this would have happened soon anyway, and nabbing Hassan al-Sidaan was a good occasion for the promotion. Aban wasn't 100% sure he wanted to manage a section of 40 agents. He rather enjoyed working in the field, interviewing people, and trying to work out the reality of situations which initially were unclear. He enjoyed detecting. Still the big rewards anywhere come from rising in the chain of command. And he was on the path for doing that.

Chapter 63

After work that day, George and Gillian met at Devon. They had invited Hampton there for a drink and discussion about their joint happenings and expected him to appear shortly. Rather than sitting at the large rectangular bar as they usually did, they were sitting at one of the tables looking out through the windows toward Rittenhouse square. That was much more conducive to general three-way conversation than everyone sitting in a row, side by side.

George could hardly wait to tell Gillian about his commendation. She congratulated him, saying with a smile "You deserved it, especially for your nocturnal visit to Front Street."

George grinned ruefully, "I never reported that to anyone other than my boss, and he was not about to pass it up the line. Also, I seem to recall that you made a nighttime visit yourself." He raised his eyebrows at her.

'Also, something that I only discussed with Gloria, and she never said anything upward either. Probably that's why I got a commendation also."

"That's terrific!" George remarked to her. "You deserved it for the way you got al-Sidaan to cooperate with us immediately. You were playing tough cop with him. Getting him to own up to things made it a lot easier for us to understand what was going on."

"The trouble is, I feel guilty about the commendation. I think most of the credit is due to Aban."

"I have the same feeling," confessed George. He told her of Dan Carolli's contention that agents or managers often get credit for things done by other people.

"My boss, Gloria Wentworth told me much the same thing."

"Gloria seems like an extremely nice person. And a good manager."

"She's great." said Gillian. She paused to sip her drink. "You know, she thinks you're sincere."

"I didn't know that and I like her even more now."

"She keeps teasing me about you being 'my young man'."

George stated, "Clearly a brilliant woman. But if I'm gonna have that designation, you must stop calling other guys 'sweetie'. You know I'm more than a little jealous that you called Hampton a sweetie the last time we saw him."

Gillian looked at him, amused. "So why does that make you jealous?"

George looked at her wryly. "You've never called me a sweetie and I've been much more involved with you than he has. And shown you much more attention."

Gillian shook her head. "You're so easily offended. How does my appreciation of Hampton's actions affect you in any way?"

"Well, I guess it doesn't," he said grudgingly. "But I still want to be called a sweetie, too. In particular, I want to be your sweetie."

Gillian smiled and said, "Careful there, it almost sounds as if you're looking for a commitment. Not at all Y of you."

George swallowed, "I guess I am not. And if it's not Y, I don't care. I like you a lot."

Gillian almost laughed out loud, "You like me a lot? So, what is this, High School? Are we gonna go steady? Do you have a class ring to give me?"

George smiled at her and said, "No ring, but going steady sounds good to me. And more refined than 'friends with benefits' "

"Since we haven't had any 'benefits' yet, it's also more accurate."

George said. "I find it encouraging that you qualified benefits with a 'yet'. It gives me hope for the future."

Gillian laughed, "You are funny sometimes." She took a long look at him. "OK, sign me up. I'm ready to go steady with you."

George pumped his fist up and down in the air, "Yes!" Just as Hampton arrived at their table.

Hampton was on crutches, so George got up and pulled a chair out for him. He also held the crutches while Hampton folded himself into the chair.

"So, George, what are you so stoked about?" asked Hampton.

"Gillian says she'll go steady with me" said George.

Hampton was bemused. He looked at George and Gillian. "Go steady? What are we, back in High School? In 1950? Don't couples in our day hook up?"

"I hate that term," said George. "It makes the whole process sound like tow trucks collecting wrecked cars."

Gillian laughed delightedly. "You know Hampton, he has a point. Who wants to hook up like a tow truck?"

Hampton smiled and said, "I have to admit that you're right George. I don't want to be hooked up like a wrecked auto."

Gillian seconded him, "Good for you Hampton, I always knew you were a sweetie."

George said "Are you saying that just to aggravate me? You know I want to be your sweetie."

"And you are, George, you are my sweetie And I'm glad I'm your steady. You're much more sensitive than the average Y."

George smiled and said, "I'll drink to that. What do you think, Hampton.?"

Hampton said to his two friends. "I will drink to that, too. I'm still trying to absorb everything's that has happened. But I do think you two make a good couple. A really good couple."

Chapter 64

Many of Gillian's girlfriends thought the same thing. Almost everyone she introduced George to was impressed by his consistency in referring to females as women instead of girls. And he never addressed them as "guys" either, although they often used the term themselves in referring to members of their group. Several expressed the thought to Gillian that if she ever wanted to get rid of George, they wouldn't mind being suggested as a possible replacement for her. Gillian laughed and assured them that she was nowhere near "getting rid of him." George himself was consistently delighted to be associated with her in any social situation. After a while, Gillian was convinced that he was "into her", as the saying went. It didn't hurt when several of her friends expressed the same sentiment.

As days went by, she found herself spending more and more time with him and thoroughly enjoying such periods. After work, they often met at his apartment, sometimes to go to a movie, sometimes to go out to eat. They drew each other's attention to things they read on the internet and discussed them. She occasionally stayed overnight at his apartment and was beginning to accumulate a number of things at his place, clothing, toilet articles, and so on. Going steady seemed to be working out well for both of them.

Eventually, Gillian thought carefully about the subject and concluded that she might as well move in with him. He was ecstatic when she suggested this and couldn't wait for her to do it. Gillian preferred to be a little more sure of things and waited a few weeks until her lease was up in SOWSO before taking the plunge. She offered to pay half the rent of his apartment, but he wouldn't hear of it.

As he put it, "I'm making twice your ATF salary as an FBI special agent. Let me pay for it. You can buy things for yourself out of what you were paying for rent."

That wasn't exactly in line with Gillian's usual desire to support herself, but she went along with it. It helped that, when they ate in, she always did the cooking. George was not a cook, but compensated for that by cleaning up the kitchen after she prepared meals. Both were satisfied with that arrangement.

Gillian also had a suggestion about their car situation. "It also doesn't make much sense for us to have two cars. I thought I should get rid of mine and then take over the expenses on yours, insurance and maintenance, and so on."

George said, "Sounds fair to me. That's a great idea. Also, it's hard to find street parking for cars in Society Hill." George was fortunate in that his apartment lease came with a dedicated garage space for one car.

Gillian was finding more and more things to like about George. She was glad she had moved into his apartment in Society Hill. It was much more spacious than her digs in SOWSO. Plus, it was surprisingly clean. Gillian had been prepared to move into a bear's den. Most of her girl-friends who were living with guys, or had lived with guys, had warned her that men were essentially bears. Occasionally endearingly affectionate, but usually just messy and given to producing trails of debris wherever they went. It was quite a relief to her to find that George put some effort into keeping things picked up, neat, and clean. She had not yet mentioned this to him for fear of causing him to lapse into bear-like messiness.

Interestingly, George had never said anything about her living habits even after she had been in his apartment for a while. Gillian, on the principle of letting sleeping dogs lie, had declined to bring this up as a subject of conversation. She was satisfied and he did not complain, so he seemed to be all right with everything as well.

One thing Gillian did take advantage of was George's underwear. Some of her girl-friends had mentioned that most guys never threw out their old underwear, simply washing the articles over and over until they were as soft as satin and eventually disappeared.

Gillian found such garments extremely comfortable and usually wore them around the apartment. It was OK with her that this occasionally caused George to get into a state where he could not keep his hands off her. She viewed this as an acceptable perk of living with a guy. It was nice to see how attractive he found her in his boxers and t-shirts. And it was kind of fun to have him chase her around the apartment until she let him catch her.

Chapter 65

Some weeks later, Hampton was off the crutches and returned to his apartment after work to find the door open. Since he knew he had locked up when he left in the morning, he was a little disconcerted about that. He entered his rather small apartment to find Jennifer in the kitchen apparently pouring herself a glass of Chardonnay. Now he was more than disconcerted, he was extremely surprised. Why the heck was she here? Whatever could she want with him now?

Still as attractive as ever, she turned to greet him. "Well, Hampton, you seem to have survived that gunshot wound with no ill effects. I'm glad for that."

Hampton said, "When you left for the commuter trains, I was sure I would never see you again."

Jennifer smiled ironically. "If you had given me the sack of diamonds, you wouldn't have. Why did you give me that sack of gravel? Did you decide to keep the diamonds for yourself?"

"At the time, I thought the diamonds rightfully belonged to Youkoumian. And I knew if you had them in your possession, no one would ever see you again."

Jennifer sipped her wine. "Somehow since we were last together, you have gotten a lot smarter. I don't think I like it. So Youkoumian got all his diamonds back, I suppose."

"Youkoumian is a Syrian named al-Sidaan, and was doing money laundering for middle east terror groups through the jewelry store. He is facing trial for his actions."

Jennifer said, "So he wasn't an Armenian for real."

Hampton shook his head, "No, we're not sure what country he came from exactly, but he definitely was a Muslim and was associated with Arabic terror groups."

"Well, that explains why he liked the story I made up about the Caliphate of Damascus. That was one of my best achievements, and all made up on the fly while I talked to him in his office. Too bad we didn't know he was a terrorist then. We probably could have got some diamonds out of him just through blackmail, without any nonsense about dimensions."

"The men in the green car were members of his group. Judging by their actions, I don't think blackmail would have been a good idea. If we'd tried, we probably would have wound up dead."

"You're probably right." She sipped her Chardonnay. "Either that or George and that Gillian somehow would have stuck their noses into it."

"Despite what we thought, George was not after the diamonds and had nothing to do with the thugs who were chasing us. In reality, he's an FBI agent in the local field office."

"And what about that Gillian?"

Hampton smiled and said, "We were also wrong about her. She's an agent for Alcohol, Tobacco, and Firearms. She was checking out the 71st VA. because of our black powder supply."

Jennifer acridly said, "I always thought she was pretty deceitful," and took another sip of Chardonnay. "She was attracted to you, but I made sure she couldn't get to you. That would have ruined all my plans early in the game." She thought about it. "So, what happened to all the jewels?"

"The Homeland Security guy who developed most of the information on the workings of the group in Philadelphia confiscated the store's portion under the Patriot act. Ironically, he is a third generation Arab-American. He's now in the process of getting the rest back to the legitimate jewelry store owners who lent them to al-Sidaan."

Jennifer shook her head. "What a waste. To get so close to millions and miss out on all of it. It's all your fault, you know. If you had given me the correct bag I would be rich by now."

Hampton shook his head, "No, there was a tracker device in the diamond bag we got from al-Siddan. If I had given you that bag, they would have tracked you down, eventually picked you up, and you would have been charged with theft. That tracker was how those thugs always were able to get close to us as we were trying to get away."

Jennifer sighed. "So, I was never destined to win on those jewels, one way or another. All that effort and planning for nothing. What a waste." She drank some Chardonnay. "You didn't hold out a few for souvenirs, did you? No, that's not something you would do, is it?"

"I'm afraid not." Hampton took another long look at her. She looked just as good as ever. The question was why was she here in his apartment? "The agent from DHS also developed a lot of background information on you. He discovered that you've never attended a university and all of the paper work you used to get into Penn graduate school was faked."

"That agent sounds like a clever person." Jennifer took another sip of Chardonnay. "Faked or not, I was still the smartest person in the Physics department."

Hampton nodded in agreement. "He guessed that your mother passed on a lot of her expertise in Physics to you."

Jennifer stopped sipping. "So, he found out about my parents."

Hampton smiled slightly to see her surprised. "Yes. And the big puzzle for everyone is, with your looks, brains, and background, why you didn't go through ordinary channels to become super successful in Costa Rica. With your looks and talent, Gillian thought you could have owned the country."

"That Gillian! I didn't like her when we first met, and I certainly don't like her now. She obviously doesn't know the first thing about what it's like to be a woman in Costa Rica! Men control everything there."

Hampton raised his eyebrows.

"Don't give me that querulous look. Even if you were smarter, I wouldn't expect you to understand what it's like to be a woman in Costa Rica. Or even in the U.S. And God help the poor women in Muslim countries.

"My mother is the smartest person I ever met and the highest position she managed to rise to was assistant professor at the Universidad Latinoamericana de Ciencia y Tecnología. Her advice to me was that the only good place for a woman was to be independently rich. Only extremely wealthy women command any respect from men."

"And so, you came up with the scheme about dimensions, diamonds, and jewelers just to become super rich."

Jennifer smiled evilly. "Of course, and it almost worked, didn't it?"

Hampton nodded in agreement and looked at her steadily. "And why are you back here now?"

Jennifer looked right back at him. "I was hoping you had scored some of the jewels somehow. But the more I think about it, the more I realize it's not something you would do. Still we came so close last time, I think we should look for another opportunity. I have some possibilities in mind. There's a ...."

Hampton interrupted her. "Jennifer, I think it's only fair to warn you that your magic won't work anymore. Fool me once, shame on you. Fool me twice shame on me. Whatever you have in mind probably involves taking something which doesn't belong to you and certainly not to me."

The eyes turned particularly flinty at that. "You weren't so particular about morality when *we* hooked up. You were quite willing to do anything I wanted."

Hampton nodded. "That's so. But circumstances have changed. The tale of the little lost girl from another dimension won't work anymore. And I certainly don't want to be involved in stealing from whomever your latest mark is now."

The flinty eyes were still sparking. "You know you're still absolutely in love with me and will do anything I want. If I take off my clothes, you will still do anything I ask you to do."

Hampton smiled ruefully. "I know I'm totally in something with you but I'm not sure whether it's love or lust or just fascination. But I do know that there are some things I just won't do, even if you tell me to. Sorry, Jennifer, I'm a little smarter now."

Frustrated, Jennifer stared at him for what seemed to him like an interminable period.

Part of Hampton was telling himself to do whatever she wanted so he could have sex with her. While a second part was quite convincing and maintained that she was just trying to re-establish her prior dominance over him. He was resolved not to be in that position again.

Finally, Jennifer shook her head, put down her unfinished glass of wine, and said "This isn't over yet." She then left and Hampton had to sit down on one of his kitchen chairs. He thought 'I wonder if that's the end. It's hard to imagine her giving up any resource that she thinks might make her rich. But I don't want to be a "resource" any more.'

Chapter 66

Later that week after work, Hampton walked over to Ritten-house Square for a meeting with George and Gillian at ev-erybody's favorite bistro, Devon. Although Hampton wasn't much of a drinker, he rather liked having an occasional drink with those he now considered to be his old friends and finding out how their relationship was progressing. It was a bittersweet reminder of the connection, such as it had been, between him-self and Jennifer. For this get together, Hampton was sure they would both be interested in the fact that Jennifer had gotten in contact with him again. As was usual, George was there first and had acquired a window table for the three of them. They had tried all sitting at the bar in a row but it was not conducive to general conversation.

"Hi George," said Hampton as he came up to where George was sitting.

George was glad to see him, "Hampton, you dog, you seem to have no after effects of your shooting. It's good to see you."

"Good to see you, too, George. I suspect Gillian will be by later", said Hampton.

"It's an interesting effect," said George. "Females never show up early and often make their males wait. I'm not quite sure why that is so, but it seems to be a recurring feature with Gillian."

"Probably has something to do with establishing dominance. Or maybe fighting back at male dominance. I suppose it won't be long before we hear more out-cries against male privilege along with all other forms of privilege," remarked Hampton.

"Except they'll probably call it Y privilege instead of male privilege," said George. "I know Gillian would."

"So, you two are still 'going steady'?" asked Hampton.

"Yes!" said George. "She's terrific! I'm so glad she likes me. I have no complaints about her. You know, she's moved into my apartment in Society Hill. Apparently, I'm acceptable enough for that."

"Congratulations," said Hampton. "I've always thought Gillian was smart and had good taste. I remember you once advised me that Jennifer was not a good choice because I said she was smarter than me."

George sighed, "Yes, in our case, I'm not sure who's smarter, Gillian or me. Not that it matters. She's sharp, and I find I can appreciate that, even if it turns out that she's smarter than I am. And I don't care if she is."

"You're a good man, George." said Hampton as Gillian showed up at the table.

"And why is that, Hampton? "asked Gillian.

"He can admit when he's wrong," said Hampton.

"Yes," said Gillian, "I've noticed that too!"

George said, "You don't have to say that so enthusiastically. If we're through discussing me and my shortcomings, let's move on. So, what's new with you, Hampton?"

Hampton smiled slowly, "Well I had a visit from Jennifer."

"You're kidding," said George.

"No, she showed up at my apartment."

Gillian came out with the obvious question. "And what did she want?"

"Most immediately, to see if I had any of the diamonds."

Gillian made a face. "You'd think she would know you well enough to know you would never keep something that didn't belong to you."

"Also, I think she wanted to see if she still could control me completely."

Gillian said, "And can she?"

Hampton smiled also. "No, it was hard, but I managed to finally say no."

Gillian leaned over and gave him a hug. "You're a good man, too, Hampton."

George protested, "Hey, if you're giving out hugs, I want one, too!"

And he got one, along with a kiss.

George recovered and said "So, Hampton, what's your take on seeing Jennifer again?"

Hampton considered this, and said "I think she has some new scheme in mind. It becomes clearer all the time that she was into getting the diamonds to become fabulously wealthy, so whatever she's into now probably involves something similar."

Gillian said, "I think you're right, Hampton, and you're right to resist doing anything she wants, especially if it involves money."

Hampton thought about that. "I don't think that's the only thing motivating Jennifer. She also has a thing about male dominance. She told me her mother was the smartest person she ever met, and the highest her mother ever got was assistant professor at her university in Costa Rica. Her mother advised her that the only way for a woman to be respected was to be independently rich."

George thought about it for a while. "I think Jennifer and her mother have a point. I don't think Gillian is into trying to dominate but she certainly doesn't put up with any guff."

Gillian said, "And what is guff?"

"My grandfather used to say it a lot", said George. "Guff is foolish nonsense. To tell someone they don't put up with it is a compliment. According to my grampa."

"Thanks to both your grampa and you."

A nicely dressed young woman walked up to their table and said, "Hi Gillian, sorry I'm late."

Led by Hampton, both men stood for the newcomer.

Gillian introduced her. "Guys, this is Katy Wakefield. I met her at an exercise dance class at George's fitness center in Society Hill. Katy, these guys are George, my steady, and Hampton Wade, our friend."

Both men expressed the usual niceties about meeting her. Hampton pulled out the fourth chair at their table for her. George tried to get the attention of their waitress so that she could get a drink.

Once she was setup, Gillian said, "Katy has a store on Antique Row."

Hampton said, "I believe I've walked past your store, Wakefield's, between 11th and 12th on Pine."

Katy looked at Hampton carefully. Her first impression had been that he was kind of cute. Now she was wondering whether he might be gay. "Yes, it's not mine, but that's where I work. What were you doing on Antique Row? Surely not shopping for antiques?"

Hampton said, "I do a lot of walking around Center City. It's amazing how many interesting things there are within a mile of City Hall. Antique Row is one of them."

Katy was wondering whether walking explained why he was so thin. He was certainly different from most young men she met in Philadelphia. She hoped he wasn't anorexic.

Hampton said, "In addition to antique furniture, you have a lot of interesting art work. I especially like the oils by Walter Emerson Baum in your front window."

George said, "And just who the heck is Walter Emerson Baum?"

"He was a 20th century Philadelphia area painter", said Katy. "Hampton, I'm amazed that you recognized Baum. Did you major in Art?"

Hampton said ruefully, "I've never attended a college."

This discombobulated Katy. She had never dated or had any interest in a guy who wasn't in college or already had his degree.

Gillian stuck up for Hampton. "Hampton works at the University of Pennsylvania Rittenhouse Physics Labs."

Surprised, Katy said "Wow, you must be quite smart to be a Physicist."

Hampton said, "Nothing so grand as that, I'm just a Lab Tech."

"And how did you learn about Baum?"

Hampton said, "I've audited a lot of courses at the University. One of them was on early Philadelphia area artists."

Katy was more than surprised. "I took that course myself! What a coincidence."

Hampton said, "So your major at the University was Art History?"

Katy said, "Yes, graduated three years ago." Initially disconcerted that Hampton had not attended college, she was feeling a little better about this striking looking young man that Gillian had suggested she meet. He certainly was smart enough to have gone to college. He was also less full of himself than most guys she had met in college or dated after graduation.

"Hampton, do you live in Center City?"

"Yes, over near Fitler Square."

"Great neighborhood."

Hampton said to her, "How about yourself?"

Katy thought he had a nice smile. "Chestnut Hill", she said.

"Another great neighborhood."

"Yes." said Katy, "I live in my nana's house. It's so big it's practically a mansion. She's also the chairperson of the board for the Art Museum."

Hampton asked, "So what street does she live on?"

"St. Andrew's Road. Don't tell me you've walked from Center City to Chestnut Hill and gone past it?"

Hampton laughed. "No, that would be a little too far even for a confirmed walker like me."

"Good," said Katy, "I was beginning to think you were super walker!" She smiled at him, and thought 'He may not be super walker but he is super cute.'

Gillian could tell that both Katy and Hampton were physically attracted to each other. That was good, since she was trying to get Hampton into a situation where both parties found each other mutually attractive. Gillian was pleased that her plan to get Hampton a new girlfriend seemed to be working well. She was glad she had invited Katy to have a drink with her and George and their "cute" friend Hampton. It had worked out much better than trying to arrange a blind date between Katy and Hampton.

After an hour, Katy said "You know, I'm enjoying this, but I promised my nana I'd be back early. I'm going to call Uber for a ride back to Wakefield's where I left my car."

Hampton said, "Don't do that. At this time of evening it will be quicker to get there by walking. I'll walk with you there."

Katy said, "How far is the walk from here."

"It's less than a mile," said Hampton.

Katy said "Oh my God, I'm not sure I can walk that far and live. If I collapse on the sidewalk, will you call an ambulance for me?"

Hampton smiled. "Don't worry, you won't collapse. We'll take it easy."

"Who could turn down such an offer from such a gallant gentleman?" Katy and Hampton stood and said goodbyes to George and Gillian.

George and Gillian watched them leave. George looked at Gillian and tried to sing, "Matchmaker, matchmaker, make me a match, find me a find, catch me a catch…"

"Stop", commanded Gillian. "You can't sing at all."

"You have to admit that it fits, you know."

Gillian looked smug. "Yes, it did turn out well, didn't it?"

"And you never mentioned any of it to me beforehand," said George. "You are a devious woman."

"I like Hampton, and, after Jennifer, I think he would be happier with a nice woman, like Katy. And I like Katy as well since she's definitely a considerate person. I thought they would make a good couple, and if you knew what I was doing, I thought you might not be as natural as you usually are."

"You're quite right. If I knew ahead of time that you had invited her I might have said something about it to Hampton", said George.

"I'll probably see her at the fitness center tomorrow and I'm looking forward to getting her reaction to him."

"She looked quite pleased that he was walking her to her store. Except for the walking part."

Chapter 67

At the exercise center the next day, Gillian was already busy spinning away when Katy arrived and took the machine next her.

"Hey girl-friend, how are you doing," Katy said cheerfully as she got started pedaling.

Gillian said, "You look and sound quite happy."

Katy said, "And I have you to thank for that. He's quite cute and quite the gentleman. My only problem is, he didn't try and kiss me good night. Are you sure he's not gay?"

Gillian said "Hampton's definitely not gay. Until they broke up, he kept his last girlfriend well satisfied."

"That's good to hear. I find him quite attractive."

Gillian said, "Yes, I felt the same way. Until I got more involved with George. There's something about Hampton that's quite appealing."

Katy said, "He told me all about his Physics lab which I pretended to understand. Then he listened to me when I rambled on about Wakefield's. I think he likes me. He took my hand as he walked me there."

Gillian said, "What's not to like? You're fabulously gorgeous with a sensational figure and naturally red hair. Guys love red hair. And sensational figures." She pedaled on for a while. "I think Hampton's a little shy when meeting women."

Katy said, "He's more than a little shy, he's a little like a schlub."

Gillian was puzzled, "What's a schlub?"

"I learned that from one of my Jewish girl friends. It's a Yiddish word for a socially awkward guy", said Katy.

"So, you don't like him?"

Katy said, "No, no, no, I like him! He's great! He's cute, just like you said. Schlubs are nice, friendly creatures who like to do things for you, like rotate your tires, or paint your kitchen, or help you move. As far as I'm concerned, I'd rather have a schlub than a macho man."

"Me too."

Katy frowned as she pedaled on. "The only thing that bothers me about him is that he hasn't gone to college."

"He has gone to college. He works at one. In the Physics Department, no less."

Katy said, "Yeah, but he's only a lab tech. How could I introduce him to my friends?"

Gillian shook her head. "How did we get to the point where a college degree is like an imprimatur needed for a relationship? Hampton is smart even though he would never say that himself. Both George and I have degrees and we always enjoy talking to him. He often notices things that we don't and talks intelligently about them. If your friends would look down on Hampton because he doesn't have a degree, maybe you need new friends."

Katy nodded as she pedaled on. "You may be right. Especially the male friends. Most of them work in insurance and investment companies and can't talk about anything else. They are more than a little boring. It's kind of nice that Hampton likes art."

"There you go", said Gillian as the bell on her stationary bike announced that she had completed the exercise she had set it for. "Let's go see what concoction they're selling at the juice bar today."

"Sounds good to me", said Katy. "I've had enough pedaling."

At the juice bar, both Katy and Gillian got the latest juice mixture they were offering, a mango-pomegranate concoction.

"Not bad," said Katy. "Sweet things are my downfall."

Gillian said "Four ounces of fruit juice is not going to hurt you. With or without it, you'll still look great."

"Wow," said Katy, "You know just what to say to boost my confidence. You're like my wiser, prettier, more sophisticated older sister."

"I'm not that old," said Gillian. "I'm just twenty-eight."

"A perfect age for my older, more experienced, gorgeous sister." They both took sips of their juice. "I'm attracted to Hampton. Do you think he likes me?"

Gillian looked at her new baby sister. "I would bet on it. It looked obvious to me that he was impressed with you. You can trust him to say what he thinks. I don't think Hampton lies about anything. "

Katy thought about it and said, "I was a little surprised that he'd never gone to college. He seems quite smart to me. I'm wondering if it's a mistake to get involved with a guy who hasn't graduated or even attended a college. "

Gillian said, "Compared to some of the college guys I've dated, Hampton is a hands down winner. I think I'd rather have honesty rather than a guy with a sheepskin."

"I'm a little worried about what my nana might think of him."

"Your nana?'

"Yes, Regina Wakefield. She's the actual owner of the store on Pine street. And I'm living with her in her house in

Chestnut hill. She's the Chairwoman of the Board for the Art Museum."

Gillian thought about it. "Well, if she's smart enough for all that, she should be smart enough to see the pluses for Hampton. And also smart enough to respect you for any choice you might make."

Somewhat mollified, Katy said, "So, do you think Hampton will call me for a date?"

"If he doesn't, he's a lot stupider than I think he is. You do like him, don't you?"

"Sure, I haven't been on a date in six months. Hampton is looking extremely good to me right now. I'm betting he doesn't have love handles!"

Gillian said, "His last girlfriend said he was ferociously firm and hard."

Katy said, "God, he sounds delicious!"

Gillian snorted. "Katy, you're a naughty girl! Are you already thinking about getting physical with him?"

"It has crossed my mind since he saw me to the store last night. Do you think I ought to call him for a date?"

Gillian laughed out loud. "Well, I think that might be moving a little too fast. Why don't you give him a chance to show his interest in you?"

"I trust you, sis, I'm gonna wait." She raised her juice glass in a toast.

Gillian clinked glasses and said, "Smart choice, baby sister!"

Chapter 68

In NYC, Aban finally got results from his phone scan requests. The words diamond, tracker, and Youkoumian had all appeared in short phone calls made from Philadelphia to phone numbers which correlated with numbers in Syria. It seemed likely to Aban that these calls originated from al-Sidaan's former thugs. To him, it seemed that there was a good chance that the men from the green car were back in Philadelphia and might well be a danger to Hampton Wade and/or Jennifer Lopez. No doubt trying to regain control of their group's diamonds would be a major priority for everyone in that group. Since Hampton and Jennifer were the last persons known to the group to have access to the jewels, they might well be in new danger from them.

DHS techies had already analyzed both the GPS display device and the wireless trackers in the opaque bags used to transport jewels. DHS now had the means to detect and locate anyone using either a display device or the tracker bags themselves. Aban decided to take that equipment and four of his best agents to Philadelphia and try to both prevent any harm coming to Hampton and Jennifer, and to apprehend the thugs who had wounded the Independence Mall ranger so that they could be prosecuted. He also decided that he would be the operations leader for the attempt. It might be the last chance he would have to get out in the field and do what he considered to be real work.

Chapter 69

That evening, Hampton was thinking about Katy and the evening before. She was certainly not as glamorous as Jennifer. If she had been, he would have been just as much out of his league with Katy as he had been with Jennifer. Katy was quite attractive to him. He was particularly fascinated by her red hair. She also seemed to be much more accepting to him and less imperious. She was apparently also more receptive to small gestures, since she took his hand when he offered it. He was certain Katy would not dig her nails into his palm, even if she got mad at him. Overall, he felt far more comfortable with Katy than he had ever felt with Jennifer.

He wondered if she was smarter than he was. Probably. She had graduated from the University of Pennsylvania. That might be another problem. Why would a college graduate be interested in a mere Lab Tech. The last time he was in that situation it had not turned out well.

Still, he thought, George and Gillian were both graduates and they seemed to enjoy his company. Why shouldn't Katy? Perhaps he was worrying too much about the situation. As George put it, what's the worst that could happen? Since Gillian clearly liked her as a friend, he thought it unlikely that Katy would turn him down in a hurtful manner. Even if she did, he thought he could live with that since she didn't appear to be as controlling as Jennifer. All in all, he thought she would be much more suitable for him. The only way to get more information would be to ask her for a date. He was wondering if calling her tomorrow would make him seem too anxious, when his cell beeped.

It was Aban Hassad.

Hampton was completely flummoxed when he learned who it was. He had never expected to encounter Aban again. And the things Aban had to tell him perplexed him even more.

Since Hampton no longer had any diamonds from Youkoumians, he had assumed no one from the Jihadist group would be interested in him. Aban was now informing him that the tracking GPS was now being used actively in the Fitler Square area and the presumption was that the thugs who had been chasing Jennifer and himself were still looking for him and the diamonds.

Aban wanted to speak to him directly about the situation and said he was just outside Hampton's building. The door buzzer buzzed and Hampton toggled it to allow Aban in.

Once Aban entered and sat down, Hampton asked for more details.

Aban explained to him that substantial fractions of digital communications in the U. S. are being recorded by the NSA. Once stored, the data can be analyzed almost at leisure to look for key words, names, and so on that would be indicative of suspicious activities. He, Aban, had put in a request for analysis of messages that included the words diamonds *and/or* tracker *and/or* Youkoumian. A few days earlier, the data analysis had begun to spit out records that originated in the Philadelphia area and were directed to destinations in Syria. It had become obvious that the group that had been working the diamond store was still active and probably still quite interested in recovering their diamonds.

Hampton, asked "Do the appropriate agencies have a plan to deal with the remnants of the group?"

Aban did have a plan. Unfortunately, it required Hampton to act as a decoy duck to entice the thugs to approach and try to extract the diamonds from him.

Hampton was understandably apprehensive about being a target for thugs who had demonstrated their willingness to use guns any time they felt like it.

Aban said, "That's the point. To be certain of putting them away in a secure prison, we need to apprehend them with the Glocks, especially the ones used in the Liberty Bell Pavilion. Then ballistic tests will prove convincingly that these guys are guilty of attempted murder. The only way to get them *and* the Glocks is if they have them in hand while trying to get their diamonds back from you."

Hampton asked, "How can you be certain that they still have the same Glocks?"

Aban said, "I can't be absolutely certain but I feel that the odds are high that these guys would not give up such tools unless they had to. Jihadists love guns."

Hampton thought about it. "How do you see it happening?"

"We have equipment which shows that the GPS location device is being used around Fitler Square. We still have the original diamond bag with the tracker broadcaster in the seam. If you walk around the area with the transport bag, they should soon pick you up and try to get it from you."

Hampton said, "It sounds pretty dangerous to me. What would prevent them from just shooting me and getting the bag from my dead body."

Aban said "You'll be wearing a ballistic vest. It's possible you might get shot, it's not likely. It's far more probable that they will be interested in examining the bag and making sure that all of the diamonds are in it. If they kill you and all the diamonds are not in the bag, they're out of luck. Also, I and four of my agents will be right in the area and will arrest them as soon as they start to approach you."

Hampotn said, "And why can't one of your agents just carry the bag around."

"Because these thugs chased you through Center City and know what you look like. Seeing one of my agents carrying the bag might throw them off."

Hampton realized that he had little choice. If he didn't go along with Aban's plan, he would always be under threat of some intervention from the thugs which had chased him.

Hampton said, "OK, it looks like that's the only thing to do in this matter. When do we try this?"

Aban said "The sooner the better. I think the best thing is to start tomorrow morning. Thanks Hampton, I know it's not easy, but I think this is the right thing to do to get rid of this problem."

Chapter 70

Despite Gillian's general contentment with living with George, there were some things he did which she let him know didn't work. George was quite happy to have her in the apartment wearing his underwear. As might be expected, he was also quite happy when she didn't wear any clothes at all. However, she let him know, when he tried not wearing anything in their apartment, that it was not acceptable.

The first time he did it, she told him "George, naked is not a good look for a guy. It just doesn't work."

He was a little hurt at this, since he was quite happy if she didn't wear any clothes at all.

"That's not fair. I don't object when you're naked."

"That's different. Women look great naked. Men, not so much."

"I don't understand. I love it when you don't wear clothes."

"George, believe me, it just doesn't work for men."

"So, you don't like my body?", he asked.

"I love your body, you have great upper body development, no love handles and I love it when we're under the sheets. But it just doesn't work if I have to look at it walking around the place." She couldn't explain any more explicitly than that, but George understood that something bothered her when he did it, and so he reluctantly went along with her opinion, without understanding. He always managed to at least put on his boxers and t shirts when they were together alone, regardless of whether she had clothes on or not. It was a small price to pay.

Chapter 71

Gloria set a date for her retirement from ATF. Gillian was the person most distressed at this, since Gloria had been her group supervisor since she had transferred to the Philadelphia Field Office. In view of the increasing evidence Gillian was finding out about ATF management, Gloria was an unusually good supervisor. The evidence seemed to be tending in the direction that working in ATF was not a good deal for her, Gillian. Perhaps she should have tried to get in the FBI earlier, as some special agents had previously suggested. She talked to George about it.

He was quite willing to help her as much as he could, but he himself had no influence in hiring choices. He also didn't think the management in the bureau was necessarily much better than that in ATF. As he put it, "ATF just seems to be caught more often with their pants down. Also, you would have to go through the Quantico Academy... a 20 week program."

Gillian made a face. "That doesn't sound like a stroll in the park either. I have been toying with the idea of going private. But Gloria made it sound like most of what private investigators do is getting evidence on cheating husbands for wives who want divorces."

George said, "I suspect Gloria is probably right. If I understand you correctly, you would be satisfied if you could do investigation on interesting stuff like what we did on the 71st VA."

Gillian said, "Yes, that's exactly what I would like."

George said, "Gillian, if you want to try private, I can support us on my FBI salary while you go for it."

"You would do that for me? We're not even married."

"But we are partners. And anyway, my long-range plan is to convince you that your only choice is to make an honest man of me."

Gillian smiled at that.

George said, "See, you're already smiling. My plan is working perfectly. We should think about setting a date."

Gillian shook her head and said, "You are definitely not a typical Y. Most guys would not even want to think about a wedding, much less talk about setting a date."

George said "Most Ys don't have the opportunity to live with you. I do, and I don't want to lose it."

Gillian gave him a hug and said "You have no need to worry. I'm not going anywhere."

"God, I love it when you hug me."

Gillian said, "OK, enough hanky-panky. Let's talk about our investigation agency."

"I don't think there ever can be too much hanky-panky," said George. "What are you going to call your agency?"

"It's our agency, and the only possible name is G and G Investigations."

George's eyes lit up. "I love it! Whose G comes first?"

Gillian said. "We can tell people whatever we want, or let them think whatever they want."

"I definitely think Gillian should come first!"

"Sometimes you are so sweet that it's close to causing nausea."

George said, "I can't help it. That's the effect you have on me."

Gillian said, "I make you nauseous?"

"Of course not! You just turn me into a jell-o cube. All sweet and quivering and shaking."

The next evening Gillian was wearing some of the afore mentioned underwear when she wanted to discuss their agency with George. It took some sternness in Gillian's approach to get his attention directed to their agency rather than to what she was wearing.

"George, stop it, I want to talk about what we need to do to set up our agency."

"But fooling around would be so much more fun!" he complained.

"We're not going to do that now! Pay attention! We'll need to incorporate our agency. You can be president and I'll be vice president. I've asked Gloria and she's agreed to serve on our board and be an officer."

George thought about that. "That's great of her. She has lots of contacts among Philadelphia movers and shakers and that might mean interesting business for the agency."

Gillian agreed. "Yes, I'm sure she could be a great help. Also, I think we can start off using our apartment here as an office for the agency."

George shook his head, no. "We need a real office with a secretary and all the trimmings."

"But that would cost a lot of money."

George said, "You need a professional office in order to be taken seriously as a competent investigations agency."

"But it will be so expensive."

"I have $100,000 in a savings account that we can use to pay for it until it takes off."

"My God, you'd blow that all for me?"

"Of course, I'd do anything for you, you should know that by now."

She said, "I do know that, and I do appreciate you."

"Great, let's go to the bedroom and fool around!"

"Not until we settle a few more details." She said.

George said "Damn, your attention to doing things makes me feel secure about our agency but frustrated about our personal lives."

"Contain yourself, we need to discuss a few more details, before we're finished."

"What details? All we need is an office somewhere around here, some furniture, and a secretary. With enough money, we can get that done in a day."

Gillian thought about it and decided he was right. She gave in and said. "OK, let's go to the bedroom."

Chapter 72

Aban assembled his team of four agents in Hampton's apartment. They fitted Hampton out with a ballistic vest which made him appear closer to normal sized instead of painfully thin. Additionally, he was given the original bag he had carried when escaping the thugs. Aban had consulted with Philadelphia detectives in both the sixth district which covered Jewelers' Row and the ninth district which covered Fitler Square. They knew he was actively working in their areas and were prepared to support him.

Two of the DHS agents were female and pushed small baby carriages. Instead of containing babies, the carriages held Winchester Super X4 autoloading shotguns. Aban did not intend to fool around in gun battles with Jihadists who probably also had ballistic vests. A 12 gauge shell at 10 feet was quite likely to knock down and stun a bad guy even if he was wearing a vest. And the results of a 12 gauge in the face were not pretty.

Hampton himself was not armed which was in accord with both his and Aban's wishes. Hampton just wanted to get through the process with no one getting hurt. The group proceeded to circulate at walking pace around the Fitler Square area. They started around 10 AM. It took several hours, but eventually Aban was notified via ear mike that his agent with the new equipment had detected that one of the GPS tracking display devices was in the area.

Sure enough, shortly after that Aban could see that two men who looked much like thugs were approaching Hampton from behind. He notified his team. As the thugs got within 15 feet of Hampton, they drew out their Glocks. The closest female agent ordered them to stop and drop them. She announced that she had a repeating 12 gauge and advised them that even if they had vests, they would not like being shot with a 12 gauge shell containing buck and a one ounce slug. The other agents converged on the pair, made them kneel with their hands behind their heads, and cuffed them with hands behind backs. Aban consulted with the ninth district detectives and they had two RMP units at their location within five minutes. The thugs were each bundled into an RMP and sent off into custody. Aban thought, 'If only the paper work could be that easy.' Aban called the serial numbers of the Glocks taken from the thugs into DHS records. As expected, the Glocks were the same as those recorded as having been bought by Hassad al-Sidaan in his Youkoumian role. They almost certainly could use ballistics to link their current arrestees to the shooting of the Park Ranger in the Liberty Bell Pavilion. Aban was quite satisfied that he had successfully cleared up the last loose string from his Jewelers' Row operation.

Hampton was quite satisfied as well. He was glad no one had gotten hurt, and that a threat he had not been aware of had been removed.

Chapter 73

The next day, Gillian talked to Gloria in her boss's office. She explained to Gloria about how George was willing to support her in starting her own investigation agency. To the extent of using $100,000 of his savings.

"Damn!", said Gloria. "I always thought he was a pretty good catch, but I would never have predicted that. This guy is beyond sincere, he's way over into seriously in love with you. What did you tell him?"

"I thanked him and told him I wanted to talk to you again."

"What did he say to that?"

"He thinks you're the best manager he's ever met, especially since I told him you liked him, and thought he was sincere. I think he wants to marry me."

"It's good that he's smart enough to see things as they are. And he's quite smart to want to marry you. So, what are you going to do?"

"I told him I wanted to talk with you again before making a decision."

Gloria said. "My advice is to marry him as soon as possible. Why wouldn't you?"

"Because I'm still trying to decide what to do career wise and marriage is a complication I don't think I can handle at the same time as trying to find a new position."

"You young people worry about things too much. I mean you're living with him now in his apartment, that's got to require much more work than living with him in marriage. Is he OK in bed?"

Gillian blushed. Gloria had no problems at all in saying exactly what she thought. With reddening cheeks, Gillian said, "No problems there. He's great in the sack."

Gloria said to her, "You're so cute when you blush. I love it. Well if bed is great, then what is bothering you?"

Gillian considered her answer. "I think I worry a lot about being supported by a guy, even one as nice as George. My father has always urged me to be independent and only depend on myself."

"Ah ha," said Gloria, "another dutiful daughter with father issues."

Somewhat alarmed by Gloria's statement, Gillian asked, "What does that mean?"

"Just that you might be trying so hard to do what your father suggests that you may be overlooking what's available under your nose."

"I don't understand." Gillian was confused.

"Look, what do your girl friends think about George? They definitely seem to think he's a great guy. I've heard them talking about you and him. In my day, girls would be fighting each other to get someone like George. All I'm suggesting is, consider him for what he is and not just what your father has always instilled in you. After all, you were dependent on your father until you graduated college and that turned out OK, didn't it?"

Gillian sighed and said, "Yes, you're right. So, you suggest I go along with George's offer and let him support me while I try to get my own agency started?"

Gloria said, "You'll never get a better chance to start out on your own with that level of support."

Gillian had to agree with that. She was still a little apprehensive about being dependent on George, but she was rather taken with his expression that they already were partners. She had to agree that the affair with the 71st VA. had in fact cemented them as more than co-workers. Besides, she probably never would get another guy whose underwear was washed as satiny as George's boxers and t shirts.

Chapter 74

In retrospect, Hampton was happy about Aban's last activity involving the diamonds. Not only had it eliminated a threat to him, it had diverted his attention from calling Katy too soon and looking too anxious. But now enough time had passed so that he could contact her and ask her out without embarrassment. He decided that seeing her in person would be even better than talking on the phone, so, the day after trapping the thugs, he skipped lunch and walked from the Rittenhouse Labs to Antique Row.

Wakefield's was a handsome looking antique shop on Pine Street. Hampton paused for a minute to admire the Baum paintings in the left window and then went in. He saw Katy immediately. She looked terrific in a Hunter Green dress which fit her nicely and complimented her red hair. When her current customer turned to leave her store, she noticed Hampton and couldn't help herself from breaking into a big smile.

"Hi Hampton, it's nice to see you here."

Hampton said, "I feel it's nice to see you again as well."

"Did you come to see the Baums again?"

"No, I came to see you."

Katy blinked. He certainly had no problem saying what he was thinking.

Hampton said, "I wanted to see if you would like to do something with me this week, like have dinner. I thought asking you in person would be better than a phone call."

Katy said to him. "You're right, it is."

Hampton said, "Would Friday work for you?"

"Perfectly. What restaurant did you have in mind.?"

Hampton didn't have enough money to take her to an upscale restaurant and he wasn't comfortable with asking her to go Dutch. "If you wouldn't mind coming to my apartment, I'd be glad to cook dinner for you."

Katy said, "Oh my God, you cook, too? Is there no end to your talents?"

"I'm not much of a chef. It's only a Blue Apron meal, and they have quite detailed instructions on how to put it together. Perfect for techie oriented guys."

"So, what time should I show up?"

Hampton asked, "Would seven work for you?"

"Any time will work for me," said Katy. "What kind of wine should I bring?"

"The Blue Apron meal I have features trout, so a white wine would be good."

"Is Chardonnay OK?"

Hampton said, "My favorite."

Katy said, "Mine too!" Katy didn't have a favorite wine, but she thought the more things she had in common with Hampton, the better things would work out. "OK, I'll see you at seven on Friday."

Katy was charmed that he had come to see her in person to ask for a date. Particularly since it was almost a certainty that he had walked from the Rittenhouse Labs to Antique Row. That had to be more than a mile. She couldn't think of any guy she knew who would make that much effort for her. Or for any woman for that matter. Hampton was looking better and better to her every time she saw him.

Chapter 75

Katy and Gillian saw each other at the exercise center on Friday morning. Katy was pleased to tell her "big sister" that Hampton had walked over to her store on Antique Row and asked her for a date for dinner. At his apartment.

"Well", said Gillian, "that should be interesting. I've known him for several months and never seen where he lives. I also didn't know that he cooked."

Katy said, "Well, he was pretty honest about that. Apparently, he'll be preparing a Blue Apron meal. He says they have pretty specific instructions on how to do that. He was quite honest about that. At least he didn't try to puff himself up into a real cook."

Gillian said, "Preparing a Blue Apron meal sounds good to me. At least you don't have to prepare something for him!"

Katy said, "That is definitely a plus. I sometimes resent having to cook for guys I've invited over. I'm pretty interested in seeing what his apartment is like. Everyone I know says you can learn a lot about a guy from seeing how he lives."

"Amen, sister!" said Gillian. "Most of the guys I dated before George just had huge recliners in front of a gargantuan flat screen TV with several game station devices close at hand. The rest of their apartment was a mess. Not a good sign. There's something immature about guys that spend a lot of time playing games when they could be paying attention to you. Thank God, the only game George is interested in now is chasing me around the apartment."

Katy laughed. "That sounds like fun. At least he's paying attention to you."

Gillian said. "That's definitely a plus. And I can always rein him in when necessary."

Katy said, "I can't wait to see what Hampton's place is like. And what he has in mind for activities besides dinner."

"My guess is that it will be neat and clean. But I'd be surprised if he chased you around the place. At least on your first date."

Katy said "You know, I wouldn't mind if he made a pass at me. He's cute and he's got that ultra-thin hard body and I haven't had any action for six months."

Gillian said "Contain yourself, baby sister. You don't want him to think you're a slut."

"I know, I know."

Chapter 76

The next evening, Katy took an Uber car and arrived at Hampton's apartment building 10 minutes before 7. She knew it would not be a good idea to appear so early, so she forced herself to walk around the block. Slowly. As she walked she was thinking about what she would like to do in his apartment. When she got back to the building door, she was practically fermenting. At 7:01 exactly, she rang his bell, and he came down and welcomed her in.

She handed him the bottle of Chardonnay and he said, "That's a great one." Katy thought it should be, considering she spent an hour on the internet sifting through wine blogs to find it. They climbed the stairs and he opened his apartment door for her.

She thought to herself, 'Wow, the living room is so clean. I hope Gillian is right and he's not gay.'

He showed her his kitchen which was clean and his bathroom, clean also. Finally, he showed her his bedroom. It was neater than her room at her nana's house. And it had a queen-sized bed, neatly made.

This was it! Her heart was beating furiously as they stood near the foot. She reached up, put her hand behind his neck, and pulled his head down for a kiss. It was quite a long one. When she came up for air, he was breathing hard as well.

Eventually, Hampton remembered the ostensible purpose of the evening. He said, "Maybe I should go to the kitchen and warm up the dinner? You must be hungry."

Katy was disappointed. She was attracted to this bony, hunky guy and was so close to the edge that she was ready to start taking off his clothes. But reason finally prevailed with her and she recognized that rushing into sex would not be a good start to a relationship.

Instead, she said, "Perhaps we should try that Chardonnay."

Hampton gratefully said, "Great idea!", and led the way back to the living room. Katy followed him.

When they got to the couch, Hampton embraced her. It was quite the most expressive hug she had ever had. Somehow, it managed to show her that he was physically attracted to her, wanted to have sex with her right now, but didn't think this was the right moment, and that they would be better off waiting. She was a little astonished at all he managed to convey. Katy's knees wobbled a bit and she had to sit down on the couch.

Hampton said, "Maybe I should just take a minute and get us glasses of that terrific Chardonnay."

When he returned with the bottle and two wine glasses, he noticed that she was breathing more steadily. Clearly, she still wanted him to look at her and appreciate how attractive she was. And he was prepared to do that for as long as she wanted him to.

Hampton opened the bottle deftly, using a server's corkscrew. He used the built in little blade to sever and remove the foil top, then rotated the cork screw into the "cork" top.

Almost no wineries used actual cork any more to close their bottles. Most used a synthetic rubbery substitute to save costs. Using the double notched lifter, he got the "cork" started, then removed it completely by using the second notch.

Katy was interested in what he was doing. "You're quite good with that. Is it a rabbit or something like that?"

Hampton laughed. "No, this is an ordinary server's cork screw ... what waiters and waitresses use to open bottles in restaurants. You can trust that what professionals use is generally the best. And often the least expensive." He poured two generous glasses for them

He tasted his own glass. "Wow', he exclaimed, "That's the best chardonnay I've ever tasted."

Katy thought, 'It should be, it cost a small fortune.' But she contented herself with saying "I'm so pleased that you like it." She thought the small fortune was worth it if it made him happy. And she did want to keep him happy, so that he could keep her happy. As he was doing.

Katy said, "I'm glad I came to your apartment. I like it a lot."

Hampton said, "I'm glad you like it. And as you can tell, I also am quite pleased that you came. I'm already looking forward to seeing you in the future."

That sounded good to Katy. Apparently, Hampton was a guy who could consider and talk about relationships.

As they sipped Chardonnay, Hampton said, "I know Gillian has told you about the joint encounter we all had with the jihadists based in Jewelers' Row."

"Yes, exciting and scary, especially for you."

Hampton said, "It looks like it's finally completely over." He described the episode he had participated in with Aban Hassad to apprehend the remaining thugs of the gang.

Katy was quite concerned about it. "My God, that all sounds incredibly dangerous! I can't believe you let yourself be used that way!"

Hampton was thoughtful. "The logic of it was pretty clear. Two thugs were around the area looking for me to supply something I didn't have. It seemed to me that working with the professionals from DHS was dangerous, but less so than not doing anything until the thugs found me. I was sure they would kill me because I didn't have what they wanted."

Katy looked at him with wonder and then gave him a hug. "You are too brave for your own good and so smart and logical."

Hampton hugged her back and said, "I think you're great also, baby."

Katy murmured, "When you call me baby, I feel Tingly."

Katy heard a timer go off in the kitchen. "Ah ha", Hampton said. "It's ready. The only place I have to eat is the kitchen table." He rose and offered her his arm. They took their glasses and went in to dinner.

Chapter 77

The next morning, Katy met Gillian at the door to the spinning machines.

"Good morning, big sister!"

"Good morning to you, baby sister! You look pretty happy. How did your dinner with Hampton go?" Both women entered the room and chose side by side machines.

Katy said "Just fine. I almost got carried away and wanted to rip his clothes off."

Gillian said, "Oh my God, did you have sex on your first date?"

Katy said ruefully, "No, fortunately Hampton showed a little more self-control than I did and we had Chardonnay instead."

"Tell me more!", said Gillian, as they both started spinning.

"His apartment is incredibly neat and clean. When I first saw it, I thought he was gay," said Katy.

Gillian said, "And did he prove he's not?"

"Practically," said Katy. "He showed me his bed room. He has a queen bed, which was neatly made. And as we were looking at it, I pulled his head down for a kiss. We were both breathing hard when we came up for air."

Gillian said, "Oh my God, did he try to get you into the bed?"

Katy said, "No, I could tell he wanted to, but he just suggested we go to the living room and have a glass of the Chardonnay I had brought."

"Incredible", said Gillian.

"Yes", said Katy "and I was disappointed until he gave me a hug before we ate. That convinced me he was completely attracted to me. And not gay."

"Oh ho", said Gillian. She spun in silence for a while thinking about it. "And then what happened?"

"Then we ate the dinner he had prepared and talked. Blue Apron has pretty tasty meals. Afterward, I helped him clean up and get the dishes in the washer. Then we went back to the living room and fooled around a little. It was a great evening."

Gillian said, "I would think so. A guy with a clean and neat apartment who cooks and cleans up and isn't gay. Sounds like any woman's trifecta."

Katy said, "I'm no longer bothered that he didn't go to college. He's cute and funny and knows almost as much about Art as I do. He reads a lot and is smart. I wouldn't be embarrassed to introduce him to anyone."

"Sounds great to me, baby sister!"

"And I owe it all to you, big sister!"

Chapter 78

George was a little optimistic about the time necessary for G and G Investigations to find a place. They did find reasonably priced and attractive office space in one day. Their new office was in an old town house on a tree lined street in Society Hill. The owner had put it to reuse as small professional office spaces. The house featured large windows, eight foot ceilings with substantial crown molding, and oak hardwood floors. Their office was one of two on the second floor with shared privileges to a bathroom. It had three substantial rooms, and included zonal control of central heating and air conditioning. One of the rooms had built in shelving and craftsman cabinets, a window that overlooked a small garden in the rear, and a front window that looked out over the tree lined street. Both George and Gillian loved the location and decided that they would share the room with front and back windows as a joint office. The first room entered from the second-floor hall could be a waiting room with space for their secretary, comfortable chairs, and file storage. They hoped that eventually they could use the third room when they reached the point of needing associates. If ever they were that successful.

Finding furniture for their office took a lot longer than George anticipated. His suggestion was to get stuff from IKEA.

Gillian vetoed that immediately. She felt they needed furniture that fit well with their 19th century house. George never knew how she did it, but she found desks, chairs, end and coffee tables, a couch, pictures, and lighting that fit the house without having to pay antique prices.

The selection of the secretary also fell to Gillian. Normally George would have wanted an attractive young woman for the position. Someone who could impress any male customers. But he passed on that since he already had an extremely attractive and impressive young woman for a partner. Gillian finally settled on an older woman, Ruth Williams, with a professional air who had been a former competent office manager for a center city law firm that went under.

George's contribution to the furnishings of the office was reduced to selecting and installing a wireless intercom to allow Ruth to contact them in their office room.

G and G quickly got incorporated as a partnership. With their government credentials, they quickly became licensed by the City of Philadelphia as a private investigation agency. They were set.

Gillian arranged for opening announcements in various legal journals in Philadelphia. George found an appropriate source to construct a web site for them. Then came the hardest part for Gillian: she had to resign from ATF.

Both Gloria and Gillian cried together on Gillian's last day there. Each, of course, promised that they would stay in touch, but both knew that the effort to keep such resolves does not always happen.

Gillian held an open house at their agency on their opening day. She invited every friend she could think of and every local professional she had ever had contact with in

Philadelphia, Pennsylvania, and New Jersey Law enforcement. Gloria supplied an introductory letter to everyone she knew with businesses in the Philadelphia area. Their new office manager, Ruth, also helped with letters to everyone she knew in center city law offices. They were ready.

George was still working at the FBI to support them. Gillian was anxious when she opened their office by herself for business for the first time. She was more than a little afraid that she had done the wrong thing by quitting ATF. She was terrified that G and G investigations would be a failure. She felt an immediate boost when she got a congratulatory telegram from her father in Cincinnati.

This was reinforced by a telegram from George with the same sentiments, which she thought something of a waste of money since he had said much the same things to her at breakfast a few hours ago. Still, it made her feel better.

It was also nice to get a telegram from Hampton. He promised to be by later today when he could get away from the labs. Gillian thought that was a nice comment on their friendship, especially since she knew Hampton did not have much in the way of spare money. Gillian thought 'Thank God, at least someone will show up.'

Gillian was hanging about in the waiting room, arranging and rearranging their brochures which extolled the credentials of the agency principals and indicated the types of problem G and G Investigations could help with. Notably, on Gloria's advice, it did not mention obtaining evidence for divorce cases. Gillian realized that if no suitable work showed up, they might have to accept such assignments.

Ruth said, "Girl, you need to stop fussing around out here. It makes you look anxious."

Gillian said ruefully, "I *am* anxious."

Ruth said, "That's understandable, but you don't want to show that to potential customers. You need to go into your office and relax. When someone shows up, I'll make sure they get coffee and rolls if they want. Then I'll notify you on the intercom and you can come out and welcome them. Go ahead, shoo, shoo."

Gillian shooed, but once she got into her office, she was too wound up to sit. Instead she marched around the desks and hoped someone would arrive. Her hope was finally answered and she heard Ruth notify her on the intercom. "Ms. Andrews, you have a visitor."

Gillian relaxed a little at that announcement. She fluffed her hair, took a deep breath, put on her best smile, and went out to the waiting area to find Gloria looking around. She immediately hugged her former boss and said, "Thank you so much for coming!"

Gloria hugged her back and said, "I told you we'd be in touch! I love your office, it's a great location, and having it in a former row house is so cool. I wish I worked here."

Gillian showed Gloria their extra room. "If we get enough business and need additional associates, we would have them in here. After you retire, both George and I would love you to work here for whatever hours you want."

Gloria admired the third room. "This is a great room! I love the big windows overlooking the back garden, and the crown molding." She looked at Gillian with an ironic smile. "So, do you think you could handle me as an employee?"

Gillian said "Sure, I would just do the same things my previous boss used to do with me." Gloria laughed at that.

Gillian's former ATF female agent friends arrived and were escorted into the third room by Ruth. All exclaimed over the new office and their former colleague who was now running her own business. All got coffee and were shown the main office and admired the room and the desks and chairs for Gillian and George. All promised to stay in touch, and said it wouldn't be hard, since the ATF offices were within walking distance of both George and Gillian's apartment and the new office.

As everyone left, Gillian was feeling much better after her friends' and Gloria's expressions of support. As the day progressed, a few former legal acquaintances of Ruth also dropped by to see her and see what G and G Investigations was all about. Most picked up and took away G and G brochures.

At the end of the day, George arrived with a cooler full of mojitos and he poured them into martini glasses for Gillian, Ruth, and himself to celebrate their first day in business. As they were getting ready to toast, Hampton and Katy Wakefield showed up and were introduced to Ruth. And they also got mojitos.

George and Ruth conducted Hampton and Katy on the short tour around the waiting room, the main office room and the third room. Hampton and Katy were suitably impressed with everything. As they were getting the tour, Gillian realized that she felt much better about gambling to startup G and G. She thought there was at least a probability that they could make it successful and that she had a chance to do what she liked best.

When younger, Gillian had read and enjoyed detective novels. She wasn't attracted to helping those who were preyed upon or by some abstract devotion to justice for victims. Rather, trying to figure out a situation, find the answer, and get some attention and reward for it appealed to her. As she read, she noticed that the most common thread in most of these mysteries involved a detective, almost always male, interacting with various people, asking questions, finding information both true and false, comparing information from different people and gradually focusing down to who was telling the truth or at least some reasonable approximation of it. Even mysteries set in different time periods followed the same pattern. Gillian had always wanted to do that as a career.

As the day came to an end, Gloria dropped by G and G again to say to George and Gillian, "I want to invite you two to my retirement party this Sunday afternoon." Spotting Katy, she said "Your nana told me you'd likely be here. I understand from her that you and Hampton are now an item. You two have to come as well. We'll have bounce tents for my grand-children and any children of my friends. Plenty of food and lots of booze. Everything necessary for a roaring good time for all."

Katy said, "Gloria, you're embarrassing me. Did nana call Hampton and me an item?"

Gloria said "Your nana used those exact words. She said the two of you had a hard time keeping your hands to yourself when you invited Hampton to her house to meet her."

Katy shook her head resignedly, "Elders have no sense of decorum. They just blurt out everything that comes into their heads whether it's true or not."

Hampton said, "Katy, I think your nana sees and describes things pretty accurately. I did have a hard time restraining my-self from putting my arms around you when she was out of the room."

Katy said, "Hampton! Stop it, you're too honest! You're not helping!"

Chapter 79

Although Hampton occasionally was too naively honest in saying things, Katy decided she much preferred his honesty, no matter how embarrassing it was from time to time.

Tonight, they were at his apartment again relaxing after he had prepared another Blue Apron meal for them. He was in the kitchen cleaning up and Katy was in the living room relaxing with a glass of the Chardonnay she had brought. She thought she could get used to this. It would be great to have a guy who regularly cooked for her. And if they lived together and he kept the place as clean as his apartment, she would be in the cat bird seat.

The only problem remaining was, he still hadn't managed to get her into a bed.

Finishing in the kitchen, Hampton brought in a glass of Chardonnay for himself, and brought in the bottle to top off her glass. As he sat next to her on his couch, she asked him "Hampton, where are we going with this?"

Hampton was a little disconcerted by this directness. He said, "You mean with our relationship."

"Yes."

Hampton decided to show her how he felt about their relationship.

Hampton started to cuddle in earnest. Presently Katy began to breathe harder and Hampton thought he was on the right track.

Hampton said, "You know, Gillian and George are going steady."

Katy took a deep breath and said, "What's that?"

"It's an old term from the 1950s. My gamps told me about it. Back then, when a guy and a girl in high school were sufficiently serious about their relationship, they sort of announced they were exclusive with each other by telling their friends they were going steady. It was sort of being engaged to be engaged."

Katy said "You're the only one I want to be with, so I'd definitely love to be going steady with you.

Hampton said, "You are also the only one I want to be with, so going steady sounds good to me, too, baby."

Katy said "God, when you call me baby I get tingly. So, let's cuddle some more."

Hampton thought that a great idea.

Chapter 80

The next Sunday afternoon, George and Gillian took their car to the Fitler Square area and picked up Hampton at his apartment. George got on Kelly Drive and made his way into Chestnut Hill to Gloria's house on Seminole Street for her retirement party. George parked and the three friends walked down the street past a large number of parked cars to a big house festooned with balloons and featuring air inflated "bounce houses" on various lawns. Going around toward the back, they found Gloria greeting guests with her husband.

Gloria was quite happy to see them and all three got Gloria Hugs and Gillian got cheek kisses. Gloria introduced her husband, Randolph, a distinguished looking tall man with senatorial white hair, a great smile, and laugh wrinkles around the eyes.

"Let me guess," he said, "This walking scarecrow must be Hampton, the other young man must be George, and this beautiful young woman must be Gillian." Gillian blushed.

Gloria said, "Don't you think she's adorable when she blushes, Randolph?"

Randolph said, "I certainly do. But I'd bet she's adorable whether she's blushing or not."

Of course, this made Gillian blush even more.

Katy Wakefield approached the group.

Michael DeMeis

Gloria said, "And you remember this beautiful young woman is Katy Wakefield, Regina's grand-daughter."

Randolph said "Of course, you used to come over to play with our son, Donald. He still regrets letting you get away."

Gloria said, "Get away, she did. That's Donald's loss. Now she's Hampton's special friend."

Randolph said, "You're a lucky guy, Hampton. Katy is something special."

Hampton said, "I can certainly endorse that."

Randolph said "Katy, were you involved in the apprehension of the jihadist group with George, Gillian, and Hampton?"

Katy said "No I didn't meet everyone until well after that. But I feel I know every detail of it from my three friends and Gloria. Everyone says Gloria was a big factor in making it happen."

Gloria said, "I didn't do much, but it did make a suitable coda to my ATF career. It made my decision to retire easier since I didn't think I'd ever have such a successful project again. And the other contributing factor was the decision of my star worker to resign to form her own investigation agency." She gave Gillian a hug.

As was usual, Gillian blushed some more.

Randolph said, "Well, I suspect all of you might like a drink. There are two bars, and one is just on the other side of the back screened porch."

Everyone congratulated Gloria on her upcoming retirement and moved away to allow additional guests to reach her.

At the bar, the young women got their favorite mojitos, and George got a vodka tonic. Hampton got his usual glass of Chardonnay.

"Katy," he said, "taste this, it's like that bottle you brought to our dinner. "

Katy tasted, and agreed that it was a great chardonnay. That did not stop her from preferring her strawberry mojito.

As the four wandered, they saw a group of young women who had become quite happy while enjoying the catered bar. They were Gillian's former female ATF colleagues, all of whom were pleased to see her and also George. The drinks they had already consumed were apparently enough to allow them to flirt shamelessly with George even though Gillian was right beside them. Gillian wasn't worried. She knew George belonged to her. George, however, enjoyed the attention.

Katy and Hampton, drinks in hand, preferred to circulate amongst all of Gloria's friends, neighbors, and well-wishers. They walked past several bounce houses filled with shrieking children having the time of their lives jumping around inside and literally bouncing off the walls. As they rounded one of the inflated tents, Hampton stopped short.

Standing less than twenty-five feet away was Jennifer. She was next to a man even more distinguished looking than Randolph Wentworth, Gloria's husband. Tall, slender, and a full head of silver white hair seemed to be a distinguishing marker for the Chestnut Hill elite. Jennifer noticed Hampton, smiled rather evilly and started to walk toward him and Katy.

Katy noticed her and asked, "So, who is this?"

Hampton said, "That's Jennifer, the one I was involved with."

"Damn," said Katy, "She's seriously gorgeous."

Jennifer came up to them. "Hello Hampton, I'm glad to see you again. Who's your little friend?"

Hampton was quite irritated at this implied disparagement of Katy, and so he tried to show his feelings by presenting Jennifer to Katy. Thus, implying Katy was the more important higher ranked person rather than vice versa.

"Katy, this is Jennifer Lopez. We worked together for a time at the Rittenhouse Labs. Jennifer, this is my friend Katy Wakefield. She has a store on Antique Row." Unfortunately, Jennifer did not even appear to notice the implied snub.

Jennifer smirked, "To be more correct about it, we didn't work together so much as Hampton worked for me, building equipment and so on." Addressing Katy, she said, "Skilled trades people, like you and Hampton, are good to know wherever they are located. I don't do much shopping for antiques, but if the occasion should arise, your little shop might come in handy."

Katy said wickedly. "You're welcome to come by anytime. Part of the mission of our store is to educate those who don't know anything about antiques, so we could probably help you a lot."

Jennifer was seriously pissed at this observation from someone she considered to be a little Wasp girl. "I suspect Hampton has been spreading all kinds of stories about me to you."

Katy said sweetly, "No, he has never said anything derogatory to me about his time with you. I did learn from Gillian that you usually described Hampton as 'Furiously firm and hard' and I can definitely endorse that observation." Jennifer did not like that comment, and showed it. "Also, he seems to have the capacity to continue many activities beyond their expected time."

Jennifer could not understand what that comment referred to, but she was sure it had implied negative characteristics that were directed against her. It was pretty clear that Katy liked her even less than she liked Katy. She's another Gillian, thought Jennifer.

It could be seen that Jennifer was seriously pissed off at both Katy and Hampton. Jennifer apparently decided that a retreat was in order "I definitely need to go back to my new boss." She indicated the tall silvery haired gentleman waiting for her near the other bar. "When you're the personal assistant for the CEO of a large hedge fund, you're always on call."

Katy said sweetly, "Jennifer, it was a distinct pleasure meeting you."

Jennifer twiddled her fingers above her shoulder as she left.

Katy and Hampton watched her return to her boss.

Katy said, "That is one nasty witch. I can't see what you ever found attractive in her, other than she's sexy as hell."

Hampton said, "I guess that's the only reason I was so involved with her, but it's something I'm not exactly proud of either." He looked affectionately at her. "Baby, you handled that well."

"Oh God, whenever you call me baby I get all tingly. I'm so glad you belong to me and not to her."

Hampton said, "I'm definitely glad of that as well."

Hampton and Katy wandered back around the caler looking for George and Gillian and saw them with Gloria and a regal looking older woman.

Hampton said "Katy, isn't that your nana with Gloria?"

"Yes, it is. It turns out they are fairly close friends with lots of connections through Chestnut Hill.

Gloria had just spotted George and Gillian and waved them over. She also waved over Hampton and Katy.

Gloria addressed her companion "Regina, I'd like to present George Bailey and Gillian Andrews. George is an FBI Special Agent and Gillian was the star agent in my ATF group until she left to start her own investigation agency. Guys, I'd like you to meet Regina Wakefield, the chairperson of the board of the Philadelphia Museum of Art."

Gillian and George were suitably impressed and expressed the usual pleasure at meeting Gloria's friend. Regina smiled at the young couple.

"I believe I saw both your names in the news reports about the apprehension of the jihadists on Jewelers' Row."

Gillian looked at George and said to Regina, "We were part of the task force, but most of the credit should go to Aban Hassad, the DHS agent who provided the information and organizing behind the arrests."

Regina considered the couple. "It's unusual to see such modesty in young people these days."

Gloria said, "They were essential parts of the task force, but they are not self-promoting by any stretch of the imagination."

Regina said to Gillian, "Do you have a card for your new agency?"

Gillian almost dropped her purse in her haste to get their cards out.

Regina said "Ah ha, G and G investigations, so you are both involved in the agency. Whose G comes first?"

George said, "It was Gillian's idea not to be explicit about that. Potential customers can decide which they prefer. I can see why quite a few men and perhaps some women would want to think of a man as heading the agency. On the other hand, it's possible that some men might prefer to deal with an attractive young woman. And some women would probably like to see a woman running things."

Regina looked back at Gillian. "That's a clever idea. I can see why you were Gloria's star agent. Smart as well as beautiful."

Gillian felt her cheeks reddening yet again. She was blushing at getting compliments from the distinguished chair-person and George.

Regina tucked the agency card into her clutch. "I will definitely see that the museum's director of security gets this. Our security people are good but not trained to investigate complex occurrences."

George and Gillian thanked Regina and then left Gloria and her friend since other friends and neighbors were waiting to engage them. Hampton and Katy joined George and Gillian in seeking a last drink.

At the catered bar, Hampton and Katy told George and Gillian that they were now also going steady.

Gillian said, "Whenever I hear that term I get a feeling I've fallen into a time warp."

Hampton said "It is anachronistic. We're probably the only young couples in Philadelphia who are 'going steady'. But as the song goes "Everything old is new again."

George said, "That song is almost as old as 'going steady'. Hampton, you are so anachronistic that I sometimes think *you* are a time traveler."

Hampton and Katy related their encounter with Jennifer and expressed their satisfaction with the day's events. Gillian said, "If Jennifer is the personal assistant with the CEO of a hedge fund, it sounds like she is on her usual track of going after the money."

George and Gillian were also extremely happy with meeting some of the Chestnut Hill elite which could potentially lead to business for their agency.

Katy was going back to Hampton's apartment for the evening, so all four would be returning to Center City in George's car.

Once started in the car, George began to sing "Show me the way to go home." The others immediately joined in and Gillian syncopated the rhythm on the dashboard. All in all, the four friends were quite pleased that coming to Gloria's retirement party was not only fun, but beneficial to everyone.

Epilogue

Indefinite detention of suspected terrorists is allowed under the Patriot Act of 2001. The circumstantial evidence found in Hassan al-Sidaan's Sansom Street jewelry store was deemed sufficient by federal authorities to allow him to be classified as belonging to a terrorist organization. However, the group to which he belonged had long ago learned how to manipulate the U.S. legal system for its own purposes. Al Tunji had been active from Syria and had enlisted the ACLU in support of al-Sidaan. They advised him to provide sufficient retainers for a certain Philadelphia lawyer to provide the necessary verbiage before a federal judge. This was done, and while there was some discussion at the hearing about whether the exemplary record of Youkoumian the jeweler could apply to Hassan al-Sidaan the money launderer, the lawyer lived up to his Philadelphia reputation and crafted enough words around the issue to convince the federal judge to grant bail.

Hassan was initially glad to be out of confinement until he exited the court building and saw the two couriers who were his former assistants waiting for him outside with a green car nearby. He immediately wanted to go back inside the federal building, but it was too late. He was marched to the green car which then disappeared into Philadelphia.

Acknowledgements

I would like to thank Tracy Shaw for reading the first draft and providing valuable feed-back which I used in improving it.

I'd also like to thank my writing coach Mark Malatesta for his support in the rather traumatic problem of finding a publisher.

About the Author

Michael DeMeis attended Stanford University as an undergraduate and achieved a Bachelor of Arts degree in Physics with departmental honors. He then enrolled at Harvard and earned a Ph. D. in Physics. He initially worked at Sarnoff labs in Princeton NJ and has spent most of his career as a software engineer on systems for semiconductor device producers.

His real passion, however, has been writing fiction and this resulted in his first novel "Diamonds to Dust" which features Physics memes driving the plot.

www.ingramcontent.com/pod-product-compliance
Lightning Source LLC
Chambersburg PA
CBHW031342070726
47496CB00017B/1457